A Kiss For All Time

For All Time, Book 2

by

Paula Quinn

Text by Paula Quinn
Cover by Dar Albert

Dragonblade Publishing, Inc. is an imprint of Kathryn Le Veque Novels, Inc.
P.O. Box 23
Moreno Valley, CA 92556
ceo@dragonbladepublishing.com

Produced in the United States of America

First Edition January 2025
Trade Paperback Edition

ARE YOU SIGNED UP FOR DRAGONBLADE'S BLOG?

You'll get the latest news and information on exclusive giveaways, exclusive excerpts, coming releases, sales, free books, cover reveals and more.

Check out our complete list of authors, too!

No spam, no junk. That's a promise!

Sign Up Here

www.dragonbladepublishing.com

Dearest Reader;

Thank you for your support of a small press. At Dragonblade Publishing, we strive to bring you the highest quality Historical Romance from some of the best authors in the business. Without your support, there is no 'us', so we sincerely hope you adore these stories and find some new favorite authors along the way.

Happy Reading!

CEO, Dragonblade Publishing

Additional Dragonblade books by Author Paula Quinn

For All Time Series
A Promise For All Time (Book 1)
A Kiss For All Time (Book 2)

Hearts of the Conquest Series
The Passionate Heart (Book 1)
The Unchained Heart (Book 2)
The Promised Heart (Book 3)

Echoes in Time Series
Echo of Roses (Book 1)
Echoes of Abandon (Book 2)
The Warrior's Echo (Book 3)
Echo of a Forbidden Kiss (Novella)

Rulers of the Sky Series
Scorched (Book 1)
Ember (Book 2)
White Hot (Book 3)

Hearts of the Highlands Series
Heart of Ashes (Book 1)
Heart of Shadows (Book 2)
Heart of Stone (Book 3)
Lion Heart (Book 4)
Tempest Heart (Book 5)
Forbidden Heart (Book 6)
Heart of Thanks (Novella)

PROLOGUE

New York City
2024

FABLE RAMSEY SHIVERED as she sat against the cold wall in a small alley on 46th Street and 9th Avenue. She pulled her knees to her chest and yanked her tattered blanket up to her chin, uncovering the only footwear she owned; the fake Doc Martens on her feet. She looked up at the night sky and saw a star twinkling at her. She smiled then scoffed at herself.

There weren't any stars twinkling in her direction. If anything, they were laughing at her up there. She was the biggest fool who believed things would get better for her once she was free of her mother. But nothing had changed. She had no skills.

Kittie Ramsey had kept her from going to school, preferring to have Fable around to help her. She'd hidden Fable from any kind of authority, and on a few occasions after being hidden, her mother had forgotten to find her for days. They lived on the streets, refusing to go to shelters in case social workers started to ask questions about the dirty little red-haired girl pulling along a small suitcase with a broken wheel.

She had watched her mother swindle and cheat anyone and any situation, and Fable had learned from her. At the age of nine she became an expert at three-card-monte and every other street game. At thirteen, she'd been jumped at the back of an alley; beaten for the money she'd won on the corner. When her wounds healed, she began to practice self-defense. On the streets of Hell's Kitchen, one needed to protect oneself. At eighteen she was arrested for pickpocketing. She was bailed out by some guy who'd hooked up with her mother and was doing her a favor, but it turned out he wanted his own favor from her and she wasn't having it. It was the one thing Fable had never given up. Her body was hers. She'd rather rot in jail than let someone use her body to get out.

Unafraid of sleeping outside, she closed her eyes and settled in. Thanks to Bernadette, one of the waitresses from Tess's Diner uptown, Fable's belly was full. She'd met Bernadette one day while she was panhandling and the woman was kind enough to buy her lunch. She began showing up after hours, traveling to Fable's little alley to bring her a bag of the latest special. She was like Fable's very own fairy godmother.

Tomorrow, she was meeting Ms. Halstead, a new social worker—whom Fable prayed was also an angel sent to help her—about finding a job. After that, she'd be handing out flyers. Maybe she could make enough to be able to stay in the shelter. She'd love to get her own apartment but it was a dream for now and nothing more.

She settled in but then something rumbled beneath her. She opened her eyes to see if she felt it again. There weren't any subways beneath her but there it was again. The strange rumbling. This time the vibration shook her and a resonating hum sounded in her ears.

She stood up, ready to run. What the heck was it? An earthquake? She looked around beneath the street light. The air appeared wavy, like when she warmed her hands near a barrel fire and she looked over the flames. She thought she should run, but she'd lived in four of the five boroughs her whole life and she'd seen plenty without running. But she'd never seen anything like a man appearing out of thin air right before her eyes. She blinked and gasped a little. What had she just seen? She doubted her eyes and backed away instinctively. Where had he just come from? He hadn't been there a moment ago. Had she fallen asleep? She had to be dreaming, right? Her thrashing heartbeat in her ears proved that she was awake. But, what she just saw couldn't be real. People don't just appear out of nowhere. She almost didn't see whatever was in his hand but it glowed like a blue flame and almost drew her out of her hiding place.

He was so focused on it, he hadn't seen her when she ducked into the shadows along the wall. He looked out of place, like he'd been part of some kind of theater company or medieval society club. He wore a tunic-like shirt and pants with leather moccasin style boots. His hair was gray and hung loose around his bearded face.

He turned and looked directly at her even though she hadn't made a sound and she was sure he couldn't see her. When he took a step toward her, she reached for her bottle of mace. She should probably carry a knife, the way her mother had taught her, but she doubted she could use it on anyone.

"I can see you," the man called out in a heavy British accent, breaking the silence as he came near. "Come out and put away that useless weapon you have pointed at me."

No way! No way could he see her! She squinted trying to see him better and then sprayed him in the face with her mace. "Good luck seeing for a while, Mister." She ran around him and then came to an abrupt halt when he clamped his fingers around her arm.

In his other hand, he clutched the glowing blue item and held his arm up to his eyes. "Wait!" he ordered as if she were under his command. "What year is this?"

"Huh?" she asked. What kind of problems did this guy have? "The year? It's 2024."

He let out a sigh of such deep relief, Fable thought he might pass out. "Then I'm in the right time."

"That's great, now let me go. I don't want to hurt you."

He didn't do as she demanded. "Who's the king here? I need to speak with him."

"Are you for real?" Incredulously, she tugged her arm. "This is America. We don't have a king. You need to take a right toward the U.K. mister"

He lowered his arm from his eyes but didn't open them. The lids were already red and swollen. Fable grimaced looking at him.

"A right?"

She rolled her eyes. "Right. You need a passport and a plane ticket on British Airways and you'll be all set."

"Can I use this?" He waved the blue trinket in front of her face. Was it…a pocket watch? A sapphire pocket watch?

"To pay?" She obviously misunderstood him and felt foolish for asking.

"No."

She wrinkled her brow at him. "How would you use a pocket watch to get to the U.K.?"

"How do you think I just arrived here from where I was?"

She really didn't know! Her eyes must have tricked her. Of course he must have turned the corner and she'd missed his arrival. "Where were you?" she asked in a quiet, uncertain voice.

"1694, but it wasn't right."

The poor guy must have dementia, she thought and patted the large hand to which she was shackled. He looked to be in his late fifties-early sixties. She smiled and spoke in a softer voice. "Maybe if it brought you here, it wants you to speak to the president, and not the king."

When he nodded, she pulled her arm free. "There we go," she said gently. He was sick and Fable knew how to care for the sick. She cared for her mother most of her life. "Now, let me just call for help with seeing to what you need."

She dug into her pocket and produced her old flip-phone. When the screen lit up, the man in front of her pulled free the long sword from the scabbard at his side and swung it, stopping only inches from her throat. She yelped and fell back on her rump. "What are you doing with that thing? Now I'm calling the cops!"

An instant before she touched the screen again, she stopped. Had she frightened him? Is that why he attacked? Not wanting it to happen again, she lowered her voice. "This is a phone. It lights up so I can see. Put the sword away. Wait..." she gave the metal pointing in her face a better look ... "is that blood?"

"Do you know her? Do you know my wife? I've been searching for her."

"What? Oh, y...yes, I might. The police station has books with pictures of people who are lost."

He waved the sword at her, though he'd moved it a careful distance away. "Send word to them immediately," he ordered as if she were his servant. She quirked her mouth at him and tapped 911. "You can't get more immediate than this." She stepped away and held her phone to her ear. After she asked for help and gave a description of him, she tried to explain what was happening. "He has a big sword and I'm pretty sure there's blood on it."

Four minutes, she thought, releasing a deep, calming breath and putting her phone away. The cops would be here in four minutes. She eyed her blanket. She was sleepy. "Okay, help is on the way. And...um...keep the sword in its scabbard."

"Miss, will you help me?"

"The police will help you," she corrected gently.

"You have to help me find her and bring her home to our children."

Fable took a step closer to him. "What happened to her?"

He held out the pocket watch in his hand. "This thing ate her up. I've been searching endlessly. I cannot go home until I find her. I finally figured out how it works. She's here. Somewhere."

Gosh, he was really not well. "We'll find her," she assured him with a gentle smile. Her expression didn't change as the distant sirens grew closer.

He turned to the whirling lights on the police car when they pulled up onto the sidewalk. He watched the doors open and the officers rush out, hands on their guns, shouting orders. His dark eyes slipped to her and sent a warning that he was capable of terrible things. "The first thing they will try to do is take this." He held up the pocket watch. "And then I'll have to kill them all, including you for betraying me."

Fable's blood ran cold. She wanted to run. What if he chased her with his bloody sword? She hadn't been this afraid since Pug Grady and his thug friends kidnapped her from her mother when she was seven and held her ransom for the hundred dollars her mother owed him. Pug had waved his gun around in her face in an effort to frighten her and make her cry. He had failed. Crying was a waste of time in her world. She had stopped doing it for good when she was eight.

She wouldn't do it now.

"Just…please, relax, Sir," she tried gently.

And then, in an instant, the cosplay soldier leaped behind her and curled one arm around her neck, close to his bloody blade. In his other hand, he still gripped the blue pocket watch.

"Is this the thanks I get for being nice to you?" she muttered under her breath and then pushed his arm holding the sword away, reached over for his wrist and began the process of flipping him. Then something strange happened when the air waved and grew distorted. The ground shook and then it was over. One second she was standing on the street defending herself against a crazy man with a sword, and in the next, she was overwhelmed by daylight, standing behind what appeared to be a barn, gasping for breath that was scented with manure. She bounded to her feet and looked around, but the man trying to hold her hostage wasn't there. What just happened? She lifted a shaking hand and found herself gripping the pocket watch. How did it end up in her hand? She almost flung it away. She squinted at the people staring dumbfounded at her under the sun. Why were they dressed like the peasants from the medieval festival in her neighborhood park every year?

Clutching the pocket watch, she looked around for the crazy 'time traveler' guy. What had he done? Her blood suddenly went cold as she blinked curiously at the small group of people staring at her.

"Where am I?" she called out.

"You're in Belstead," one of the onlookers replied.

"Belstead?"

"That's right, Miss. Belstead in Ipswich."

Ipswich? Where was that? Her heart pounded so hard she grew queasy. Did she have the courage to ask the same question the time-traveler guy had asked her? "What…what year is this?"

They turned to one another with curious, concerned faces. Then, one woman stepped forward. "It's the year 1718."

This was some kind of trick. A terrible one, at that. But the vibrating pocket watch in her hand proved her theory wrong. The time traveler must be coming. She had to run.

Chapter One

Colchester, England
The year of our Lord 1718

"I know I promised not to meddle in your personal affairs, Ben, but the *season* begins in six days and you're the *ton's* most eligible bachelor!"

Benjamin West, His Grace Duke of Colchester, glanced up from his wooden pawn to his sister, then, without a word, returned to the chess match.

"Ben!" she shrieked loud enough to startle his opponent and long-time friend, Simon Hamilton, Earl of Sudbury. "Just think about attending my ball. All the *ton* will be here, and they all want to see you."

Ben closed his eyes and called for patience. The very last thing he wanted to do was meet a dozen ladies and their mothers all bent on snagging him as a husband. "Prudence," he said with a tinge of steel in his gaze. "I'm not going. I've told you dozens of times. I want no part of—"

"I'm doing this to help you," she lamented. "Do you want to fulfill Father's last wish or not, Benjamin? Besides that, you're eight and twenty! You're only going to continue to get older!"

At this, Lord Sudbury smiled.

"She isn't amusing," Ben murmured, watching the earl move his knight.

"I disagree," Sudbury replied and looked up to smile at her.

Everyone in Colchester House knew Sudbury was in love with Lady Prudence West. Only Ben knew that Sudbury planned to ask her to wed him when his tour of fighting for the king was over the following year.

Ben moved his pawn to black to drive back the knight, also securing an outpost square to defend against enemy knights.

Sudbury sighed and dropped his chin into his palm. "I was distracted."

"I know," Ben looked the board over and then lifted his dark gaze to his friend.

"And you went straight for my throat," Sudbury accused playfully.

"Throat, heart…" Ben shrugged his indigo velvet-clad shoulders … "whatever takes you down."

"Benjamin!" his sister shrieked.

He rolled his eyes just before he closed them. He should let Sudbury win the game since the poor sot had to be mad to care for her.

"You've attracted the attention of the most elite," the meddlesome wench wore on. "I hear that even the king's niece is interested in you. Think of Father's will, and of how proud he would be of you if you wed the king's niece! You're rich, handsome, and unwed. I'm sure she would fall right into your arms."

Prudence knew he didn't want a wife, but she didn't know why. There would be some time to tell her.

"Colchester," his friend said and shook his head, staring at the board. "How did you capture my knight again! How do you do it every time, and while your sister distracted you?"

"If you truly want to learn, study your surroundings and what I'm doing. We've played enough times. I won't just tell you my strategy."

"Benjamin," his sister sniffed. "I don't have peace because of you."

He turned his cool gaze on her. "Why would you say that?"

"Because it's true." Now, tears streamed down her face. "How can I have peace when my brother will disappoint our father's unfortunate spirit by not marrying into an influential family? When my brother, the only family I have, has no one to care for him?"

Ben drew in a deep breath, having heard it all a thousand times, and mated Sudbury's king, pushing it to the edge of the board. "Let's end this," he told his friend. "Your heart isn't in it."

The earl rubbed his fingers over his throat while Ben rose from his chair. "You're speaking of the game, eh?"

"Pru," Ben addressed his sister instead of his friend. "I'll attend your ball—" He had to stop and wait until he could pry her off him. "But, if I don't find anyone there to my liking, you'll forget this matchmaking obsession of yours and let me live how I wish to live, as we agreed."

"Alone?" Her big eyes, the same color chestnut as her hair, grew rounder.

"If that's what I want," he said woodenly. He gave her a slight smile, then waited for Sudbury to join him and left the solar.

When he shut the door behind him, he shot his friend a menacing look. "I should have let one of her other suitors wed her and take her from under my feet instead of waiting for you to finish your duty to the king. Before taking her to her new home."

Sudbury shook his head in disgust. "Think of how your sister would feel if she heard you say that."

"She's heard me say it a dozen times," Ben let him know and then left his friend to go break his fast.

Part of the reason he allowed his meddlesome sister to stay was she didn't want to leave Colchester House. He understood that she loved it here where they grew up, where the memories of their parents lived on no matter how many years passed. He loved it the same way.

Turning to look down the torchlit hall on his left, he saw the ghost of his father, Lieutenant-colonel Richard West of the Royalist Army on one of the rare times he was home. He walked slowly, barely looking up from a pamphlet while his children scurried around him, his mother hurrying after her children to keep them from disturbing their father.

Ben knew his sister had the same memories. He was too compassionate. That was his problem. One of the conditions of him agreeing not to marry her off was that she wouldn't interfere in his personal life. Well, he scowled, she'd gone back on her word. He growled low in his throat. A ball. A ball with every marriageable woman from Colchester to London attending. All hungry and willing to do or say anything for a nibble.

He hooked his finger under his cravat and pulled. He didn't want or need a wife, especially not just because she came from a rich and powerful family. Still, he didn't want to disappoint his father, who had included his wishes in his will.

Ben was also a little insulted that his sister thought he needed someone to take care of him. Had she forgotten that it was him who looked after her, though she was two years older than him, when they were made orphans by radical followers of James Stuart? Ben didn't need any help. What he needed was to go back to the chaos of the battlefield. It was the only place exactly like him. He missed it. He needed it after being forced to retire after almost losing his arm while saving King George from the rebellious Jacobites three years ago. It was the third and last time he saved the king while fighting for him. Ben still had hopes of returning to the king's military service once his arm was strong enough to fight again. Being idle had almost cost him his purpose, which he believed was to fight. It had to be to fight. With all the darkness he felt inside himself over his parent's death, there wasn't any room for happiness or love. All he felt was hatred since he was eleven years old. It's what drove him, joining Queen Anne's army when he was sixteen, training and fighting under the brilliant strategist the Duke of Marlborough for the next eight years, after which time he fought for the new king, George of Hanover. The army had helped relieve the roiling pressure of his anger. He needed to go back.

He headed to the dining hall for some refreshment. Around him, servants scurried about, but he didn't stop or pause. He merely nodded an acknowledgement to some and barely that to others.

"Your Grace," said an older man who appeared at his side when he entered the Great Hall. "I trust you beat Lord Sudbury."

Ben glanced at Stephen, his long-time steward. "I should lose next time just to perplex you."

Stephen followed him but stood at his side when Ben sat at the largest of three trestle tables and called out for water.

"You look as if you need something stronger," Stephen remarked, sizing him up.

"The sun just came up an hour ago."

"And at night, you don't partake because you say Tories might attack. Sir, if I may say, you are no longer in the military. There's no need for such rigidity."

Ben shot his steward a cool look. "I'm not rigid, Stephen. I'm disciplined. There's a difference."

"Good morn to you, Your Grace!" called out one of his vassals.

The greeting was repeated six more times by others. Ben had learned long ago how to drown out most voices else he'd never hear the important matters.

"And you have to meet with the Earl of Ardleigh, Lord Brambley about escorting his daughter to London next month for the—"

Ben held up his hand to stop him. "Yes, yes, I know." Ben's father had desired a union between his family and the Brambleys. Or, according to his will, any high-powered family. His father had given him until the age of nine and twenty to find a well-bred wife. After that, half of his inheritance would go to Prudence if he didn't fulfill the stipulations of his will. Let her have it all, he thought to himself. He wanted the battlefield. He didn't want to take Louisa Brambley for his wife, whether his father wished it or not. She was stuffy and said little, yet somehow she made Ben feel less than enough. He'd agreed to escort her to a new playhouse in London for his father's sake but this was the last time. After this, he would inform her father that he didn't wish to see her again.

He raked his gaze over the people occupying his dining hall. They were his men and the wives of those who were wed. There were troubadours set up in the northeast corner, hired by his sister. They weren't playing, but eating his food. No matter, they would play during supper or they'd be kicked out on their arses.

He reclined in his seat when the female server brought him a jug of water and two cups to go with it. She leaned over to pour his and let her gaze drift to him. She was pretty, with plump cheeks and blonde braids swinging over each shoulder. Briefly, he wondered what Prudence would think of him wooing a servant.

She smiled into his eyes and let out a little sigh, then knocked the cup over into his lap. He sprang to his feet, wiping a few droplets of water from his lap.

"Oh, forgive me, Your Grace! Forgive me!"

He held up his hand to stop her from crying. It didn't work. He slipped his gaze to Stephen for help.

"Now there, Miss…" his steward comforted like a father—the way he'd always comforted Ben. They'd met in the early years of Ben's enlistment. Stephen wasn't a soldier or a noble, he was the queen's scribe, who traveled everywhere with the royal army. They had become friends. When Ben was injured and had to leave the current king's army, Stephen went with him. Ben was glad he had, for he was there in Ben's darkest days of being away from the battlefield.

"Patrice, Sir," the server informed them while her cheeks filled with blood.

"Yes, of course, Patrice," Stephen said, a master at putting others at ease.

Well, it seemed his steward was doing what he did best. There was no reason for Ben to linger about. While Stephen convinced the girl that the duke wasn't angry, Ben slipped out of the Hall without eating, and then strode directly out of the house before anyone stopped him.

It was a warm day without even a breeze to stir the hundreds of flowers when he opened the gate to the garden. He liked it here, where the calls of birds took the place of the mundane duties of an idle duke, where he could be alone deep in the garden, nestled on a bench draped with vines festooned with small peach-colored roses. Pity he didn't bring a book to read this morning.

His ears picked up the sound of a cat meowing. He liked cats. They weren't needy animals. He took a step forward, then paused. It was a human voice. He turned to it and the direction of the huge cross memorial he'd built for his parents.

"Please. Ooh, please, Lord," a woman begged, "bring me back to the twenty-first century. I'll do anything. And please stop that man from chasing me. He scares me—"

Ben came upon her kneeling in front of the memorial. Standing behind her, he could only see her long waves hanging to her waist. In the sun, gold and autumn bronze puddled in soft copper waves. He could see her wrists and hands as she lifted them in prayer. She appeared as delicate as the lilies around her. Someone was chasing her. She was afraid. He took a step a little closer.

He moved his gaze over what he could see of her clothing. Her legs seemed to be bare but for her torn black hose beneath pants that only reached her thighs. She wore odd boots that came to mid-calf and appeared to be made of some sturdy material.

"I don't know how I got here but I can't stay here," she continued to pray. "That man scares me. Don't let him find me, Lord. I'm afraid that if he does, he'll—"

She must have sensed him behind her because she stopped praying and turned slowly to look over her shoulder at him.

Ben was prepared to offer her help, but when he looked at her every other thought but one fled from his mind. She was beautiful and...oddly clothed, as if she didn't come from Colchester. Perhaps even from England. She stood to her feet slowly and turned around to face him fully, confounding him further. She moved with caution, like a feral kitten, ready to flee.

Ben couldn't take his eyes off her. She was petite, more like a mythical garden creature than a human woman. Her skin was milky white with smudges of dirt on her cheeks and chin. She stared at him with large, pale blue-green eyes that slanted upward at the outer corners like a cat.

"What do you want?" she asked him, ready to spring away.

Ben had the ridiculous urge to smile at her. No. She deserved a scowl for entering his garden uninvited. "This is my garden."

She eyed him suspiciously then took a step to leave. "Oh, sorry for trespassing. I didn't mean to—

"Is someone following you?"

She nodded and gave him a desperate look. "He…he put his sword to my throat. I've been running for days." Her belly made a loud sound, and she rubbed her palm across it. "I'm starving, Mister. I've been hungry before but not like this." She lifted the back of her hand to her forehead and closed her eyes. "Maybe just a little water?"

He didn't want to get involved.

"Follow me," he muttered and began to turn toward the house. He saw her falling from the corner of his eye and reached for her, catching her in the crook of his arm. She felt fragile and weak and he was overcome with the unwanted desire to protect her.

He pulled her a little closer.

"Please," she whispered weakly. Her eyes were beginning to close. "Don't hurt me."

She closed her eyes and her head lolled back over his arm.

"Damnation," Ben breathed out. Now what was he supposed to do? He lifted her, in both arms, ignoring the pain to cradle her.

"Miss? Miss?" He gave her a little shake but she didn't respond. He looked toward the house and then hurried to the back door.

"Stephen!" he called out. The steward appeared while Ben carried the woman to the back of the kitchen and the empty cot in the corner, half hidden by pots of herbs and spices, along with sacks of apples. "Bring water," he told the steward as he set her down and then stood over her. Her fiery hair spread out around her head as if it were the sun behind her.

"Who is she, Sir?"

"Water first," he ordered, then found a wool blanket and covered her with it. Yes, he thought while Stephen hurried to his task, who was she? She was clothed in nothing his eyes had ever seen before. Who was following her and why? His curiosity was piqued—and nothing had piqued it in so long, he'd almost forgotten what it felt like.

He lifted one of the kitchen torches from the sconce on the wall and bent beside the cot. He held the torchlight near her face, over the alluring curves of her jawline and the pert tilt of her nose. Studying her made him feel something warm and inviting. Who was chasing her? Why would anyone want to hurt such a fragile being? He'd prefer it if she didn't die. He wanted her to open her eyes again so he could ask her why she had asked the Lord to bring her to the twenty-first century. No. He didn't care why. He shouldn't get himself more involved than he already was.

When Stephen returned with the water, he helped Ben sit her up. Ben had to sit at the head of the cot and nestle her head between his chest and his arm to keep her steady while he wet her lips and then her tongue. He told Stephen and his sister, when she joined them, where he'd found her and what she had been doing.

"It doesn't look like there is much we can do for her," Prudence said, "Benjamin, I don't know why you would lay her in our food supply seeing how filthy she is. We should put her out."

"We're not putting her out," Ben rested the woman's head on the cot and stood up. "I'll decide what to do with her when she wakes up. For now, Stephen, assign someone to watch over her."

"Yes, Sir," the steward said as his lord left the kitchen.

Ben left the house again and surveyed the area around the

house and garden for any sign of a man lingering about. After almost an hour he was satisfied there was no man close by who didn't belong here. He returned to the kitchen and went to the back where she still lay sleeping on the cot. One of the servants, Edith was her name if Ben remembered correctly, was sitting with her. When she saw him, she leaped back and almost fell over backwards in her chair.

"Oh, Your Grace, I didn't see you," she told Ben as he righted her.

"Has she improved at all?"

Edith shook her head. "She's cold, Sir. Cold as death. Here, feel for yourself."

She snatched Ben's hand and deposited the sleeping woman's hands into it.

He stared down at them, small, slender, delicate—like her. Edith was correct, the mysterious woman was freezing. Ben covered her hands with both of his and rubbed. "Get her more blankets, and have braziers brought in."

"But, Sir, I have been putting braziers in her bed all morning," Edith told him. "She still has not warmed."

Ben closed his eyes for an instant and then looked up to heaven when they opened again. He was never going to hear the end of this from Prudence. No matter. He was heir to his father's estate. The money was mostly his.

"Call for the physician. Tell him it's urgent."

"Yes, Sir," Edith bowed and hurried away.

Alone with the sleeping beauty behind piles of fruits, grains, and fresh herbs, Ben sat in the chair Edith had left empty. He let his dark gaze rove over the woman's form, her face. Her complexion was paler than it had been earlier. Was she getting sicker? Why had she chosen his garden to pray and then to faint in his arms? Why had he taken her in? Was he responsible for her now? He ran his hand down his face. He was responsible to the king. He touched his hand to his shoulder as he rolled it. That was enough. He didn't want to take this woman in, as if she were some helpless cat that needed a home, and protect her from a man who was chasing her. What did the man intend to do if he caught her?

"No."

He leaped up at the sound of her then leaned down with his ear close to her lips. When she remained quiet and still, he turned his face to see her and felt her breath blend with his. He was too close. "Don't try to speak. Rest."

He didn't know if she heard him or not, or why his voice had gone soft when he spoke to her. It made him want to grumble under his breath, but Stephen told him he did it often and it was unbecoming to a soldier.

"No! Leave me alone!" She didn't cry out, seeming to only have enough breath and strength to speak quietly. "Stop! No…you can't have it. I have to find…a way home."

"Lady?" he said just as quietly. But she didn't respond. Who was she running from? Her husband? Father? Whoever he was, he'd put a sword to her throat. Bastard. Where was her home?

"Your Grace," Edith rushed back to the bed. In her arms, she carried four folded blankets. "The physician is on his way." She dropped the extra blankets onto the bed, then unfolded the first to spread over the woman. Her gaze fell to something on the bed and she cast him a curious look.

He followed her gaze to where his hand grasped the mystery woman's own hand. He pulled it away. For a moment, he felt as if he were standing on a ledge and his next step could be life or death. What was wrong with him? A woman in trouble falls into his arms and he can't seem to leave her bedside? He needed more purpose, he told himself. He'd gone from the frightening thrill of being on the battlefield, blood rushing through his veins from his constantly pounding heart to being idle for a large part of the day. Either boredom or—

"Do you think she could be ill and it could be contagious?" he asked.

Edith blinked and took a step back.

"Leave the diagnosis to the physician, not to a servant, eh?" Barnaby Greeves, the town's physician, entered the kitchen and strode to the back of it. Prudence and Sudbury followed behind him.

"Are you going to pay for a physician for her?" Prudence gave him a slight sneer while the physician examined the woman in the bed and removed her footwear.

"Yes."

The sneer faded and worry creased her brow. "Why? Who is she? Who is her family?"

He clenched his jaw and kept his gaze on the patient. "Should I toss her to the side of the road?"

"Why wouldn't you?" she asked, sincerely perplexed. When it came to helping others, his sister only helped those who could benefit her. There was no use trying to answer her question.

"Benjamin?" she demanded when he didn't answer her.

"Prudence?" The Earl of Sudbury stepped forward. "What are you doing? You will not badger him about his code. Not another word or I'll carry you out over my shoulder." He stared down at her from all six feet seven inches of him. He never used his size to intimidate her before. Ben was glad he stepped in now.

"Her body temperature is very low," the physician announced, stepping back. "But I don't think the cause is anything nefarious. She seems to be suffering from hunger and severe fatigue. She has traveled a great distance. Look here at her feet." The physician pulled back all her blankets and exposed her bare legs and feet. The latter were rubbed raw. Both feet suffered the same blistered, bloody condition. Ben's stomach knotted and his chest felt tight. Prudence sighed and looked away.

"I'd like for her to stay rested," the physician continued. "Don't move her, save only to try to get her to eat. Begin with soup today. Her stomach is weak from not eating and anything other than liquid could do more harm than good."

Edith nodded.

"How long must we care for her?" Prudence asked the physician and was promptly hauled over Sudbury's shoulder and taken away.

Ben looked down at the sleeping woman. He'd done everything he could. There was nothing left for him to do but trust her to Edith's care. As he was practicing his swordplay, he couldn't help how often he thought about her. But he tried with all his might to refocus on his task at hand. He needed to become stronger, and he wouldn't deviate from it. The old hatred clung on tight and wouldn't let him forget. He needed to fight.

Priding on himself on his self-discipline, he forced himself not to think of her while he practiced, swinging and ducking, blocking and parrying, nor when he ate supper that night alone in his room. As he laid down to sleep, he was plagued with questions about the beautiful stranger that left him restless as he got up and began to pace his chambers. Her clothing was strange, where did she come from? What happened to her petticoats and what were her boots made of? They were as strong as thick leather with especially thick soles. Who had been chasing her? And why?

He groaned. He had to stop troubling himself with her. To prove that he could, he returned to his bed and closed his eyes, vowing not to open them again until he had slept. But all he could see was her face behind his eyes. Finally, he left his bed and went to the kitchen.

She was still asleep. He stood over the bed until the sun broke through the window. He hoped she would live. He thought he might be the only person cheering for her. Maddeningly, it made him want to reach out and run his fingers over her hair, her face. She was far from home. Her feet testified to it. But as each moment passed, his head talked his heart out of whatever spell he'd fallen under. "There's no place in my life for you," he whispered. "I must rein in my intrigue and my desire to protect you and stay away. So, get well, my lady. Get well and live."

Chapter Two

FABLE OPENED HER eyes and saw a man turning away from her. She didn't scream because her throat was on fire—and also because of his words, spoken in the softest of masculine voices, still echoed around her ears. His desire to protect her? That wasn't something a guy who chased you through time said. It seemed to be something no one said in 1718. She'd been here four days now or was it five? Alone and impoverished—running from a man who was trying to catch or kill her, stuck in the eighteenth century. No one would believe her if she made it back. But worse was the hunger. She was starving. Literally. She couldn't sell the pocket watch since she'd hidden it in the wall of a church in Ipswich. She was sure it was the only way to get back home, and whoever was chasing her wanted it. She led him away from it and she knew how to defend herself but he wasn't some homeless, hungry guy on the street. He carried around a bloody sword and Fable had no doubt he could use it. She also wasn't sure if she could actually kill him once she got him down. So she did what she did best. She ran. She didn't know how far she'd gone. Someone told her she was in Colchester but how far was that from Ipswich? She had no idea. She'd needed to get her stalker off her back and then, once she was well again and her feet could withstand it, she'd get back to that church.

But the first thing Fable needed was food. No one had helped her. No one had even looked at her since she arrived. No one but this man. She wanted to reach out and stop him from moving away. But the only thing she caught was a glimpse of his profile, his strong, square jaw and raven brow low over his eye. He was going to stay away. That was fine with her. She just needed food to feel better and then she would be on her way. She was used to being alone. No big deal. Sleeping outside on the streets of New York City had prepared her for the worst, but at least at home people offered a hand to help her eat. Here, everyone was basically as poor as she was.

Everyone except this man. Was she safe here? Was the man chasing her close by? Were those apples she smelled?

She didn't open her eyes again for the next two days. When she did, a thin shaft of sunlight streamed through a narrow window to her right, providing light for her to see the bundles of apples stacked behind her head. She was hungry. She looked around. Where was she? Did she dream of the man's voice telling her he had to resist his desire to protect her and stay away? She almost laughed out loud at herself. Of course it was a dream. Who had ever wanted to protect her?

"Oh, my lady, you're awake!" A short older woman with pink cheeks and graying hair hurried toward her. "His Grace will be pleased. How are you feeling? I'm Edith. I'm here to serve you. Don't try to get up. Just stay right where you are and I'll bring you some soup."

Before Fable had a chance to respond, the woman left her sight. Fable could hear her busying herself preparing her soup beyond the storeroom. What did the woman mean by "serve her"? Who told her to do so? Fable's belly gave a loud growl. She wasn't sure soup would be enough. Then again, the thought of actually eating turned her stomach.

"Thank you," she said when the woman returned to her beside carrying a tray with a bowl on top. "May I ask…you mentioned His Grace. Is there a man…a lord here?"

"Yes, the duke," the woman told her and spooned some soup into her mouth. "He's away in Ardleigh, but he should be returning today. I think he'll be pleased to see you awake. He was concerned for you."

"Me?" Fable asked, and then closed her eyes to stop her tears from pouring out. She never tasted anything as good as the carrot soup Edith was feeding her.

"Yes," Edith confided with a sly smile. "I have never seen His Grace give a fretful thought to anything. He even paid the physician to come see you."

"I don't remember him too much," Fable told her, though the foggy image of a man cradling her in his arms invaded her thoughts.

"You were quite ill, lady. His Grace ordered Stephen and I to feed you clear soup so you wouldn't die of starvation. It was quite difficult since you were asleep."

Fable wasn't sure what to say. She'd never met anyone with such a kind heart as this "His Grace" guy.

Everything was going fine until another woman came forward and eyed her as if Fable were the filthiest creature she'd ever seen.

Fable agreed that she probably was. But it wasn't easy staying clean while being chased down dirt paths, getting struck by another woman on the street with three missing teeth and an even dirtier face than Fable's. Oh yes, and she'd never forget the guy who had promised her a bowl of stew and then tried to capture and sell her as a slave.

"So, you've decided to wake up," the woman breathed in disgust. She was dressed in a pretty, dark brown gown. She would have appeared plain, especially in the candlelit space where they were, if not for the gold earrings dangling from her delicate lobes and the pearl encrusted choker around her neck.

Fable thought they would be worth a pretty penny on the streets.

"Will you eat all our food now?"

Fable turned away from the spoon Edith held up to her. She hated imposing on these people. This woman was probably the wife of the guy who had helped her. She obviously didn't want Fable here.

"Prudence," a man's voice said, his husky pitch reverberating in Fable's blood. "Will you leave on your own or should I have you removed again?"

Fable stared at the man striding toward them. He was tall and lean and dressed completely in black. He reminded Fable of a wild stallion. Guys didn't look like him unless they were in the movies. And she knew after walking from Ipswich for four straight days and not seeing any cars, trains, or planes that this wasn't a movie.

"How are you feeling?" he asked, taking a step closer to her and then stopping himself.

She was tempted to smile at him, though he offered her an aloof scowl. She didn't think he would hurt her—and she had no other choice but to be friendly. "Hungry, and very displaced and disoriented."

The woman in the pearl choker glared at Fable first, and then at the man standing between them. He stood as straight as an arrow, with quiet power, and didn't seem to mind her.

"Benjamin, how can you treat me with such contempt because of someone you just met?"

His name was Benjamin. Fable thought it was a manly name. He looked like what she imagined a Benjamin would look like. Tall, dark, and handsome. Who was the villainess? His wife? They had money if this was their house. She needed money to live until she could get home. She would hate to rob him since he helped her out but one of the many things she had not learned to be when she was growing up on the streets, was loyal.

She wondered if it was rude or gluttonous of her to ask for a third bowl of soup. "My lord—" Fable began.

"You'll address him as Your Grace," the evil villainess of Fable's Harrowing Adventure Into the Past snapped at her.

"I will?"

"That's correct. He's the Duke of Colchester, His Grace Benjamin West."

"Wow, that's a mouthful," Fable let her know, glancing off to the side, doubtful that she'd remember it all.

"Your Grace will suffice," the duke told her in a gruff voice.

A duke. Wasn't that pretty high on the social ladder? Fable smiled at him. He didn't smile back.

"I'm Lady Prudence West, His Grace's sister. Who are you?"

Oh, good. Not his wife. "Fable Ramsey."

"Ramsey?" The duke's sister hissed. "You're a Jacobite?"

"A what?"

"Supporters of the Stuart Pretender," she went on. "A wild, rebellious lot that should be dealt with with more force."

Oh, Fable thought wryly while the villainess spewed. She really was lovely then, wasn't she? "No, I'm not one of those. I'm on the same side as you."

The duke's sister folded her arms across her chest and glared at her. "And what side is that?"

Fable tried desperately but she came to the same pathetic conclusion she'd been arriving at for at least four days. She didn't know anything about British history.

"Prudence, that's enough questions," the duke said in his sorcerer's voice. "The physician wants her to rest, and so do I."

"What about where she—"

"Leave," he said with a low, warning thread that moved his sister's feet.

"Miss Ramsey." He moved closer to the bed when his sister left. "If you're here to cause any trouble, you'll make an enemy of me."

A cold thread trickled down her spine, cooling her blood. She doubted this man didn't mean what he said. Maybe he wasn't such a nice guy.

"I'm not here to start any trouble," she assured him. "But just so you know, I'm also a pretty scary enemy to have."

He said nothing but stared at her good and long, then he finally turned away.

Fable thought she saw the slightest trace of a smile on his lips.

She felt Edith take her hand and then slip it into the duke's hand. "She feels warm now, Your Grace."

Fable thought she should pull back, but she wouldn't reject the hand that fed her. Besides, her heart was pounding too much for her to move without him seeing her trembling. His hand was large, his fingers, broad and elegant. "You're warm," she told him while he cupped her hand in his.

He lifted his eyes to her. Were they dark blue or black? "So are you," he said without giving away a clue about how he felt about his conclusion.

"Edith, continue to see to her," he ordered then pivoted on his heel, leaving the alluring scent of sandalwood with hints of papyrus and violet behind. "When she's well enough," he called out, turning at the door to set Fable's blood on fire with his gaze. "Send her on her way."

"Yes, Your Grace," Edith responded.

"But..." Fable murmured when he left. "I have nowhere to go."

She wished he wouldn't throw her out, but in case he did, she should fill up on food to keep her going. "Umm, Edith?"

"Yes, my lady?"

"Is there any chicken? Umm, what kind of meat do you eat here? Venison? Pork? No." She shook her head when Edith scrunched up her face. "Any kind of meat, really. I need protein. Eggs are good."

"Yes, my lady. But the physician said—"

"I have an iron stomach and that was two days ago. I'll be fine," she assured with a smile. "Please, I'm starving. And also, don't call me my lady. My name is Fable."

The older woman tilted her head at her "Are you a servant?"

"No. Of course not."

"Then 'my lady' it is."

"Is there nothing else to be then?" Fable asked her. "Either you're a lady or a servant? There's nothing in between?"

Edith looked her over, knowing what she wore under the blankets. "A prostitute, or a thief."

Fable laughed. "A prostitute or a thief. That's a terrible 'in-between'. I should be insulted. I don't give myself to anyone."

When Edith waited for more, Fable remained quiet. Then, "I won't steal from him."

"See that you don't, Miss."

Fable looked away, hating who she was for the zillionth time in her life. Actually, she was lower than a servant, not higher. Even servants had roofs over their heads. Even servants were loved by someone.

Edith left her alone but returned a little later with two whole roasted chickens, a braised duck, three cooked fish, and six hard-boiled eggs.

"Where have you traveled from, Miss?" Edith asked her while she ate.

Fable remembered where she'd 'touched down' in the eighteenth century because she must have asked fifty people where she was. "Belstead."

Edith drew back with her hand on her chest. "In Ipswich?"

Fable nodded and bit into a hard-boiled egg. She realized her torn tights and boots had been removed. She'd taken a look at her feet while Edith was getting her food. She wasn't going to be walking anytime soon.

"You have a strange accent though," Edith pressed on. "It doesn't sound like anything from Ipswich or anywhere I've heard."

Fable took a bite of a drumstick and then licked her fingers. "Oh really? I thought I sounded like everyone in Belstead."

Edith shrugged her shoulders. "Why did you walk here?"

"My father."

"Your father? Did he mistreat you?" Edith asked. "Were you escaping him?"

Fable stopped eating and held the serviette Edith had given her to her dry eyes. She sniffed and nodded. She didn't feel guilty for lying. Her father had run off before she was born. He deserved to be made out to be a monster.

"It's difficult to talk about, Edith."

"Of course. Oh, there, there," the older woman comforted.

It was nice to be comforted. Her mother hadn't been the comforting type. Fable didn't know how to react to such physical contact as embracing and broke away first.

"I'm fine."

"Yes," Edith said softly. "Of course." She smoothed out her apron and smiled at Fable. It seemed she no longer mistrusted the *thief*. "Well, the duke won't allow your father to hurt you again."

"Oh?" Fable looked up from a bowl of fowl. "What will he do? Is he very powerful?"

"Oh, yes," Edith let her know. "He merely has to ask the king for a favor and it will be granted."

"Really?" Fable asked. The king? Could he bring her to visit the king's castle? She wondered if the walls were really made of gold as believed amongst the poor. If so—

"The king is in his debt. The duke saved his life three times."

"What? Wow! Is the duke a soldier?"

Edith nodded proudly as if it were her son she was bragging about. "The people of Belstead have an odd way of speaking."

Fable agreed and they both laughed. Fable continued to eat while Edith told her all about the striking Duke of Colchester and his mean sister, Lady Prudence.

"Miss?"

"Hmm?" Fable's eyelids felt heavy and her stomach felt on the verge of eruption.

"You don't look well," Edith said and pressed her palm to Fable's forehead. "Oh my, you're burning up."

"I need the toilet....the...um...a bucket. Edith, hurry, please."

Edith disappeared for an instant then returned with a bucket and shoved it in front of Fable's face. And just in time.

Later, after Edith washed her down and cleaned her up behind a curtain. Fable fell into a deep sleep. She dreamed that her rescuer, the duke, came to the kitchen and lifted her from the thin bed. She even dreamed that he held her close to his chest, cradled in his arms while he climbed the stairs. She'd never felt so safe in her life. When he entered through a few doors and set her down on a bed of clouds, she knew he was going to let her go. She clutched his coat. "Don't leave me," she whispered into his shirt.

She woke several hours later, more disoriented than before. Where was she now? She pushed herself up on her elbows and looked around the room lit by hearth fire and candles scattered about on wooden tables. She was no longer in the kitchen, but someone's…bedroom. And oh my, what a bed it was! It was at least queen-sized with four thick wooden posts and a wooden frame around the top. She saw loops to hang curtains, but the loops were empty. There were layers of wool blankets covering her, along with a fur skin. There were three wardrobes in polished walnut. Paintings hung on walls that were lined with bookshelves. It was very cozy. Was it the duke's room? More like one of the royal rooms in the king's castle. She'd never seen anything like it. She'd certainly never slept in such a majestic bed.

Her dream flashed in her mind. Had it been a dream? She was still trying to decide when the duke stepped into the room with his nose in a book. Earlier, he'd worn a coat, waistcoat and cravat. Now, absent of all three, with his shirt unbuttoned at the throat, he looked more like a brainy rogue than a duke. When he looked up from what he was reading, his gaze, eclipsed by his inky hair, went immediately to her and his feet stopped moving.

"You're awake," he said, his voice like a rumbling drum in her ears, through her blood.

She nodded and sat up. "How long have I been asleep?"

"Seven hours," he told her, closing his book. "The physician had ordered no solid food. Do you remember him saying that?"

Oh no! She'd eaten a lot! He looked angry—which was only slightly different than his impassive resting face. There was nothing warm or soft in his eyes—which were black as coal, by the way.

"No. I'm sorry I don't remember that."

He raised a doubtful eyebrow. His lusciously full lower lip needed very little provocation to pout. "Well, I can understand that. Your mind wasn't in the right state to follow instructions. It was Edith's respon—"

"It's not her fault. I convinced her to feed me."

"Two whole chickens, a duck, and a fish?" he asked incredulously.

"Three fish…and six eggs," she corrected quietly, looking at her fingers. Why lie to him? He seemed like a decent guy. He hadn't left her, after all. "I wanted to stock up on protein," she told him, still not looking up, "so that after I left here, I wouldn't starve so quickly."

He didn't say anything for a few torturous seconds. She glanced up to find him looking at her, his book forgotten in his hand at his side.

"You don't know how to take care of your body," he pointed out in a dispassionate drawl. "Your assumption made you very ill. You said you weren't here to start trouble."

She let out a little laugh of disbelief. "I wasn't trying to start any trouble."

"But you did. You troubled the physician, Edith, and the cooks. Are you a liar as well as a troublemaker?"

She ground her jaw and her hands balled into fists on the bed. "Why are you trying to push my buttons?"

For the briefest of instants, she thought he looked amused. He took a step closer to the bed and the chair beside it. "What does that mean? What buttons? And why would I try to push them?"

He certainly knew how to insult her. He took enjoyment in it. Well, let him. She was quickly beginning to form a new opinion of him. "Forget my buttons, and forget what happened in the kitchen. I was simply trying to look out for myself before you see me out."

He stepped around the chair and sat in it, keeping his eyes on her. "Stay."

"What?"

"Are you on your way somewhere?"

"I'm trying to live. Same as always."

He bent forward in his chair, resting his elbows on his knees, his gaze boring into her. She felt as if she were exposed on a mountain cloaked in foreboding clouds. He appeared to be fighting some kind of battle in his head, tightening his jaw, thinning his lips. "I won't have you starving on the streets of Colchester. Stay here. Serve me."

For a fleeting instant, her blood ran scalding through her veins. Serve him? What exactly would that entail? Would she still sleep in his bed? "Thank you, Your Grace, but I'm not a servant."

"Then you must enjoy striving to live," he concluded, rising from his chair.

"Must I serve you to stay?"

He nodded and scoffed. "You want everything for nothing at all? Even a wife wouldn't ask that of me."

A wife? It was all she could think while she watched him leave the room. With his long, straight legs and breeches that hugged his backside perfectly, along with the beguiling flare of his shoulders, the back of him clouded her thoughts as much as the front of him did. So then, he wasn't married. How in the world had women let him slip by? Was his personality really that bad? Was she just as foolish to let an opportunity slip by her?

"Your Grace?" she called out as the door was closing.

He popped his head back inside the room and set his gaze on her.

"I'll stay."

"And serve me?"

She rolled her eyes heavenward as if she were sparing him her last shred of patience. "Fine."

Chapter Three

Fine.

Ben huffed out a breath as he left the guest bedchamber and entered the small sitting parlor. He looked back at the door as he closed it. When his parents were alive, these rooms had been reserved for visiting guests. But Colchester House no longer received guests. Not until last night. Strange how she could breathe life into that stuffy old bedchamber. Her presence seemed to brighten every corner.

When he'd heard how ill she had become and what had caused her malady, he went to her. Instead of her wide heaven-colored eyes staring back at him, she was barely awake, weak from expelling the contents of her belly, which, according to Edith, was much. He still didn't know what had come over him when he bent to her small cot and lifted her limp body in his arms. All he could think about on the way up the stairs to the room she now occupied, had been that she was obviously a street urchin who probably begged or stole for money, and he didn't care. She piqued his interest. Who was she running from, and why? He intended to find out. She amused him. What made her a fierce enemy to have when a heavy gust could sweep her away? She was quick witted and had honestly told him how much she'd eaten. And what had she meant by him trying to push her buttons? Edith had changed her odd clothes to a gown. There were no threaded buttons attached. She spoke in an odd manner—like the rest of her. Her hot temper made him want to dominate her, but it was an instinct. Nothing more.

Because he was alone, he let himself give out a short, quiet laugh as he fell onto a quilted crimson settee. He opened his book and held it up. She didn't want to be his servant but she hadn't asked what her duties entailed.

"What shall I have you do for me first, Miss Ramsey?" he mused into the book.

Suddenly, the book was yanked from his fingers, the ship on the cover turned upright, then shoved back into his hands.

"You can start by asking me to have mercy on you."

He looked up into those fathomless ocean-colored eyes he couldn't seem to shake from his thoughts. "Or what?"

She snatched the book from him again and slapped his recovering arm with it, then dropped it on him and turned away.

For at least ten breaths, Ben couldn't do anything but stare at her in quiet shock that she dared to strike him. It hurt his pride more than his arm, though he clutched the latter as if the opposite were true. This was a first. What should he do?

"Miss Ramsey."

She stopped and turned to him.

"Do you want to be thrown into prison?" he asked.

"Oh, yes, Your *Majesty*, who doesn't want to be thrown into prison?"

He gave her an admonishing look laced with humor. She had a saucy spirit and a viperous tongue. She—his gaze dipped to her stockinged feet.

"You shouldn't be walking." Before he had time to think about what he was doing, he leaped out of the settee and scooped her up off the floor.

He made the mistake of looking down, so close to her face, her eyes. She was staring up at him with a dreamy look.

"Did you… Did you carry me to your bedroom yesterday?"

"It's not my bedchamber," he answered. "But yes."

She began to smile and he was glad when she caught herself

and pushed against him. "I'm fine. Put me down."

"No walking, Miss Ramsey," he said sternly, carrying her back to bed.

"I walked all the way here on these same feet, Your Grace."

"I know." He hadn't set her down but stared steadily into her eyes. "What in the world was so bad that you had to run so far from it? Were you running from *him*? The man you were praying about in the garden?"

Her eyes seemed to grow rounder, more fearful. Ben found himself hating the man who frightened her so. "Why is he after you?"

"It's better if you don't get involved."

"I involved myself when I took you in," he told her, then asked his question again.

"I have something of his," she answered.

"Did you steal it from him?" And what if she did? Would his rigid code demand that he toss her on the street?

She shook her head against his chest. "He wasn't there and then...and then he was. He had a pocket watch in his hand. I called the police and when they came he grabbed me from behind and held a sword to my throat, threatening to kill me. He did something with the watch. I don't know how, but one minute I was near my alley on 46th Street and 9th, and the next, I was here in 1718. I think he followed me. In fact, I'm pretty sure he did."

What was she saying, Ben wondered as he bent with her to the bed. "Where did he take you from?"

"The twenty-first century."

A man wasn't there and then he was? A pocket watch with the power to send her back in time? It was madness.

"You almost make me believe you can protect me from this," her voice was low against his ear while he set her down on the mattress.

He'd be a fool to involve himself with her further. She obviously wasn't right in the head.

He stared into her eyes, calming the turbulent seas within

her. "What makes you think I can't?"

The faintest hint of a smile played around her coral lips but then she looked away. "Your confidence can be dangerous for you."

"Let me worry about myself." He stepped away, already feeling the emptiness of not having her in his arms.

"Why don't you sit?" she invited like a fiery temptress too irresistible to ignore. "Share a word with me. I'm lonely."

He backed up and fell into the chair close to the bed as if he had no power to stop himself. He didn't.

She laughed and tossed back her head. "You believe my story just like that. Do you like me or something, Your Grace?" She stopped to cast him a curious smile, and then rattled him senseless when she winked. "Would you try to protect me from something you don't even understand?"

Would he? He blinked. Why was he hesitating? He wanted to tell her of course not. He wasn't a mad fool, putting his life in danger for someone he didn't know, but when he opened his mouth to tell her, his tongue deceived him.

"What does my understanding of it or not have to do with anything? If you're in danger, I can protect you."

"I'm not helpless."

"I disagree."

She frowned at him with suspicion narrowing her eyes. "Who made you my protector?"

"You did when you fainted in my arms in my garden and when you made yourself ill by eating my food." *And the first time I looked at you and every time after that.* He clenched his jaw. Was this his voice he was hearing in his head? This odd little prickling feeling he felt when he wasn't around her was both curious and alarming. His feet brought him to her even while his head was commanding him not to go.

Even now, commanding his eyes to shift away to something other than her did him no good. He took in every nuance of her myriad of facial expressions. Her hair, with its waist-length coppery curls lent to her enchanting appearance. Her peach-colored lips tempted him to lean forward and steal a kiss. But he was no thief. He told his traitorous feet and legs to move, leave the chair, the room, and her. But he remained where he sat.

"You're a nice guy in a cold, aloof sort of way."

He tilted his head at her, wondering if she just complimented him.

The door to the bedroom burst open and Prudence strode inside. She stopped when she saw him sitting by the bed. Her face turned red and Ben was reminded of a bull about to attack. His facial expression didn't change as he pulled his gaze from Miss Ramsey and set it on her.

"What are you doing here, Benjamin?" she asked in a trembling voice. Her scornful gaze flicked to Miss Ramsey. "With this…this creature from the streets?"

Did he even want to argue with her? Wasn't it better to shout for Stephen and have her removed?

"What are you trying to prove by spending time with her?" her venomous tongue continued. "Are you doing this to spite me because I want you to fulfill Father's wishes to marry into a family that will expand your lands and your power? You constantly rebel against me by not attending any marriage balls and by refusing the dowries of the most elite nobles. You don't give a whit about the interest the king's own niece has in you! Why? Do you mean to tell me you've been waiting all this time for a pauper?"

He could have replied with a hundred different things, but he looked to Miss Ramsey and found her smiling with her chin to her chest. She glanced at him, her amusement clear in her eyes. When he smiled back, she giggled silently and looked away.

"What's this?" Prudence stared at him in horror watching him smile at his guest. "Oh! Oh, I think I'm going to faint!"

"Prudence," he said calmly. "Gather your wits and see yourself out, since you came here to do nothing but insult her."

"Benjamin—"

"When you can behave like the gentry you represent, you may return."

When she opened her mouth to refute him, he rose from his chair as if to escort her out. She snapped her mouth shut and hurried out.

Alone with her again, Ben turned to Miss Ramsey, who was staring at him as if he just dissolved all the worries in her world. He had the insane urge to smile back. This time, he didn't.

"Have you eaten?"

Still smiling, she shook her head.

"I won't have you starve under my roof," he said gruffly and strode to the door without looking back. He wanted to look back. But he didn't.

"PRUDENCE TOLD ME that you and Miss Ramsey were laughing at her," the Earl of Sudbury said over a cup of wine in Ben's private parlor. "You know how she exaggerates. I don't believe it. You don't laugh often, and especially not with women you hardly know."

"We mostly just smiled," Ben let him know. He'd left Miss Ramsey's food to Edith when Sudbury requested a word with him.

"You…smiled? With Miss Ramsey?" Sudbury asked, sounding as stunned as he looked.

Ben nodded. Memories invaded his thoughts of her covert amusement and silent giggles at a time when a dozen other women would have wept or snapped back at his sister. She giggled, vanquishing the sting of Prudence's words, and by doing so, she made him smile too.

"Don't make more of it than what it was, Sudbury," Ben told him with a scowl that had little to do with what he said, and more with how he felt saying it. "She found humor in my sister's barbs, and that pleased me."

"Where are you going?" Sudbury asked, looking up from his chair when Ben rose to his feet.

"I told Edith to feed her. I want to make certain she followed my orders."

Sudbury rose and eyed him with a knowing smirk. "You rush to see to a servant?"

Ben clenched his jaw instead of answering. What was he to say? That even while he was denying her, he couldn't keep his feet from hurrying to her? He didn't want any women to get attached to him since his goal was to return to the battlefield. He might not live beyond his thirtieth year. He didn't want to leave behind a widow and possible children. But even feeling the pull of his dream of fighting, he couldn't help his desire to see her again.

"What about your rule?" his friend asked.

Sudbury was the only one who knew the true reason Ben refused to take a wife. He never breathed a word to Prudence. If she knew her brother planned on returning to the battlefield she'd never get over it, and she'd make his life a living hell trying to stop him.

"What about it?" Ben raised his brow at him. "I don't plan on taking Miss Ramsey as my wife."

"Your bed then."

Ben glared at him. They had known each other since they were boys of eight, when their fathers were friends. He'd been visiting Sudbury when he learned of his parents' murder by the Jacobites. They'd remained friends and even fought side by side on the battlefield. Sudbury was his closest friend, but Ben didn't want to discuss Miss Ramsey with him anymore. "That's not your concern, brother."

Sudbury smiled and held up his palms. He walked off without another word, and for a moment, Ben spared him another thought—one of appreciation for always knowing when to quit. Then he turned and went the other way.

"Your Grace, there you are!" his steward called out and hurried down the stairs to reach him. "Lady Prudence is turning my hair white, and not just me but the cooks, and all the servants on the estate with her extravagant plans for a ball here. Sir, have you allowed it?"

Ben nodded.

"Well then, thanks to you, I'm about to pack up and leave for Scotland to escape her."

"Where is she now?"

"In the kitchen, ordering the cooks to prepare an array of dishes and delicacies that will surely use up half of Your Grace's wealth."

Changing course, Ben led the way to the kitchen. He found his sister where Stephen said she'd be, ordering the cooks to gather her list of needed ingredients.

"Prudence?" he interrupted her, straightening his spine and squaring his shoulders. "I'll look over and approve everything you're planning from now on."

"Your Grace," she said with a pleasant smile in the presence of servants, "I wouldn't dream of burdening you with such trivial matters. I know how busy you are in your charity work for the less fortunate."

He knew she was trying to engage him in one of her little battles. Perhaps they were battles that, like his own, she needed. Today though, he wasn't willing to engage.

He set his hard gaze on the head cook. "Not a thing will be purchased, hunted, or traded on her list unless it bears my seal. Understood?"

"What do you mean?" she practically screeched. "You have no idea what it costs to host a ball, Benjamin!"

"Prudence," he said in a low voice. "If you insist on spending every pence I have, you'll add Sudbury to the list of eligible bachelors. Since he is one.

She went pale. He knew she had her own eyes on his unfortunate best friend. After shooting him a murderous glare, she stormed off.

"Thank you, Sir," Stephen said reverently.

Ben held his wrists behind his back and stared at his steward. "Next time, do as she says and don't involve me."

Stephen nodded obediently but looked as if he wanted to say more.

"You take each of her demands and decide which are feasible and which are not." At the last, he motioned casting things away over his shoulder.

This time when Stephen nodded, he smiled.

Ben was led away next by Lieutenant Frenton of his private army. Frenton fought alongside Ben at the Battle of Blenheim in Germany. "I've returned from scouting the surrounding towns and burghs. No one recalls a woman running or hiding from any man, but..." He quirked his mouth and shook his head.

"But? Tell me."

"I went as far as Ipswich," the lieutenant continued. "A few folks in Belstead claimed to have witnessed a woman appearing before their eyes."

He wasn't there...and then he was. Ben remembered Miss Ramsey's story.

"She asked them where she was, and..." Frenton paused to laugh. "...what year they were in."

"What year?" Ben asked, trying not to sound as if he was more familiar with this matter.

"They didn't have a chance to question her further because she became hysterical and ran off. An instant later they claim a man appeared out of nowhere and demanded to know which way she went. They gave him the wrong direction, and then they too ran off." The lieutenant gave him a sheepish smile. "I didn't think it credible, and didn't know if I should waste your time telling you."

"Yes," Ben agreed. *So then,* he thought, *her outlandish tale had witnesses. And the man chasing her is here.* "It's ridiculous for certain. Good work, Lieutenant. Keep it up."

"Yes, Your Grace."

"Frenton," he called, stopping him as another question came to him. "Did you get a description of them: the woman and the man?"

Frenton gave him a surprised look. "I didn't believe the story, so I didn't—"

"You're quite right," Ben told him.

"There's one thing," the lieutenant said after he thought about it. "She had red hair. They said the woman had hair like flames flickering around her face in the wavy air." The lieutenant laughed. "It's quite a tale."

Yes, Ben thought, it was. "I wonder why tell it if it wasn't true?"

Frenton sobered, then shrugged.

They parted and Ben set his course toward the guest room. He had to re-route twice more to settle a dispute between two landowners. He'd had the fleeting thought of strangling them both when they stubbornly refused to settle their disagreement. But he left them both alive when he departed his receiving room a short while later-the dispute settled. Nathan, one of the stable hands, caught up with him next.

"Your Grace! The black mare has delivered! The foal is well and resembles its mother!"

The black mare was one of Ben's favorite horses. All the stablehands knew he favored her and they all looked after her well. He was happy the mare and her foal were alright.

"Kevin and Peter are waiting for you now to come greet the newest foal, Sir."

Ben turned to give the stairs a solemn look over his shoulder then followed Nathan out of the house.

By the time he set his feet to his course again, supper was approaching. Had Edith served Miss Ramsey yet? How could her story could be real? She'd said a man appeared out of nowhere and with the aid of a pocket watch, brought her back to 1718 to escape the police. It was mad and Ben was mad for considering it.

Hair like flames flickering around her face.

It was her. It was her. He shook his head. It was too fantastical. People traveling through time? No. But... the woman in Ipswich matched her description.

He reached the door to her room and stared at it. What was this enchantment with her that he'd fallen under? Was his life so pitiful that he would find such amusement with a woman who was out of her mind?

Or was she?

The sound of male laughter seeped through the door and pricked Ben's ears. He knew that laughter. He pushed open the door and gave his best friend, sitting on the chair across from her, a dark scowl.

CHAPTER FOUR

THE EARL OF Sudbury was very informative. Once Fable learned that he was the sulky duke's closest friend, she set about finding out what she could about Benjamin West. There wasn't much else to do. Her afternoon was turning out to be pleasant though. So far, Lord Sudbury had told her that the captain once killed eighteen men without any help. Some high-ranking guy called Captain General Marlborough sent him to infiltrate enemy ranks and thanks to Ben, in the end, the king's army won a decisive victory.

"He's the king's favorite," Lord Sudbury told her, sitting in a chair across from where she sat on the settee. His eyes shone with sincerity, his smile wide with each word he spoke. It was evident that he felt very strongly about his friend. There was no trace of jealousy in his words, his voice, or his smile. From the moment she had asked about the duke, he gladly boasted about him.

"He has never lost in battle—or a game of chess. Do you play, Miss?"

She smiled and looked down. "A little. Tell me," she said, lifting her gaze to his again. "Lady Prudence mentioned marriage balls." In truth, this was the real reason she'd agreed to speak to him. Maybe Edith could have shed some light upon the matter, but the duke's friend would have insight Edith didn't.

"Yes," Lord Sudbury said, smiling and waiting for what she said next. "She's hosting one here in a few days."

Hmm, Fable wondered if the king's niece would be here. "Is it something like speed dating to music?"

The handsome earl's smile didn't falter despite looking a little lost. "Speed dating?"

"A ball to meet your wife?"

His dark eyes warmed on her. "Not mine. The duke's."

"Just…the duke's?" She didn't want to ask, but she needed to know.

"Yes," the earl told her. "His sister is determined to wed him off to the daughter of a prestigious family—hopefully a royal one."

Fable almost choked on the air she took in. It wasn't that she thought she had any chance with the dispassionate duke, but he'd been nice to her—and generous. She was grateful and felt the urge, as he did for her, to protect him. "So by next week, he could be betrothed to the king's niece?"

"He could be—"

"Has he met her?" What if she was beautiful and elegant and everything he liked in a woman? Fable's belly knotted. It worried her. Was she going to be sick again? Why? This time she hadn't gorged on food.

"Yes, he's met her. Twice, I believe."

Fable held her breath. The niece of a king definitely wouldn't want her husband to be friendly with a pauper. So what? There was no reason why she should feel sweaty, like she had when her fever broke. Was she still ill, or did talking about the duke make her feel bad? No, it wasn't thoughts of him that made her feel bad, it was thoughts of him getting married, of losing his protection, his roof, and his food.

What does my understanding of it or not have to do with anything? If you're in danger, I can protect you.

Who in her life *ever* promised to protect her? And so unconditionally? There was no one. How could she not be attracted to such a man?

"Does he like her?" she asked the earl quietly.

"The duke has no interest in her."

Relief swept through Fable and made her question her rationality. "But he'd marry her because his sister wants him to?" What did she care, really? She laughed at herself silently. She didn't even know the duke. She certainly didn't have a prestigious family.

"It's what his father wanted," the informative earl told her. "But, in the end, I don't believe he'll ever marry. As for his sister, she wants what she thinks will make him happy."

"She's wretched."

"She loves him," he defended.

"You know," she said, trying to ignore the pain in her feet. "I'm no expert on it but I think if you love someone, you want what they want. Does he not have enough wealth to live a comfortable life until he's old?"

"He has enough."

"Will it be taken from him if he doesn't do what his father wanted?"

"Not all of it and not enough for him to care," the earl told her.

"I see. Then, is he lacking in power? He's a duke, that's pretty powerful, isn't it?"

"Yes."

"Is he always so serious and melancholy because he's lonely and wants a wife?"

His responses had grown quieter with each one. Now, he practically whispered, as if he knew where her questions were leading and he couldn't do much but answer truthfully. "No."

"Then, when it really comes down to it, the duke's marriage and who becomes his wife is for Lady Prudence's benefit, and not her brother's."

His smile slowly widened on her, but he didn't say anything.

"Has anyone even asked him what would make him happy?" she demanded, then cleared her throat and smiled repentantly.

"Three years ago, while saving the king's life from a Jacobite attack, Colchester almost lost his arm." Lord Sudbury sighed and stretched out his long legs in his chair. "The thing that will make him happy is to return to the battlefield. He practices every day in the hopes of returning."

The battlefield? Fable thought, suddenly feeling even more anxious about the duke leaving. She needed him...and there was something more...something that made her heart feel too heavy to beat, that made her very curious and a little jealous.

"Don't worry," the handsome earl reassured her as if reading her thoughts. "King George won't let him fight."

"Then his hopes are for nothing."

The earl stared at her for a moment, and then with his smile fading, he nodded. "You're correct."

"He deserves more," she said.

"Yes. He does."

Fable liked the duke's closest friend.

"What about you?" she asked him. She'd been surprised when, after she'd washed her hair, Edith told her the earl was in the sitting parlor outside her bedroom door, waiting to pay her a visit. Her feet still stung but were otherwise healing nicely. She was able to walk to the other room on her own. When she first saw the earl, she was surprised at how tall he was and how small the room appeared with him in it. He wore his dark chestnut hair slicked back from his handsome face. His nose was sharp and his lips, full and red, as if he'd just polished off a basket of strawberries.

"I fought alongside the duke for many years, but these days have been peaceful, so I hunt, travel back and forth between here and Sudbury, and lose to my friend at chess."

"Is Sudbury far?"

He gave her a curious look, and she guessed she was supposed to know where Sudbury was. Then shook his head.

"Why don't you just live there, if it's where you're from?" she asked.

"There's a lady here that I enjoy spending time with." He

smiled and his eyes danced, gleaming from within. There was something different between him and the duke. Lord Sudbury was more open, more cordial, easy-going and warm.

The door opened. Fable turned to see the duke and her first thought was that Lord Sudbury might be friendlier, but he wasn't *him*.

For a second he did nothing to hide the fact that he didn't like them alone together. Dark brows dipped low over his eyes, lips drawn tight and closer to a snarl than a smile. But after expelling a deep puff of breath, he quickly pulled himself together and strode into the room.

"You should be in bed," he said, coming to stand over her.

"It's better that I'm sitting, isn't it?" she asked, looking up and then watching as he sat beside her on the settee. "Or am I expected to greet guests in bed?"

"You're correct," he quickly conceded. "Forgive me."

In his seat, the earl stared slack-jawed at his friend.

Fable's breath felt warm going through her and made her heart flutter. The duke was close. Close enough to stare into his eyes and see the soul of a brooding warrior, leashed by an unhappy knight in shining armor. He turned those dark eyes on his friend across from him. "I wasn't expecting to see you here."

"I came to see you actually," Lord Sudbury told him, his smile quickly restored, appearing even warmer than before. "When you weren't here, I thought I would stay for a bit and get to know your guest. But she cleverly avoided speaking about herself by asking an endless array of questions about you."

Fable's heart went still. Why would the earl say something like that? And he was still smiling! And...did he just wink at her? There was no time to react to that. From the corner of her eye, she saw the seemingly possessive duke facing her. Oh, she could scratch Lord Sudbury's eyes out. Reluctantly, she turned to the duke, her cheeks on fire. She didn't say anything. What was there to say?

He didn't say anything either—and yet, his dark, expressive

gaze seemed to say much, like, *don't be embarrassed. I don't mind.*

She heard Lord Sudbury stand from his chair and the duke broke eye contact with her and looked up, then stood with his friend.

"I'll walk you out," he offered, though Lord Sudbury didn't mention leaving.

After a flowery farewell, the earl left with Duke Colchester speaking softly as they went.

When the duke returned, he went to her and without a word, slipped his arms under her and lifted her off the settee and into his arms.

"What are you doing?" she asked, feeling surprisingly light in the cradle of arms.

"Putting you back in bed." His voice was deep like an ocean, seeping into her flesh.

"I'm fine, Your Grace." She didn't know what to think. No one had ever concerned themselves with her care. Why would he? *Because*, she answered herself, *he doesn't know what you are.*

He stepped into the bedroom, his gaze steady ahead, his voice softer, huskier, but marked with command. "When we're alone, you'll call me Ben."

"That's very casual of you," she remarked lightly, neither agreeing to it, nor disagreeing. One of the million other reasons she didn't have a boyfriend was because they were all jerks who thought she was put on this earth to please them and do what she was told. They were wrong.

"You've been in my arms since I've known you," he pointed out, neither scowling nor smiling, making her heart flip. "Formality when we're alone is no longer genuine."

"So, you value honesty," she said, more seriously.

He looked down at her and nodded as he set her on the bed. Too bad, she thought. He was too straight and narrow to accept what she was. An illiterate street urchin, as the duke's sister had called her. Not a thief as Edith suspected, but a reformed hustler. There was a difference.

"Why did your face turn glum?" he asked, pulling up a chair and sitting close.

"I was just thinking of my life before."

"Was it a difficult life?"

She shrugged her shoulders. She'd never complained about it before. What good would it have done?

"I'd had hope of finding a job, saving up and getting my own place. But no one would hire a homeless illiterate who couldn't even sign her name." She glanced at him to see his reaction. If he was going to throw her out, she'd rather he do it now, before she grew to like him too much.

"Where were your parents?" he asked, leaning in closer.

She told him about being abandoned by her father and about her mother who raised her on the crowded streets of New York City.

"You never had a home?"

Fable didn't like the pity she saw in his eyes. "I was okay. I didn't miss what I never had." Of course, she would have loved a warm bed and a hot meal but she'd rather lie to him than have him look at her this way. "It's okay, really. I'm used to being alone. In a way it's easier. You don't learn to depend on anyone, so no one can let you down."

She watched his Adam's apple dance along his neck as he swallowed. "Not everyone will let you down," he answered coolly, but Fable heard traces of something warm.

Edith arrived soon after with Fable's dinner. When she saw the duke there, she hurried to bring him food, as well.

"This is the second time I've eaten with you," Fable told him, feeling an unfamiliar warmth rise from her belly and heat her face. The first time, he hadn't eaten with her, but he was there. He'd fed her.

"Does how many times we eat together mean something?"

"Well, yes," she told him, surprised that he looked so innocent right now. "Not for us in the same way, but...now then, haven't you ever had a girlfriend?"

He blinked his beautiful, obsidian eyes. "A what?"

"A woman in your life? Someone who meant a lot to you?"

He shook his head. "I've been on the battlefield since I was sixteen. Before that, I fought on the streets to live. I never had time for a serious union."

What did that mean *he fought on the streets to live*? Why hadn't she asked the earl more about his friend's past?

And honestly, he never had a serious 'union'? Fable could hardly believe it. Why, the more her eyes took in the sight of him, the kinder he was to her, the more magnificently beautiful he became. What a pity.

"Why did you spend your life in battle," she asked him in a quiet, curious voice, "risking yourself for so many years?"

"I had to," he told her, in his low, steady voice. "One way or another, I would have killed others around me, possibly myself. Battle saved me."

She stopped eating and stared at him. What did that mean? And why did it make her want to cry for a week? What had made him want to kill?

"Are you okay now?"

He looked up from his tray of food. He wasn't smiling, but something pleasant and pleasing covered him like a veil. He nodded, and then tilted his head doubtfully. "I assume by okay, you mean well or good? If so, then yes, I'm well."

"Good," she said and went on eating.

She was certain he smiled, but it was gone too quickly.

"You said eating together meant something, but not for us," he reminded her. "What did you mean by that?"

"Well, because I'm not your girlfriend and because that's not why I brought it up. I just meant it was the second time I've eaten with anyone besides my mother."

He put his spoon down. "Do you mean to tell me that not only did you never have a home, or a bed, but you were alone your whole life but for your mother? You didn't even share a meal with anyone?" He blew out a deep breath and almost groaned looking at her.

"Duke—Ben. I won't tell you anything else if you continue to pity me. It's just my life. Everyone has one, and none are good all the time. Not yours, and not mine. It's just the way things are. We deal, you know?"

He didn't answer but she felt his eyes on her while she ate.

"I'll teach you to read," he said, breaking his silence.

She stopped eating and looked up.

"I'll teach you everything I know if you wish," he promised, breaking eye contact with her, looking a little bit awkward to her untrained eye.

She couldn't help but smile. He'd already done much to help her. Would he really teach her to read? But wait, didn't she have to serve him? "What do I have to do for you?"

"Hmm?" he asked, biting off a piece of bread.

"As your servant?"

He looked a little lost as to what her duties would entail. Fable watched him think about it and chew. She liked how he chewed. He had a strong, squared jawline and good teeth—another thing most homeless guys were lacking.

"You will wake me in the morning—"

She smiled.

—and bring me my breakfast."

Her smile faltered, then faded.

"Very well then, Helen can continue to bring it to me."

Helen? "Who's Helen?"

"One of the servants."

Fable wanted to ask him if this Helen was young or old. Was she pretty? What did she care? The duke was just a guy who helped her. She had to get back to the future, or wake up from the coma she'd fallen into in 2024. Why? Why did she have to? What was waiting for her there? Not even a bed. At least here, she had a bed and food. But here was the eighteenth century. She didn't belong here. She certainly couldn't let herself get attached to a guy who was good enough to possibly marry the king's niece, and she couldn't slow down because a sword-wielding maniac was after her.

"You'll stay by my side and be there if I need anything. You'll eat with me every day," he continued when she didn't protest.

Fable considered that this didn't sound so bad. Temporarily. She basically had to stick around him. Who'd complain about that? "Anything else?"

He thought about it for a moment then shook his head. "Perhaps later I'll think of more."

"What about your sister?"

"Once she understands there's nothing between us, she'll back off."

Nothing between us. He was right, of course. When she mentioned to him that she wasn't his girlfriend, it made her think of it as a crazy possibility. No. She was confusing gratitude with some other affection. She almost laughed at herself. She wasn't a fool. She wouldn't become one now. She'd take what he was offering then leave. Even if she didn't find a way back, she'd leave the Duke of Colchester the way she'd found him. She wouldn't take anything from him. He'd been too kind to her. Besides, she was trying to live a more honest life. It didn't matter which century she was in. If she made it back to Ipswich alive, she'd try to figure out a way to use the pocket watch and get back to her century. If she couldn't, she'd sell it and live on her own, depending only on herself, just as she'd been taught. She wouldn't ruin her good mood by thinking about the man searching for her from the future.

"Okay then, when do you want to begin teaching me?" she asked him enthusiastically.

"I'll have one of the rooms prepared for tomorrow."

She wanted to smile, to be happy about finally learning how to read. She tried to teach herself many times, but hunger often ruled, safety after that. She'd just never gotten to it. Now, she finally found someone to teach her. But it was going to take weeks, maybe months.

"Today..." he leaned forward just a little. Just enough for her eyes to open wider, thinking he might kiss her. He didn't, but excitement danced across his eyes and lifted one brow with beguiling playfulness. He made her forget running. "...I'll teach you a game."

She felt like smiling—no. She felt like giggling. It wasn't anything he said, though playing a game did sound like fun, it was more that spark of fire in his eyes that she hadn't seen in him before. Oh, she didn't mind him stoic and serious. He was like a statue called *The Epitome of Man*, but did he really possess a playful side? She wanted to find out.

Fable heard the outer door shut next and wondered where he was off to. She found herself feeling happy. Her face even hurt a little from smiling so much. What was it all about? Was the duke the reason? She hadn't smiled this much in the last five years. She thought of how she'd even giggled at Lady Prudence's slew of insults. She wondered if she was going nuts. What was funny about an evil villainess' foul mouth? But the duke had smiled when she found his sister humorous. And oh, it awakened thousands of butterflies in her belly and chest. If gracing her with a rare smile wasn't enough, he'd protected her from those hurtful words.

When you can behave like the gentry you represent, you may return.

Fable had worried about what he would think of her when he discovered she was exactly what his sister had called her. But it didn't seem to bother him at all. He hadn't insulted her once.

So what? He was thoughtful and handsome. It didn't mean anything. She couldn't fall for him.

She lost her heart to a guy once. Eddie had been more like a boy at seventeen who wanted a mother more than a girlfriend. Fable didn't know how to be either, so he went searching elsewhere and left her at a shelter. She lied about her age so the shelter didn't call the authorities and left with nothing but the clothes on her back. Staying still got you caught and taken away. It was the lesson her mother had drilled into her the most—and she'd learned it well. She'd stopped running when she was no longer a minor. This time, though, she wasn't hiding from authorities. Could she avoid the man chasing her? Maybe lay low here for a while, but not for too long.

Her ears perked to the sound of the door outside the bedroom. She patted her hair and wrestled to pull her finger, or more like her broken fingernail out of her tangled curls when it got stuck.

When the short battle was over, she looked up to see the duke watching her. He let out an incredulous snort and moved toward the bed.

Carrying an empty tray, Edith had entered the room with him and when she saw Fable's struggle, she hurried to a table and plucked up a comb. After setting the tray down on the bed over Fable's lap, the servant began to comb Fable's hair.

"This is Chess," the duke told her, setting a polished wooden box on the bed. "Have you heard of it?"

"Of course. I'm from the future, not another planet."

Above her, Edith listened, then tsked pitifully while she combed.

The duke opened the box and removed a hinged, wooden chess board with 64 squares of oak and onyx.

Fable never had anyone comb her hair before, but she was distracted from that pleasure by another: the sight of his long, broad fingers while they spread the board open on the tray. What were his hands capable of?

"Choose your color," his voice seeped into her pores like a mist.

"Which one is better?"

He sat in the chair by her bed, moved in closer, and set his doubtful gaze straight on her. "You don't know?"

The deep cadence of his voice held the power to entrance her so that she couldn't look away from him. She managed to shake her head.

He gave her a flinty snarl. "It doesn't matter. No color is

better than the other."

She chose the shiny onyx and waited while he set up the board with their pieces. "By the way," she said with a hooded gaze as Edith's comb stroked her as if she were a cat. She felt like purring, "this isn't what I was thinking of when you said we'd play a game."

"Chess is a game," he said, sounding a little breathless. She opened her eyes and saw him staring at her.

"Yes, but it's not like…a fun game."

His fingers paused, setting down a carved oak king.

"Alright! Alright!" She waved her hands in front of her, erasing what she said. "Teach me what you know."

He set down the last piece and looked up as a handful of her hair fell over her shoulder. Edith's comb had done little to tame the long, loose coils tumbling onto the board. Fable smiled coyly and brushed it over her back and out of the way.

The duke blinked, seeming to breathe again, then began to explain parts of the game. She asked questions and let him explain every move they made. Twice, she suppressed a yawn.

"Your knight is your most important piece, protecting the most valuable, the king. They all move differently. Do you want to go over it again?"

She shook her head. "So, your pawn can jump over pieces?"

"No," he told her patiently, and explained it all again. "Only your knight can jump."

"Right. Right." She smiled and cracked her knuckles. "Okay, let's play."

Edith finished untangling her hair and per Fable's request, left it hanging loose, not altogether curly, nor altogether straight, just a handful of soft spirals amidst gentle waves falling beyond the board and the tray on her lap. If nothing else, she had pretty hair. Her mother had even thought so and made her wear it in a braid or ponytail not to draw attention to it. Especially the attention of men. But Fable learned as she had grown older, the best way to hustle someone, especially a man was to distract him. Her best tool was her hair. She glanced at the board and moved first and quickly, smiling at Edith when the older woman promised to return soon.

"Miss Ramsey, pay attention to what you're doing," the duke scolded, moving his pawn.

She nodded, liking the sound of him when he was so serious, and in six more moves captured his bishop. He was too stunned to move on his turn. He stared at her, seeming to look through her, as if trying to figure her out. He came to a conclusion that curled his lip in a sneer, and then he returned his attention to the board and positioned his knight to take her.

She knew it was coming. It made her heart accelerate. It seemed he'd been going easy on her, but he was through with that. She wiped her brow. He was clever and dangerous, and it made her want to smile at him. He'd survive on the streets of New York.

She ran her fingers down her hair and coiled a strand around her finger, then held it up to examine it.

He reached for his cup and took a drink while she moved her bishop.

While she waited for him to move, she picked up his captured bishop and rubbed it against her fingers.

"Miss Ramsey, can you remain still?"

"Oh!" She opened her eyes wider. "Am I distracting you?"

"Yes, and why did you tell me you never played chess before?"

"I never told you that," she corrected him, studying the board. "I was having a little fun with you. Is that a crime?"

He didn't answer but in four swift moves, set up her king to be checked in his next move.

What? No! She had thought she had him. She had played this game hundreds of times. Old Hank the Shark had taught her. He liked her mother and let them sleep on his old couch for two months until her mother robbed him and he threw them out. But Fable had learned his game, and she'd learned it well. By the time she was ten, she was unbeatable on the streets.

How did the duke beat her? Lord Sudbury had told her the duke never lost a game. She'd been sure she could beat him. He'd obviously distracted her while she thought she was distracting him. Or maybe he was immune to her wiles. Well, she could be immune to his, as well.

When he tossed her a triumphant smirk before taking his winning move, she jerked her legs up, sending the chess board spilling into the duke's lap.

"Hmmph," she complained, making no apology for ruining his victory.

He remained seated with kings and rooks in his lap, his fingers clutching his beautiful wood and onyx board. It only took one look at him without her competitive temper, driven by fear of losing a prize, be it money, food, a place to sleep for her and her mother. Every game had a cost for losing. But today it didn't. She swallowed. "I'm sorry."

His stoic face transformed before her into a knowing grin accompanied by an almost silent chuckle she found thrilling to her ears.

"You're a sour loser."

"You mean a sore loser," she corrected with a chuckle. She stared at him and then inhaled deeply. "Why aren't you angry?"

"Who says I'm not angry? What should I do? Have you beaten? Throw you out?"

She shook her head. Her eyes grew rounder. "No. Please don't."

He shrugged his shoulders with a lackadaisical smirk. "Tell me why I shouldn't."

"Okay, but first tell me if you're planning on marrying the king's niece."

His smirk faded but when he set his gaze on her, it was anything but angry. "I'm not swayed by her title or her beauty,"

"Oh?" Fable asked quietly, tucking her hair behind her ear. She knew many people didn't like red hair. Was he one of them?

She hoped not. "Is she beautiful?"

"Yes, very," he answered. "But I'm not swayed by it."

She wanted to ask him what he was swayed by. But what if he said only a dark haired beauty could sway him? So she didn't ask.

"Tell me, Miss Ramsey," he said softly, "why shouldn't I throw you out for tossing my board around?"

There was no reason. He should throw her out. In fact, she wished he would. She foolishly had a crush on her rescuer, and she needed to be away from him before her crush became something more. But she smiled at him, and when she opened her mouth, it wasn't to tell him to toss her out. "Because I want to beat you at chess, Your Grace."

CHAPTER FIVE

BEN STOOD ON his terrace in his burgundy silk robes and looked out over the rolling hills illuminated under the pale, full moon. As was the case most nights, he couldn't sleep. But tonight he wasn't awake because of a haunting desire to fight. Tonight he was lost in thoughts of how Miss Ramsey won three games of chess against him. He'd won four, but she'd beaten him three times! She was clever and tactical. When one was raised on the street, they either became warriors or they died. He wasn't unfamiliar with the choices. She'd purposely distracted him with her hair, her eyes, her lips, her fingers, her skin, her breath…

He ran his fingers through his hair. What was she doing to him? He'd met plenty of women, thanks mostly to his meddlesome sister. The best bred, most beautiful, courtliest, most courteous women in the whole of Great Britain. And none of them had ever affected him the way the enchanting Miss Fable Ramsey did. No matter how hard he had tried, he often found himself staring at the way sunlight pooled in the cradle of one of her curls, igniting fires of coppery-gold and all the shades of autumn, and the way her slender fingers stroked the smooth wood of his chess pieces. He blew out a deep puff of air. He thought of her now. What was he to do about it? He couldn't run off to battle. His arm wasn't healed enough. Even so—and here was the worst part—would she haunt him on the battlefield? Even his trip to Ardleigh to see Lord Brambley was plagued with thoughts of the woman in his kitchen.

What was wrong with him? Should he just toss himself over the side of his terrace? He likely wouldn't even die. He had no idea what to do about her. She left him feeling completely out of control of his own thoughts and desires.

Is this what being fond of a woman did to a man? He didn't like it. He would put an end to it and as soon as she was well he'd send her on her way. Look what she was doing to him. He didn't mind spending time with her. It wasn't fair to her. Even if he didn't dream of returning to battle, did he truly want to ignore his father's wishes? Hell, why was he even letting his thoughts wander down that road with her? He had no intentions on becoming a husband—anyone's husband.

His head snapped to attention when there came a rapping on the outside door. He went to it and opened it quickly. Stephen stood on the side with Edith. Both of them were pale and their eyes were wide with concern.

"Forgive me, Your Grace," his steward said, "Edith found me and informed me that Miss Ramsey is having trouble in her sleep."

Ben hurried off without changing his night clothes. Her rooms weren't far from his and he reached them quickly. He heard her cries before he saw her.

"No! No! I…I can't!"

He rushed through the sitting room and reached her beside. "Miss Ramsey?" He kept his voice non threatening and steady. Judging by the way she was shaking and perspiring, she needed to wake up in calm, not fear. "It's Ben. You're safe. You're safe."

He sat beside her on the bed and instinctively reached for her. When she felt him near, she clung to him.

Without thinking—what was there to think about—he closed his arms around her. "Don't be afraid," he whispered into her hair as she trembled. Her soft whimper against his neck made his blood go warm. He held her closer. She didn't say his name but she woke up fully and began to cry.

He sat with her wrapped in an embrace he'd never offered to anyone before. Ignoring Edith's and Stephen's shocked expressions when they saw him, he dismissed them for the night. Whatever Miss Ramsey needed, he would provide.

They sat in the dim firelight of the hearth. He wouldn't push her away or force her to talk about her dreams. He was patient and quiet, an immovable rock, there to protect her, despite the alarms going off in his head to run. She wasn't for him. He didn't care. He'd seriously consider what was wrong with him tomorrow, when he had a clearer head. Tonight, with her in his arms, his head was somewhere lost in the clouds.

"I've been nothing but trouble since I got here." He heard her soft voice rising to his ears.

"That's true," he agreed, "though I don't know why you always bring it up. Are you testing me to find out how much trouble I'll take from you before I ask you to leave?"

"Maybe," she snapped back, breaking contact with him.

"What if I won't ask you to leave no matter how much trouble you cause?" he asked, still close enough to hear her breath.

"Why would you do that?"

"Because no one ever has before."

He didn't mean to bring tears to her eyes. He reached for her again. This time, he was afraid she would pull away, reject him. What if she did? He'd never been rejected by a woman before. He'd never been with any of them. She didn't move away but closed her eyes when his fingertips brushed over her teary cheeks.

"How do you know me so well already?" she sniffled.

"Parts of you are not difficult to understand," he told her, "It just takes an ear."

"A compassionate ear," she corrected.

He narrowed his eyes on her and warned playfully. "Shh, don't let word of my kind heart get around."

He caught her smile before she rested her head against his chest.

He closed his arms around her again and spoke softly into her hair. "My father used to say that if you want to forget your nightmares, you should tell someone about them."

"Why did he say that? Were you having nightmares about something?"

He scowled above her. This wasn't about him. He meant to help her by listening if she wanted to tell someone what made her so afraid while she slept. How did she turn it around on him so quickly?

She bent her head back to look at him, taking with her the light scent of flowers. "You must have been afraid of something for him to go around making up memorable quotes."

If she didn't beguile every one of his senses, it wouldn't have been so easy for her to vanquish his scowl and produce a smile in its place. He closed his eyes for a moment and shrugged a shoulder. "Everyone's afraid of something."

She didn't answer or respond in any way. Finally he looked down at her. She was waiting for more.

He exhaled. Should he speak of what frightened him? Why was he even considering it? Even Sudbury didn't know. "I don't usually speak of things like this with anyone."

"What if your father was right?" she suggested. "You would still be having nightmares. Are you?"

Strangely, he felt comforted here with her in his arms. "My fears have changed from when I was a child."

She returned her cheek to his chest, letting him continue in the silence.

"Now, I dream of my mother." He felt his heart swell up with deep emotion he hadn't released in a long, long time. He drew in a sharp inhalation, as if to keep it inside. "She and my father were killed seventeen years ago by Jacobites. My father, Richard West, was a lieutenant-colonel in the Royal Army and an enemy of the Stuart supporters. My parents were away at the time so I didn't witness their deaths but I dream of her dying. It happens in different ways each time, but she always dies, and there's never anything I can do to stop it. I dream of the Jacobite men I've killed to avenge her. But none of their lives brought her back." He stopped and wiped a tear before it fell into her hair. "I couldn't protect her."

The woman clinging to him remained silent but her embrace tightened.

Again, a wave of warmth coursed through him, misting his eyes, though he kept them closed. He wondered if he'd ever stopped like this and just pondered everything. He realized he hadn't. "What about you?"

"In my dreams," she began quietly. "I'm running from something, someone—it's always different. That's all my nightmares are about. Me running. I understand that the dreams have to do with insecurity. I've never been safe in my life. My mother was a vagrant and most nights we slept in dark alleys, places no normal person would want to be. So sure, as a kid I dreamed of running from monsters. But now, something different is coming after me."

"Maybe now it's time to stop running," he told her. "If whatever it is finds you, I'll help you do away with it."

She sat back, out of his arms and stared at him. "That someone chasing me is real and he has a sword."

"I have a sword too," he let her know with a gentle smirk. "I'll help you no matter what it is, Miss Ramsey."

"You want to protect me because you couldn't protect her...your mother," she said softly, understanding him a little better.

"Why does it matter?"

"Well, because..." Because it proved he wasn't protective of her because he liked her. It was from a sense of failure to protect his mother. "I guess it doesn't matter," she said and fell into his embrace again.

"I've been fighting for a long time," he told her. "I know there are those who can't fight to save their lives. That's who I protect. It may have begun because of my mother, but it's filled me, branching out like a summer tree into every part of me. I fight to protect the king, who should have the people's interest at heart. But all that protection is obscure." While he spoke, he wondered if she could feel his heart beating fast and hard against her body. "With you it's different. The first time you fell into my arms you begged me not to hurt you. That's when I decided I would protect you."

"I don't want you to be responsible for me," she said into his nightshirt, and then pulled back. "I really can take care of myself."

"My lady—"

"Call me Fable."

He dipped his brow. "An odd name." Like her.

"My mother read somewhere that fable means a legendary story of supernatural happenings like animals speaking and acting like human beings. I grew up spending much of my time in my own fantasy world of pretending I could communicate with animals." She laughed softly, rendering him senseless. "I was a silly child."

"Duke," she whispered after a moment, "all your talk of protection tempts me to depend on you. That will make me lazy and slow, and..."

"And?" he urged in the dim light.

"And it would break my heart when we parted." When he opened his mouth to speak, she cut him off. "If there's one thing I've learned in my life, it's that nothing is permanent."

It would break her heart when they parted? Why? The food, he guessed. But was there more? It didn't matter if there was more. He thought of his father. He didn't reply but let her go and rose from the bed. It was time he left her room before rumors started against her. "You're well," he said, motioning her to lay back down. When she did, he covered her with her blankets and let his gaze linger on her for a few extra breaths. "I'll be going."

"Ben?" she called out as he headed for the door. He stopped and turned to her. "Chess tomorrow?"

"No," he told her. "Something more *fun*."

He paused once more before he left. "Fable?"

She rose up on her elbows. "Yes?"

He pointed to himself, though he was sure it was too dark for her to see it. "Me. I'm permanent."

He returned to his bed and dreamed of a fiery haired woman running into his arms.

BEN REMAINED STILL while his servants helped him into knee breeches and Enis dressed him in a silk suit with gold thread buttons and a dark green velvet coat. He slipped his feet into his square-toed shoes and headed for the door.

"Your Grace," Enis called out, "your cravat."

"I'll find Stephen to tie one of his elaborate knots."

He didn't wear a periwig nor did he color his face. Running his fingers through his natural hair, he thought he looked pleasing enough. Enough for who? Her?

He thought about how she'd just swooped down into his life bringing a little ray of light and warmth with her. He'd easily opened up to her. They shared their lives with each other as if they'd been waiting all their lives to do so. He thought about how she made him want to smile. He wasn't even sure he remembered how. How was she breaking down walls it had taken him almost two decades to build? Besides, she was a Ramsey. She could be a Jacobite spy—if she was a spy he'd have to admire how good she was at it—before he killed her.

Could he kill her?

He stepped out of his rooms and spotted a little kitten racing by him. The kitten was followed by Miss Ramsey hot on its heels.

With her gaze fixed on the feline, she ran straight into Ben's arms. He closed them around her and gazed into her eyes.

"You're making a habit of this, Miss Ramsey."

"Just keeping you on your toes, Your Grace," she replied with a bright smile to start his day.

"Looking for this?" Sudbury appeared at the top of the stairs carrying the kitten in one hand.

With a squeak of joy and a little jump that left Ben's bones trembling, Miss Ramsey left his arms and ran to his best friend.

Ben watched her take the kitten and kiss and hug the tiny beast. He felt the beginning of a smile.

"Your Grace." Prudence's voice snapped across his back like a whip. She stood beside him with another lady on her arm. When she had his attention, she softened her voice and smiled at her brother. "Look who's here to pay a visit, Lady Charlotte, daughter of the Duke of Nottingham."

Ben had met Lady Charlotte on a number of occasions. He wasn't interested in getting to know her better. He spared her an uninterested glance then returned his gaze to Miss Ramsey and Sudbury standing together and stroking the kitten between them. He felt his belly rumble. Was it his belly?

"Your Grace," Lady Charlotte curtsied low and looked up at him from under her long lashes, "it's always a pleasure to see you."

Did Miss Ramsey just smile and pet Sudbury's arm the same way she stroked the kitten? "Sudbury!" He called out to the one he was certain would obey him. "A word."

He stepped away from his sister and her guest and met Sudbury halfway.

"Are you trying to start a war?" he demanded quietly.

"Pardon? Ben, I'd never dream of fighting you."

"Not between us," Ben corrected, even though what he told Sudbury was only half true. "Look at Prudence. On whom do her eyes burn?"

His friend looked over his shoulder at Prudence glaring with hate-filled eyes at Miss Ramsey, who, by now, was also looking toward the women. Mainly, Lady Charlotte and her golden curls shimmering around her ears.

Sudbury appeared thoroughly repentant, but then said. "You know I'm in love with your sister, despite her sometimes unattractive traits. I have no thought of turning my heart in another direction. It's no longer mine to give." He smiled at Ben, and Ben nodded. "But brother," the earl added. "I like the little flower you found in your garden. The more I get to know her, the more I believe she's the one who will heal you. I'll support whatever you choose to do. Your sister will get over it." With that, he patted Ben on the upper arm and stepped around him to go to Prudence—God help him.

It left Ben facing Miss Ramsey. He was glad his friend had cleared that up. Unfortunately, it spread light on the fact that he was jealous. Possessive too, he reasoned as he went to her without hesitation.

"How are your feet?" He glanced down to see her feet covered by hose beneath her nightgown.

"All better." She gave him a wide smile that rendered him weak for a moment…or two.

He laughed silently at the pitiful fool he was becoming over her. He had to fight it, keep his head on straight. He had a goal. He wanted to fight again. He needed it. He was born for it.

"I'm glad," he told her. "I'll have you measured for shoes."

"Oh, no, don't go through the trouble, Ben—Your Grace."

He turned to see what vanquished her delightful smile. It was his sister's snarl up close. She'd dragged Lady Charlotte to him with Sudbury coming up at a leisurely pace behind them.

"Yes, *Ben,* don't go through the trouble," his sister said through clenched teeth. When she turned to Lady Charlotte, she managed a smile. "His Grace has a large heart. He's always taking in strays." She looked toward the kitten, which he'd found on the road and brought home last week…and Miss Ramsey.

"Prudence," he said, straightening his spine, folding his hands behind his back, and stepping in front of Miss Ramsey, "surely Lady Charlotte doesn't wish to subject her delicate sensibilities to your unkind temper. Perhaps you should arrange for her to visit with you another day." He turned his unregretful gaze on his sister's guest.

"Good day to you, Lady."

With just a look toward Miss Ramsey and a slight motion of his chin, she came to him. Ignoring the slight commotion behind him, he took the kitten from her arms and kissed it.

As he left the hall with Miss Ramsey at his side, he made a note to thank Sudbury for stopping Prudence from following him.

"Why aren't you in the kitchen, Desdemona?" he asked the kitten.

Beside him, seemingly unfazed by the goings on, Miss Ramsey smiled. "Is that her name, Desdemona?"

"Yes. She was Othello's wife in Shakespeare's play Othello."

Her pretty, aqua eyes opened wider. "I've heard of Shakespeare!"

"Of course you have," he let out a short snort. "Everyone's heard of him."

"Even people in the twenty-first century."

He cut her a curious side-glance. "Does his fame live on then?"

She nodded and reached over to pet the kitten asleep in the crook of his elbow. She was oblivious to the many stares and whispers going on from the other inhabitants of Colchester House. Ben wasn't, and glared at every one of them.

"Where are we going anyway?" she asked.

"Back to your room. We'll find you something decent to wear and shoes, and then we'll go have breakfast together in the dining hall."

He swore her face lit up, warming his heart and his blood. He suddenly had the odd desire to make her happy all the time. Was he enchanted? Possessed? He wasn't himself. But then, who was he really? At the tender age of eleven everything in his life had changed, including him. He stopped being thankful and happy, and began living for revenge. But this woman claiming to be from a lonely future was luring him with fiery light, joy, and...peace. The peace wasn't comforting. It was foreign and it made him confined and unsure. But the more he basked in her light and watched her smile, the more he wanted to smile with her. He dropped her off in her room and set out to find Edith.

"I'll take care of everything, Your Grace," the servant promised.

When he began to return to the room with her, she stopped and smiled at him. "I'll bring her to you when she's ready, Sir. It would do no good to her reputation if you were in there while she was getting dressed."

"Of course," he said, feeling his pitiful face grow flush. He turned away and listened to her footsteps as she walked off.

"Edith," Ben called, stopping her momentarily. "What do you think of her, of Miss Ramsey? Is she unkind to you when I'm not nearby?"

She laughed softly. "What does my opinion matter in such things, Sir?"

Her opinion was the most important one in this matter. Many ladies pretended to be patient, kind, and generous when others were watching. Servants knew them best. "I wouldn't ask if it didn't matter."

She bowed her head in reverence. "I think she's a bit peculiar and uncommonly charming. I like her, Sir."

He let out a breath he wasn't sure why he was holding. Yes. She was a bit peculiar. She didn't conform. Somehow, she remained true to who she was. Not some copy of a hundred other *ladies*. She was certainly uncommonly charming, enchanting him without him even knowing, until it was too late. Too late for what? he asked himself on the way to the kitchen to drop off Desdemona. Too late to stop thinking of her when he wasn't with her. Too late to care about anything but her. Too late to live his dream of returning to the battlefield. Who was she that she tempted him to seek peace and forget killing? He turned to look over his shoulder, toward the way from which he came.

He'd gone against everything he'd promised to his parents—himself. He'd let trouble in, and now he was doomed.

Chapter Six

Fable didn't have much of a figure. She was basically straight without a voluptuous curve to her, so she was glad that the fashionable clothes of the time created ways to make her look more womanly. Of course, a corset made of pastel peach silk and pieces of whalebone was pretty but painful as it pushed up her bust and slimmed her waist, but one suffered to be beautiful, didn't one? The attached sleeves, despite being a bit long, fit her slim arms as if they were made for her. They weren't. According to Edith, the clothes belonged to Flora, one of Lady Prudence's head servants.

Fable didn't care where they came from. She'd learned in her life to be thankful for whatever came her way. So, she let Edith dress her in voluminous petticoats that Edith had to pin up so Fable wouldn't trip over them. There were actual wooden hoops placed at her sides to widen the silhouette of her hips. Covered in petticoats, they looked wider than a linebacker's shoulders. According to Edith, they weren't half as wide as those of the noble ladies. Nor was the fabric as fine. A tight bodice decorated with ribbons stopped her from breathing when Edith pulled the laces tighter from the back.

"So, I guess breathing and sitting down isn't an option," she said wryly while she lifted one foot at a time to be fitted with shoes from Edith's friend Rose from the west wing. They were made of coral silk and wood. Cotton pads were placed inside the soles for comfort. She was a servant, not a noble woman so she wasn't invited to wear a wig, powdered or otherwise. There wasn't time to pin up her hair and she didn't want it braided, so she wrapped it up in a loose bun on top of her head. She loosened a few tendrils that curled around her face. Edith showed her approval with a circlet of babies-breath that she wrapped around the bun. When she was finally ready to leave her rooms and see the duke, Edith led her to the dining hall.

Her heart felt as if it were beating in her throat. She thought of him telling her he was permanent. Why would he say such pleasing things, things that made her heart dance if he didn't like her? She wanted to squeal with happiness and twirl her way to the entrance.

When she reached the doors and stepped inside, every eye turned to her. Every eye but the duke's. Fable scanned her gaze over all the faces but he wasn't there. For a second, she felt panic rising in her. She didn't belong here, dressed like something she wasn't. She wasn't a servant. She wasn't a noble lady. She didn't know where to stand or what she should eat. She thought about turning back around and running to her rooms.

"Come, Miss," Edith appeared again at her side and urged her forward toward the tables.

"Where's the duke?" Fable leaned in and whispered to her.

"Bryce from the kitchen said he saw the duke ride away without a word to anyone."

He rode away? Where did he go? Fable worried. Why would he leave now when he told Edith to dress her and bring her to him, when every mouth she passed set whispers to the air?

"Who is she?"

"I heard the duke found her on the streets of the city."

"I heard the duke was fond of her. But look at her, she's much too plain to interest him."

"How fond of her can he be? He's not here to even greet her."

"I saw him leaving in a hurry," one of them said. "Or I should say he was running away."

Those particular whispers came from a group of ladies standing around the large fireplace. They sneered at Fable when she glanced their way. Usually, she let jabs and jibes slide off her. They mostly came from unhappy, insecure, hateful people. She tried not to let these girls bother her, but the more they laughed, holding dainty, gloved fingers to their mouths, the angrier she grew at the duke for not being here.

"Get me more tea," one of them called out to her.

"And be quick about it!" shouted another.

"Ladies," Edith intervened. "I beg your pardon, but—"

One of them stepped forward and held up her palm to quiet Edith. Lady Charlotte. Fable remembered her when she stood with the duke's sister earlier. At the time, she hadn't taken her gaze from the duke for a second.

"Are Lady Prudence's guests to be scolded by a servant?" She did nothing to mask her contempt for Fable when she set her burning gaze on her. Then she turned her smug smile to the others. "I saw this one earlier running around the halls in her nightdress and stockinged-feet."

The others gasped and sneered some more.

But Lady Charlotte wasn't done. "She brazenly ran to Lord Sudbury and laughed with him in the face of Lady Prudence, behaving like nothing more than a street prostitute."

A what? Fable lifted her head and clenched her teeth. She'd listened to enough. With her hands balled into fists at her sides she strode toward them, Lady Charlotte in particular.

"Who the fu—"

"Lady Charlotte!" They all turned to the duke standing in the doorway. Somehow he appeared taller, more like a storm, a gleam of lightning in his eyes as unyielding as the cut of his jaw. As he came near, the women took a collective step back.

Everyone but Fable. She stared at him while he glared at the others.

"Get out," he ordered Lady Charlotte in a quiet, chilled voice.

"Don't let me see you here again." He raked his gaze over the others. "Miss Ramsey here is my guest. I won't tolerate vicious rumors against her. If they continue, you will all be asked to leave, as well."

He turned to Fable now and let his gaze warm over her face.

She looked away and then stormed out of the dining hall.

She couldn't breathe. Did women back here in the eighteenth century die from their corsets and bodices being too tight?

Fingers closed around her wrist, stopping her. She spun around to see the duke. She couldn't say that in any other time, he'd be a dream come to life, because all the centuries were the same. People barely tolerated the poor. If you were street poor, you were worth as much as a sewer rat.

But he was different. He was a dream come to life in *any* time.

"Where are you going?"

"Where were you?" she asked, barely hearing his question. "You keep claiming to want to protect me, but you *told* Edith to dress me and bring me to the dining hall. You threw me to the wolves and left me to protect myself."

"I didn't know they would be there," he said, attempting to defend himself.

"Whatever," she threw at him and ignored the way he mouthed the word contemptuously. "Why did you leave? Where were you going?" She wanted him to tell her he wasn't running away.

"I...I...It..."

"Really?" she mocked. "You can't even talk about it? Were you running from me?"

When he didn't answer, she yanked her arm free, but he grasped her wrist again. "I asked you where you were going, Fable."

"To my room."

"Did you eat?"

Oh, how could his voice alone tempt her to forgive him anything? But she'd been unprepared for so many critical eyes and spiteful tongues. He'd dressed her up, put her on stage alone for all to see and laugh at. She yanked her arm away. "Don't concern yourself with me anymore, Your Grace."

"I'd like nothing more than to do that, Miss Ramsey," he told her in a voice strained with control.

A dream come true...for someone else.

"Oh? Is that so?" she demanded, feeling her temper rising. "Fine. I'll make it easy for you."

He'd heard the things Lady Charlotte had said to her. Why wasn't he telling her that he didn't see her in those ugly ways? Was any of it even his fault? She wasn't sure about anything! She didn't even know if the life she was living right now was real!

"I'm leaving." She wondered why she couldn't look at him while she said it.

"I don't think you're well enough—"

"I'll be fine, My Lord Duke." Now she lifted her chin and met his gaze. "I know how to survive on my own."

It pierced her insides that he wasn't asking or telling her to stay. He'd made his feelings clear. He wanted to stop concerning himself with her.

"Thank you for everything." Unlike her mother, she would thank her host. She turned on her heel and left him behind.

He didn't stop her. He didn't call out. He let her go. She would never forgive him for that.

She stepped into the guest chambers and bolted the door behind her. She knew how to walk away from a person who really didn't care one way or the other if she was around—or if she was a burden. So, her silly fairytale was over. They always ended. So what? What was so special about Benjamin West anyway? she asked herself, swiping foolish tears from her cheeks. So what if he walked with the rigid arrogance of a prince? He wasn't one. So what if he was as detached as a statue of a warlord? He was just a man. So what if he was always reluctantly warm and caring toward her? She swiped a tear away from her cheek and reached behind her for the laces of her bodice. She pulled off everything Edith had dressed her in except her hose and found the clothes she arrived in. She slipped on her black shorts and boots, along with her top, thankfully cleaned by someone who worked here. Lastly, she tugged the babies-breath from her hair and pulled her locks free.

She'd head back to Ipswich and get the pocket watch from where she'd hidden it. Whoever was chasing her wouldn't think she'd go back. Would he? She prayed he wasn't outside the front doors right now. Come to think of it, where *were* the front doors? She shrugged and peeked outside the guestroom door for any sign of the duke. There wasn't any. She swore an oath and set out on her way.

Unfortunately, she met over a dozen people on her way to the exit. At least six of them were stately looking ladies with powdered wigs and faces. Fable knew the white facial powder was in. Of all the fads, that was the one she understood the least. Why would anyone want to look like the walking dead? Each lady had a mother beside her to match. Fable felt as if she were in some drug-induced dream. The ladies all stared at her obscene way of dressing, shaking their heads disapprovingly. The men stared for other reasons.

She hurried out. Good riddance, Colchester House!

The door slammed shut behind her.

SHE WALKED FOR about an hour after the rain started, swearing at the torrential downpour—and at Benjamin West, His Grace the Duke of Colchester for not being the things he said he was, dependable, permanent. She had to find shelter but she didn't want to run into a barn or someplace without people, especially since she had the feeling someone was following her. She turned twice to confront whoever it was, but her vision was severely impaired in the heavy rain.

She considered that it might be the duke keeping pace behind her, but he wouldn't have let her get drenched before stopping her. Would he? No. He was considerate.

Something fell behind her. She spun around. "Who's there! Ben? Your Grace?"

She saw a shadow move in the downpour and shielded her eyes. A man moved closer. "You call for the duke," a vaguely familiar voice rang out. "Do you know him?"

She caught the flash of metal in the moonlight. A sword? His voice! It was the time-traveler! She fought the urge to scream. Who would come to save her? There was no one. Nothing had changed. She braced herself as he approached. If he put a finger on her—Her heart thumped in her chest and made her feel lightheaded and dizzy.

"THAT'S IT? YOU'RE really going to let her go?"

"Simon!" Prudence gasped. "What would you have him do? Chase after someone lower than a peasant?"

Sudbury turned to her, his usual easy smile replaced by a disapproving scowl. "I don't like this side of you, lady. It's most unattractive."

When she stared at him as if he'd slapped her and then began to weep, he looked pained, but turned back to Ben. "Don't just stand there, Brother. You need her."

"I can't give up on…my dream," Ben answered quietly.

His sister looked up. "What dream? Is it to be known as the rudest duke in the kingdom?"

Ben clenched his teeth remembering Lady Charlotte, along with her other cackling hens, belittling Miss Ramsey when he wasn't there. He was sorry he hadn't been there. Sorrier than he cared to be. He'd had to use every ounce of strength he possessed not to pull her into his arms in front of all, and hold her. He hadn't known his sister had invited her five friends. When he told Edith to bring her to the dining hall, he hadn't known they'd all be there, or that they would behave so ruthlessly. Still, it was no excuse for running away and leaving her at the mercy of others. Miss Ramsey had depended on him and he'd already let her down. He wanted to apologize to her. He wanted to beg her forgiveness for leaving and not protecting her. But she wasn't what he needed to heal. Leading men into battle, fighting, and avenging his family was what he needed. Why had he let her make him sway in other directions? Why had he made himself her protector? Why should he stop her when it was better that she left?

"Lady Charlotte deserved to be thrown out," he told his sister. "Make sure you don't bring her back or I'll throw her out again. And if you think for one moment that I would wed a woman like her, you're mad."

He had nothing else to say, and though they had barged into his private sitting room, he was the one who left. If Miss Ramsey was gone, he didn't want to think of her or where she was going to go now.

When thunder shook the foundations, he looked toward the window and scowled darker than the skies outside. No. Not rain. Of course the trouble maker would choose to leave on a night when it was pouring rain.

With a low growl he ripped his cloak from Stephen's hands. Without giving a thought to how his steward was always a step ahead of him, he opened the door and strode into the coming storm.

He went to the stable and quickly saddled his horse himself. He found a lantern, lit it, and looked around. The heavy charcoal clouds were almost upon them. Which way should he go? He looked toward the northeast, toward Ipswich and started that way. He called out her name, and then heard others calling as well. Sudbury and Stephen, along with six other servants.

Turning to watch them approach, he drew in a deep breath then proceeded to give them all direction like a high-ranking soldier.

He watched as they spread out then turned to his own path.

After a quarter of an hour, they still hadn't found her. When the rains started, Ben's vision did him little good. He called her name, hoping she had found shelter and was keeping dry. She'd said she knew how to survive on her own. But when he'd found her in his garden, she was starving and she could barely walk.

He called out again, holding up his lantern to see.

What if there truly was a man chasing her? And what if he found her? Ben's heart thumped with such force, he thought he could hear it. Why had he let her leave? What happened to his iron control?

And then, he saw her out of the corner of his eye. A liquid flame wavering in the flashing lightning. Another figure appeared to huddle in the downpour before seeing him and taking off. Was it a trick of Ben's eyes?

Letting the figure flee, he thundered toward her on his horse. He leaped from the saddle before the mount stopped—before Fable's body hit the ground. He caught her and clutched her to his chest, her hair dripping over his arms like streaks of blood. "Miss Ramsey? Fable? Fable?" He shielded her face from the rain but she didn't open her eyes.

Lifting her in his arms, he bent to listen for her breathing. He couldn't hear anything but the alarms going off in his head. "What are you trying to do to me, Lady?" he asked, scooping up her limp, cold body. He had to get her back to the house and the physician. Letting that one mission lead him, he secured her to his horse and leaped up behind her and raced home.

He burst through the door, calling for the physician and Edith, giving orders to the latter to send out some men to bring Sudbury and the others back.

He brought her to her bed and set her down in it. "Does she live?" He'd tried to keep his voice calm and steady when he spoke to the physician. He was a master at remaining calm, but when it came to her, he lost control over his senses.

"She lives," the physician assured him.

"What's the matter with her? Why isn't she waking up?"

"Your Grace," the physician told him with a slight sigh while Ben paced. "You will be the first to know once I figure it out myself."

"You can survive on your own, hmm?" Ben asked over her unconscious form. "You didn't last two hours!"

The physician wisely pretended not to hear him and continued to examine her. Twice, Ben glowered at him impatiently. Edith returned to tend to her and practically pushed him out of the way. He glared at her as well.

Finally finished with his examination, the physician looked up. "She needs to be kept warm. She wasn't completely recovered. She never should have gone out in the rain." He handed Edith a packet of herbs with instructions on putting it in her tea.

"Perhaps," he paused on his way out and said to Ben, "you should try to keep her out of trouble."

Ben would have laughed if he wasn't scowling so hard until the physician left.

"Why did she leave, Your Grace?" Edith asked him quietly when they were alone. "I thought she liked it here."

Yes, she did seem to like it here, Ben thought. Did she like him, perhaps? "I was careless with her." He gazed at her sleeping face. He wanted to get closer but Edith worked around him. He saw that her hair still dripped over her face. He wanted to pick up a cloth and wipe the droplets from her forehead, her temples, around her eyes and over the curve of her cheek and jaw. His heart raced, yet he felt as if the world had slowed, giving him time to bask in her. He looked away. He brought her back. He didn't regret it. Despite her claim, she couldn't survive well on her own. What was she doing just standing there getting soaked through to the bone? Did she have no sense at all? Was there no place nearby to seek shelter? What was the shadow he'd seen? Was it her sword-wielding time traveler?

"I'll dry her hair, Sir," Edith told him, seemingly unaware of his warring thoughts. "And I'll have to change her out of her clothes."

"Oh, of course," he said. "Just one moment."

When Edith nodded and went off to busy herself with something else in the room, he bent close to Miss Ramsey's ear and said in a low voice. "I'm afraid that if I let you, you will become all I care about. The one I put first before all else. The reason I live or the reason I die. I can't allow that, Miss Ramsey. I'm drawn to a different calling, and one day, when I die on the battlefield I don't want to leave you behind."

He went still when her fingers reached for his temple and traced through his hair, her touch as light as butterfly wings before her arm fell limp again at her side.

"Fable?" he whispered. Had she heard what he said? He bit his lip as if to silence himself.

When she didn't respond, he felt relieved and stepped out of the room and into the path of another storm.

"You went after her!" his sister said through clenched teeth, approaching him in the hall. "And this time you dragged Simon with you."

Ben kept walking, paying no attention to her. When he passed her, he closed his eyes and let out the troubled sigh he'd been containing. He'd found Miss Ramsey and brought her back.

It wasn't long before Edith called him to return. He didn't go right away but finished his chess game with Sudbury. A game he almost lost. He had to make her less important to him. He didn't know how she'd crept inside his defenses, but she was there, in his heart like a thorn.

When the servant came looking for him in the fencing house, where he was practicing, his defenses nearly crumbled.

"Forgive me, Your Grace, but nothing I do is warming her!" Edith lamented. "I fear she is freezing to death."

He yanked off his mask and laid his sword aside and hurried back to the house. To her chambers. He was torn between never forgiving himself for causing this condition in her, or for caring what condition this *trouble* was in. It was all she ever caused. Trouble.

She had been changed into dry, warm clothes, but Edith was correct, she was still as cold as death. After Ben had his clothes brought to him, he changed out of his fencing uniform and sat by her bed long into the night, long after he sent Edith to her own bed.

No amount of warming her bed raised her body heat. When her teeth began to chatter and she shivered in her slumber, Ben saw no other option but to get into bed with her. He remained still for a moment. What if she woke up and slapped him? He'd suffered worse wounds than a slap in the mouth by a dainty hand.

Emboldened by his desire to warm her, he slipped his arms around her and pulled her closer against him. He felt his heart thundering against both their chests as he covered her beneath the warmth of his leg.

Should he hate himself for being so bold with her? So intimate? He closed his eyes and rubbed her back. He worked his hand over her shoulder, down her arm. Was his heart so traitorous that he liked how she felt pressed close to him? She made him feel warm and oddly content. He hoped to spread his warmth to her. When he came to her hand, he held her fingers to his lips and breathed his warm breath onto them, on her wrist and pulse. He thought he felt her move. A tremor down her spine that made her shift ever so slightly between his legs. As if she were responding to his touch.

Or had he imagined it?

"Miss Ramsey?" he asked in a quiet voice.

He must have imagined it. She didn't respond now. But she did feel warmer to the touch.

"That's my fighter," he said into her hair. "Rest now. I'll keep you warm."

He closed his eyes, fearing the trouble she brought. Every time he thought of some sort of defense against her, the feel of her in his arms overwhelmed him and he could think of nothing but how she had started off there and how much he wanted to keep her there.

Chapter Seven

Fable's eyes fluttered open as dawn broke through the unshuttered windows of the second floor guest chambers. She was alone in the bed. Had she dreamed of him holding her, warming her, their arms and legs tangled together?

What was she doing here again? Had she really left last night, or was it all a dream? What had happened in the rain? How had she gotten back to Colchester House? She remembered the duke saying he would like nothing more than to stop concerning himself with her. Yes, she'd left. Who brought her back?

She didn't wait long to find out when Edith entered her bedroom with a basin of fresh water. "Who brought me back?"

Edith set the basin down and looked away. "Why, it was the duke, of course."

Why would he bring her back when he didn't want to concern himself with her? "Where is he?"

Edith looked around. "I thought he'd be here."

"Edith," Fable tried to sit up but a wave of dizziness washed over her and she lay back down. "Was he here with me last night?"

"Where, Miss? In this room?"

Fable didn't answer.

"No, Miss," Edith told her. "I didn't see him."

Suddenly Fable was overcome with loneliness. Oh, she'd experienced it before, plenty of times. But this time was especially painful. Benjamin West was a man she could have loved passionately, madly. But she was poor—and poor wasn't a good thing to be. So much that a father reached across the grave to make certain his son never married beneath him.

Fable had been poor all her life. It never hurt as much as it did now. He'd never be with her. Even if he defied his father's last wish, his sister wouldn't give him a moment's peace.

He went and brought her in from the rain. It didn't mean anything except what she already knew. He was a good guy. He was staying away now, wasn't he? She sighed with frustration. How long before she was well enough to leave?

She asked Edith to ask the physician, who informed the duke of her question. He finally showed up by her bed when night settled over Colchester and she woke from a fevered dream of being in her bed with him, safe in his arms.

He wasn't in her bed, but standing by it. Light from the hearth-fire and the many candles surrounding them provided Fable a clear view of him.

When he saw her eyes open, he let out a sigh. Then, "How are you feeling?"

She might be delusional but the quiet gentleness in his voice was missing, leaving his question cold.

"I think I'll live."

He was silent for a moment, then, "What do you mean by asking the physician how long before you're well enough to leave?"

"Listen, Your Grace, you've done enough for me. I need to be going."

"Going where? I don't want you going off alone again at the mercy of someone unpleasant."

She froze as an icy fissure ran up her spine, to her head, bringing back the memory of being followed in the pouring rain—and the time-traveler's voice.

You call for the duke. Do you know him?

Why would he ask that of all questions? Did *he* know the

duke? She set her gaze on Ben's face. "I heard his voice."

"Who," he asked.

"The one who brought me here. The time-traveler. That night in the rain…he was following me and then he asked me if I knew you."

"You saw him the night you left?" His voice quavered a little and the blood drained from his face.

"Yes."

"I thought I saw…something. When I reached you, you were alone."

She nodded her head. "He was there before you. He may have still been there when you arrived. It was almost impossible to see him in the rain. Otherwise, if he had more time, he would have probably tied me to his horse and taken me to Ipswich. Why else would he have followed me here?"

He stood over the bed, grinding his jaw and balling his hands into fists at his sides. "I should have come for you sooner. I shouldn't have let you go."

She remembered his words before she left. "Your Grace, I know you don't want to have to concern yourself with me."

He grimaced as if her words pained him. "I misspoke. Forgive me."

She nodded easily, but then shook her head. "You're not responsible for me."

"I said I would protect you."

"Well, I release you from that obligation."

"I can't be released from it," he told her. "Though, I can't promise how long until I'm called back to fight for the king. It's what I have been waiting for. It's what I need."

She tried not to let it prick her in the heart that he couldn't wait to return to battle. That he would rather possibly die than stay here—with her. He said he needed it. She knew all that silent darkness in him needed a way out. She knew now what had put it there—Rage toward his parents' murderers and the inability to save his mother.

I would have killed others around me, possibly myself. Battle saved me.

"What if he doesn't call?"

"Why wouldn't he?" he asked, his tone laced with alarm.

"How badly were you injured?"

He sat at the edge of the bed and loosened the laces at his throat, then pulled down his collar to show her his shoulder. She almost gasped at the sight of it. For it wasn't simply a scar. It was more like a carved out web of smaller scars left from reattaching what muscles and tendons they could.

"I practice strengthening my arm every day," he told her. "It's taken hard work."

She ran her fingers down his shoulder. "Can you wield a sword?"

"Yes," he answered in a low murmur. "I'll show you how well I wield it if the traveler comes here."

She decided she loved the sound of him. She also decided something else. "I'm not going to give him the pocket watch. When you go back to war, I'll find out how to use the watch and go back to the twenty-first century. You don't have to worry about me."

He was quiet for a while, until she wondered if she'd said something wrong. She was still so sleepy.

"I just mean I understand you have enough to worry about. I don't want to add to it."

"If I want to worry about you, I will," he told her with a stubborn tilt of his chin.

She never wanted to kiss anyone more. She felt feverish. Was it him who made her so hot? "What did you say? If you want to kiss me, you will?"

"What?" He looked lost, but only for a moment, then he smiled, looking as feverish as she. A full seductive smile and Fable felt her body going weak facing him. "Oh, yes," he amended silkily. "I did say that." He leaned in closer. Fable's heart crashed against her chest. But wait, no! She wasn't staying here. Was she?

She didn't pull away when he fit her chin in his fingers and tilted her head for her to look at him.

She wanted to tell him so many things, promise him everything—though she had nothing to give. She closed her eyes and parted her lips, hoping he would kiss her. When he didn't, she opened her eyes again to see him smiling at her in the candlelight.

"Fable," he said her name in a deep, needful voice, "you don't have to run anymore. You are safe here."

She closed her eyes again and smiled at the thought of such protection and safety that she could stop running. She wanted him to kiss her but his arms coming around her sent her head to the clouds, and her heart to the safest refuge she'd ever known.

Later, she fell into a fevered sleep and dreamed of kissing him. She dreamed of smiling when his kisses crossed her mind. She'd seen her mother kiss her boyfriends and it always sickened her. When she grew older the only boys she ever kissed were Ed Drake and Bobby Hudd. They were nothing to dream about. But she was sure Benjamin West's kiss could make her dream when she was awake. She thought he may have wiped down her forehead and face throughout the day, but she wasn't sure. All she could do was pray for the night to come when she could hold him in her arms again.

"Are you hungry?" he asked, sitting by her bed.

Had he been waiting for her to wake up? She smiled to show him that she was awake and also because it was nice to see his face when she opened her eyes. "More soup?"

He nodded with the slightest expression of pity on her, then he stood up and called out for Edith. A servant Fable knew as Kevin appeared instead.

"Where's Edith?" the duke barked.

"She…she…" the servant stammered.

Fable could see why he would. The duke was quite an imposing man with his arrow straight spine, and eyes that could penetrate even the most formidable defenses.

"She what?" His quiet words were laced with impatience.

"She was ordered to tend to your sister."

The duke went still and silent.

Witnessing him turn so seemingly unaffected, so guarded and cold was almost more frightening than his dark scowls and booming shouts.

"Bring Miss Ramsey some soup. Then go tell Edith that if she isn't back here in—"

"Your Grace?" Fable interrupted. When he turned to her, she smiled and softened her brow, motioning him to lighten his tone. He caught on and did as she bid.

"Bring the soup. That will be all."

When they were alone, he returned to the bedside and gave her a concerned look. "You look pale."

She crooked her mouth at him and felt her lips crack. "Hmm, I don't feel so good."

Without waiting for another word, he dashed out of her rooms. She heard him shout for the physician to be brought to Miss Ramsey immediately. Then he rushed back to her and took her hand. "You're on fire!" He brought her basin of water closer and wiped her down, behind her neck, in front, over her forehead.

"Come now, dear Fable. You're not going to let a thing like a fever defeat you. Hold on to me."

She had enough strength to reach for him and take his hand. But that was all. In her head, she scoffed at her weakness. He was right. She'd fought worse things than a fever. She'd been stabbed by one of her mother's enemies, she'd had pneumonia, chicken pox, and the measles. She was allergic to strawberries and barely survived on the sofa of a friend of her mother's. There was more but she couldn't remember all of it. Fever. Schmever.

She held onto his hand while another man poked and prodded her, took her pulse, and fed her horrible tasting "tea".

She was vaguely aware of the second man leaving, and then the duke's steady voice that made her insides rumble. "I'll be right here."

FABLE WOKE TO the sound of music permeating the walls. She opened her eyes to Edith scurrying around her bed. When the older woman saw her, she stopped and let her grin fill her face. "It's good to have you back, Miss."

Fable hoped she was back for good. "I dreamed that I woke up back home in the future, so I was afraid to open my eyes."

Edith came closer to the bed. "Oh, Miss," she lamented, "you're not fully well yet then."

Right, people didn't travel through time. Edith didn't know what Fable knew. She decided the best thing to do was try to forget it. But it had truly frightened her. She didn't want to go back to a life alone on the streets. Not ever.

"It was a dream, Edith," she managed a soft laugh. "Oh, and what's that music? It's pretty…and loud."

"It's the musicians downstairs in the ballroom," Edith told her, hurrying over to press her palm against Fable's forehead. "Thank the good Lord, the fever seems to have broken."

Yes, Fable agreed. Her head seemed to be clearer. Streaks of crimson washed across her face when she remembered how she'd held onto the duke and then held his hand. She wanted to kick herself. What was she? Some pitiful soul without an ounce of pride? Ugh. She disgusted herself.

"Wait," she said after a moment of consternation at herself, "the ballroom? Is today Lady Prudence's Marriage ball?"

Edith nodded. "And today is over. It's tonight, Miss."

"How long have I been asleep?"

"Two full days," Edith told her with a sigh, then leaned in and whispered. "Had His Grace worried sick."

Two days. It echoed in her head. It was the night of his sister's ball and he wasn't here.

Good.

She'd told him not to worry about her anymore. It seemed

that's what he was trying to do. But Edith said he'd been worried sick over her. She didn't want him to be. Did she? Somewhere deep inside she wanted to take joy in the fact that someone cared for her, but she knew better. She'd come here via supernatural forces. None of this was permanent. She'd wake up for real and in a flash all this would be gone.

Or he'd come for her. *You call for the duke. Do you know him?*

She pushed the time-traveler out of her mind and let Ben take over.

"Is His Grace at the ball?" She really didn't want to know—but she had to know.

Edith nodded. "Yes. He promised Lady Prudence he would attend if she would stay out of his private affairs. But he hasn't left your bedside before that."

Fable smiled and asked for Edith's help propping her up against the pillows. When Edith served her chicken broth and carrot soup, she drank every bit.

"His Grace will be pleased that you ate."

"Edith," Fable said, putting down her spoon. "I've asked myself this question over and over. Maybe you can answer it. Why would a duke care one whit about a street urchin, except for pity's sake?"

"What's wrong with pity's sake, Miss? I'd proudly serve a compassionate master rather than a merciless one."

Fable agreed, although she had no intentions of serving *any* masters.

"Is the duke compassionate then?" At least he seemed to be—

"No, not usually," Edith told her. "This is the most I've ever seen of his warmer side. None of us knew it existed."

"C'mon now," Fable shooed her away. "Don't you try to tell me you didn't know the duke was so kind."

"He's only been back to Colchester House for three years—"

"Three years is long enough," Fable told her.

"Miss, I can tell you this. He is the king's soldier first and foremost. He's never had us beaten, but no one has ever disobeyed him."

"Well," Fable said, confidently. "I'm sure if any of his servants was injured or ill, His Grace would do anything in his power to help."

Edith went about her work with a smile while Fable's mind raced with a million different images of the duke dancing downstairs. Who was he with? Was he really choosing a wife down there? Fable's heart faltered. Was he? Would she lose him forever to some nobleman's daughter?

The longer she sat there without him coming to her, the more restless she became. The second Edith left, Fable hurried out of bed. She swayed a little, feeling lightheaded from not being on her feet for days. She waited until her head cleared and then padded out of her rooms.

She had to get to the top of the stairs to see into the ballroom. She just wanted to take a peek. She stayed down low to remain unseen as the guests filed into the house.

There were very few men entering. Most of the guests were young ladies with their mothers, though she could scarcely tell who was young and who was older thanks to their powdered faces and high powdered wigs. They were all here to snag the duke as a husband. Fable was reminded of a documentary she saw once about animal auctions. The duke was the animal up for sale to the highest bidder.

It fired Fable's blood.

Then she saw him. He stopped in her view, just a side view, but, oh, her gaze fastened on him in an aubergine-colored, velvet justaucorps worn open to reveal his tight physique in a silk-velvet vest and breeches. He stood with his hands folded behind his arrow-straight back. Of course, he wore a high, elaborately-tied, uncomfortable looking cravat beneath his square chin and carved jaw. He wore a black wig with two horizontal rolls above his ears and a ponytail tied with a black ribbon at the back of his nape.

As if sensing her, he turned to look outside the open doors of the ballroom.

Fable quickly hid in the shadows. But she watched him look her way. Her knees almost gave out with the threat of being caught spying on him like a fool. But…it was more than that. She felt weak at the sight of him, the way his eyes promised her deep, intimate things and said: *You're all I care about. First before all else. The reason I live or the reason I die.*

It tempted her to step out of the shadows so his eyes could find her and pour out things he couldn't say.

Edith entered the ballroom and beckoned the duke for a word just out of Fable's sight. It didn't matter. He came into view an instant later and left the ballroom with Edith following behind. And headed for the stairs!

Fable held her hands over her mouth while she gasped and took off running to her rooms. She almost made it to her door when her slippered foot stepped on something small and shot a hot streak of pain through her leg. She went down like those pitiful women in the movies who fall while they're trying to escape.

"Fable!" his voice reached her when he called out.

She swore and tried to get back on her feet.

"Miss Ramsey!" the duke commanded while he sprinted to her and scooped her up off the floor.

She wanted to disappear into the woodwork.

"What are you doing out of your room with no shoes?" he asked, carrying her into her sitting room. He sat her down on the settee and knelt to examine her foot.

"Are you choosing a wife tonight?" she boldly asked as if that was a sufficient answer to his question.

"No," he let her know. He looked up from her foot and covered it with his hand. "I want no wife."

She chewed her lip. "But you never know. You might meet that one woman who makes you change your mind—" Was he smirking at her? It was subtle, but it was there. "Oh," she smirked back, "you don't think you'll ever meet her, Your Grace?"

"I've no doubt I will. She might turn my head, but my heart

remains steadfast to a cause bigger than love and devotion."

"Nothing is bigger than love and devotion," she corrected him with a soft laugh. "You can live without revenge and anger. But without love and devotion, you become an empty shell."

"Is that what I am, then, an empty shell?" he asked her.

"Yes," she answered without hesitation. "You need someone to fill you up. If you choose the right person, you can be happy for the rest of your life. If you choose the wrong woman, your misery will be unmeasured."

He chuckled softly. "That's a very important choice then."

"It's nothing to laugh at, Ben."

From the door came a collective gasp at her familiar use of his name—or that he chuckled—Fable didn't know which. She looked up to see Edith and a number of the guests at the door, watching them.

With a glare that sent most of them running, the duke rose up, went to the door and slammed it shut.

Fable watched him return and sit on the settee with her.

"Do you feel up to a dance with me?"

"What?" she asked, with a series of short blinks.

"Your foot isn't cut," he told her quietly, close enough for her to lose herself in the fathomless depths of his eyes. At first impression one would say he was stoic and emotionless, but staring into his eyes right now, Fable could almost feel the intensity of many passions buried deep beneath the mask of indifference he wore.

"Do you want to go to the ball?"

She laughed and leaned back a little. It wasn't that she didn't want him to try to kiss her. It was because if he kissed her, she'd probably faint. "No. Thank you but—"

"I ordered some dresses to be made for you. I'll check if they're ready."

"No, Ben, really," she said, stopping him. "I don't think I can stand those women."

"Come and stand by my side."

She laughed a little, but then grew serious. "Are you ill?" She lifted her hand to his forehead.

He took hold of her wrist and slid his fingers to hers. "You should be there."

Did she hear him right? Would she faint even if he didn't kiss her? "But why?" she said, sincerely astonished.

"Because I won't find the woman I might lose my heart to—that is, if she exists—if she's not down there."

Fable stared at him for a few seconds, unsure of what to do—what to say. Was he teasing? He had to be teasing. Should she laugh? What if he wasn't teasing and she laughed? She knew nothing about this. She had no one to ask. And why was he trying to start something when he just professed that he didn't want a wife, when he knew that if the king called he'd be gone without a thought? Would she wait for him? She felt like she was in a historical romance novel, like the one Olivia, her mother's friend, read to her and the hero was going off to war soon. If he went he might not return alive. She pushed away the thought of it. Should she let herself get attached to a guy who, despite his rigorous training, might be denied his dream? What would happen to him then? Would he be alone, too hard for one of those pansy rich ladies to handle?

She let out a deep breath and rolled up her sleeves. This wasn't the smart thing to do, but she was moved by him. Moved by her own emotions for another person for the first time since she could remember. She decided to ride them out and see where they led, even if it was all temporary. What else did she have to do? And who safer than Lord West to ride them out with? She straightened her shoulders. "Fine. Go get me a dress and send Edith to do my hair—" she almost lost her breath and couldn't go on when his smile broke through the gloom and shone like the sun—"and let's play the game."

He blinked his dark, dusky eyes. "Game?"

"Yes, the game of me showing them all the only kind of woman you need."

"Or want," he added, his tone surprisingly silky.

Someplace below her navel burned. Burned for him.

"But I'm immune to your charms—"

His smile, along with his gaze turned doubtful, stopping her.

She cast him a challenging smirk. "You think your charms faze me?"

He scrunched up his nose and squinted his eyes to offer her a sympathetic smile and a nod to go with it. "I'll go get those dresses." He slipped from the room before she could gather her wits and reply.

She was glad he was gone. Was he kidding her with that playful smile? Maybe she couldn't handle him either.

Before she had too much time to think it all through, Edith returned to her carrying an armful of skirts, Beth, one of the servants, followed behind her with bodices and corsets filling her arms, and Helen—who turned out to be very pretty, and married—carried her new shoes.

Three women dressed her in a *mantua,* a dress draped and looped over beautiful yellow floral silk petticoats and a stomacher. The laces were tied so tightly her shoulder blades almost touched. When she complained about it, Edith told her that it and the high bustle in the back were to enhance her silhouette.

Fable didn't care about her silhouette. She shifted and tugged at the dress even while her hair was brushed. She didn't complain while fingers pulled and pinned her copper locks to the back of her head and secured it with a thin ribbon. Tiny yellow flowers were woven through her ponytail and through the long, coiled strands falling over her shoulder.

"Oh my," Edith said, stepping back to admire her when all was done. "You look splendid indeed."

Fable felt like a fool in a puffy dress. At least she didn't have to wear a wig. She covered her flushed cheek with her palm and smiled at her. "Thank you, Edith."

"I checked his whereabouts this time," the older woman confessed with the hint of a smile. "He hasn't moved from outside your door."

Fable closed her eyes, unable to believe this was her life right now, dressing like some princess for the ball—with the handsome prince waiting to escort her. Her heart pounded in her chest. Lord Benjamin West was too dangerous to her head, her heart, and her body.

She had to tell him the truth about how she survived on her own for so long without giving up her body. How she hustled and robbed people of their money in cards, and games like chess. He knew she was poor and he didn't seem to care, unlike his sister. But his father cared…even from the grave. She closed her eyes to stop the burning and bit her bottom lip.

"What is it, Miss?" Edith asked her softly. "Don't you see how his eyes warm on you alone? Why, in three years I've never seen the man smile or worry over anything. But he does those things where you are concerned. And only you. Since the Lady Charlotte incident, no one can stop talking about the mysterious woman living here and how His Grace protects her like an angry lion."

Fable's eyes widened, and then her smile grew with it. Edith grinned right along with her and nodded, encouraging her to be brave.

Fable sniffed. Was Edith her first friend? Her mother didn't let her play with other kids for fear they would tell their parents about her. She just grew used to being alone so that even after her mother died, she didn't make any friends.

She walked to the bedroom door and opened it. He was there in the sitting room waiting for her.

When he saw her, he rose from the settee. No one in her life had ever looked at her the way he was looking at her now. As if she were all that mattered. First, even before battle.

Chapter Eight

SHE WAS HERE, swaying him! How could he keep his heart steadfast to his cause, which he'd boasted was bigger than love and devotion when she made him think of everything *but* fighting?

"Fable," he said moving closer to her, "you look very pleasing in your boots and short pants, but you were born to be dressed in finery."

When she blushed and looked away, he moved closer, using caution, lest he startle her and she run away.

"Are you ready, Miss Ramsey?" he asked, offering his elbow to her.

She nodded, and without a moment of hesitation, she took his arm, held up her chin, and faced the outer door.

He wanted to smile beside her. He feared he'd be smiling all night. He wanted to flick his coat lapel, suck in his bottom lip, and smile like a boastful prince who'd just snatched the damsel from the mouth of the dragon. In fact, he'd sent his men out in every direction and tripled his efforts to find the traveler. He had no doubt he would be found any day now.

"If your feet hurt at any time, let me know and I'll carry you."

She looked up at him and laughed softly. "I'll stay on my own two feet if I have to wear them down to the bone rather than have you carry me in front of those women."

"You're stubborn and strong-willed."

"Too much for you, Duke?" she teased.

"No. I like it."

When she laughed softly again, he wondered by what miracle did she find him so humorous? He didn't really care how. He liked it. He liked making her smile and laugh. It made it easier for him to do the same.

"Are you hungry?" he asked. He also liked eating with her. She enjoyed her food, even sometimes speaking while she ate. The noble ladies he knew wouldn't be caught doing anything but nibbling at their food. And never speaking at the same time. Men knew not to even ask questions to ladies while they ate.

But Fable appreciated every morsel of food she put in her mouth. And Ben enjoyed watching her.

Now, he led her to the ballroom, stepping with her through the open doors and into a myriad of pastel-colored gowns and the sweet sounds of violins and guitars, cellos, and harpsichords. He felt the eyes of every guest on him…on Miss Ramsey. He turned to look at her on his arm. She appeared like a graceful flame, a daughter of royalty. She was delicate, strong, and confident when her cerulean gaze met his and the hint of a smile hovered around her lips.

Yes, she swayed him from concerns he thought were bigger, more important than thoughts of…love and devotion. He scoffed at himself and turned away.

She'd insisted she wasn't affected by him. He intended to prove to her that he disagreed. Even if he lost, he'd still succeed in trying.

He led her to a table with a slanted bench, meant for a lady with a hooped gown to lean against and rest her feet, or eat comfortably.

Ben positioned her on the bench and lifted his hand for a server to bring him some food and drink.

"Your Grace." An older woman pounced before he sat. "It's so good to see you again."

Lady Witham, wife of the Viscount of Witham. She was here

with her husband and daughter. Ben almost groaned out loud.

"We enjoyed your birthday celebration last year," she continued, ignoring the woman he came with.

"Lady—" Ben began.

"You remember my daughter, Miss Gwendolyn Hollister?" And as if on cue, her daughter appeared and stepped under her arm.

Ben stared at the girl's mother, unprepared for her rude behavior. But it only took him an instant to recover. "No, I'm afraid I don't. Let me introduce Miss Fable Ramsey, my…" He blinked at her, not sure of what to say.

"…his guest," Miss Ramsey supplied, smiling straight at them, making him feel a little feverish. He tugged at his cravat.

His guest, he thought pensively. It meant nothing—or it could mean everything. Neither the mother nor her daughter knew.

"Where is your family from, Miss Ramsey?" Lady Witham asked her with narrowed eyes.

"Ipswich," Fable supplied, putting down her spoon.

"Oh? What brings you to Colchester?" Miss Hollister asked her.

"I often wonder the same thing," Fable told them candidly. "I think it's the same reason you're here. His Grace."

Both women gaped and scoffed until they coughed. "You're quite bold, Miss Ramsey," Lady Witham said with distaste.

"She's delightfully honest," Ben was quick to defend her.

But he didn't have to, for with her most radiant smile, Miss Ramsey put out the fire before it started. "Miss—"

"Lady Witham," Ben interrupted in a low voice and with a warm smile aimed at Fable.

"Lady Witham," she corrected herself, "Let's face it, His Grace the Duke of Colchester knows he's the most sought after unwed duke in all of Britain. He knows why you're here with your daughter. It's for him. He values honesty. So let's be truthful, ladies, shall we? Our dear duke deserves that."

"Our dear duke?" he repeated when the mother and daughter left them alone again.

"Of course." She glanced up at him with a smile. "Should I have said *my* dear duke?"

His heart jumped and skipped. *Yes, you should have said that.* He kept his mouth closed for another moment—just to steady his voice. "You did claim to be truthful, after all."

Her smile slanted into a smirk. "Are you saying I lied by not claiming you as mine?"

"No," he answered smoothly. "I'm not yours." Did he want to be? "What you said was correct."

Her suddenly easy smile returned. It made him light-headed. If one believed in magical beings, like faeries, she was what one would expect to find after peeling back the petals of a peony or a rose. He smiled back. He couldn't help it if he wanted to, which he didn't.

"So I'm still 'delightfully honest' then?"

He nodded, watching her take a sip from her cup.

"How can you be sure that there are still things about me I haven't told you?"

She was correct, but he didn't want to admit it. What could she be hiding?

"Ah, there you are, Brother. Where did you disappear to?"

Ben downed the wine in his cup and stood up again as his sister approached. When Fable turned to see her, Prudence paused her steps. Her face flushed. Her jaw clenched. Ben flashed her a warning glare before she opened her mouth.

"I didn't know your guest was attending," she said, pretending to rein in her anger. "Does this mean Miss Ramsey's name will be added to your list of candidates for a wife?"

"No—"

"Good because—"

—"because there are no candidates."

—"I would never allow a marriage between you."

He scowled, caught between astonished disbelief and anger.

"You would never allow it? What ever led you to believe you had that kind of power over me?"

She stared up at him with her hand at her chest, and stepped back from the detached soldier she'd been living with for the past three years, and many years before that.

"Do you realize how much I put into this ball…for you?" she accused quietly.

"What does who I wed have to do with you?" he demanded just as quietly. Still, his tone drew others' attention.

"When you wed so beneath you that it awakens father asleep in Sheol and he turns over in his grave from the shame of his son."

Nothing seemed to have changed in the ballroom. The musicians still played, people still danced and laughed, but something was different. It was as if the familial veil was lifted from Ben's eyes and he looked a haughty, heartless woman in the face, disgusted at what he saw.

"Ben…" she tried, somehow knowing she'd stepped over a line carved in ice. "I didn't mean—"

He held up his palm to stop her and looked at Miss Ramsey. This time she wasn't smiling. "Come." He held his elbow out to her. "The tables have been moved. No one can dance until I do. Let's dance and then leave."

He knew Prudence was biting her tongue to stay quiet. He was choosing Miss Ramsey as his first—and only dance.

Miss Ramsey fit her hand into the crook of his arm and kept her head down as he led her past his sister and to the center of the ballroom.

When he slipped his fingers beneath her chin and lifted her head, he saw tears spilling down her alabaster skin.

"Shall we go?" he asked in a quiet voice and pulled her closer.

"Of course not." She smiled lightly and swiped her fingers across her cheeks. "I didn't suffer with bones jabbing me everywhere from my clothes for not even one dance with you."

He should feel pity for her—and he did—but he smiled, then

laughed softly. He held her while the music played and she learned the steps to an English country-dance called *The Romance.*

"Sir," she told him when he twirled her out and then pulled her back. "I think I should go back to my room."

"Why?" He stopped immediately and bent to pick her off her feet. She swatted his hand away.

"I'm tired. Really. That's all. There's no need for you to escort me there."

First he looked at her as if she'd gone mad, and then he asked her if she had.

"Ben," she leaned in closer so only he could hear her. "Send someone else to bring me back. I insist. Do what you promised your sister you would do. Get to know these ladies a little. Emphasis on a little, okay?"

"Fable, I know you jest because I have no intention of getting to know anyone."

"But how will you know if you've really found her if you haven't met everyone?"

He dipped his brows and feigned a glare, but it didn't last long before it disintegrated into something much warmer.

"How much better than you can anyone be?"

"She could be the king's niece and can put in a good word for you with her uncle."

He chuckled at how pleasing she was to him. "I don't need her for that."

"She could come from a family with money and you could live comfortably."

"I'm used to sleeping in tents and dirt ditches," he let her know.

What was he doing? Was he truly thinking of taking her as a wife? No! He didn't want a wife. This was a game. She said so herself. He was supposed to be charming her and here he was thinking of marrying her! It was because he liked her, He couldn't deny it.

"Stay and keep your promise," she told him, already breaking away. "The peace you get from it will be worth it."

He frowned at Prudence then reached out to pull Sudbury in from his path toward Ben's sister.

"Escort Miss Ramsey back to her rooms," he requested of his friend.

"Of course," Sudbury said, turning his gaze to Ben. He smiled at Fable next and motioned for her to follow him.

"Lord Sudbury!" Prudence stopped them before they reached the door. "Where do you think you're going with her?"

"Your brother asked me to—"

"I don't care what he asked. Don't you dare leave this hall."

"Prudence." Now Ben stepped forward. "She insists on going back to her room and making me keep my promise to you by not going with her. I won't send her back alone. So either Sudbury escorts her or I will. Which is it?"

Prudence clenched her jaw but then looked worried and rubbed her forehead while she decided which of the two men she was less concerned with losing to Miss Ramsey. "Simon, you escort her."

Sudbury stared at her for a moment. Ben dipped his gaze knowing Sudbury long enough to know when his friend was angry. It didn't happen often and when it did, Prudence was usually the cause. She was stubborn and prideful, though not always as mean-spirited as she'd been since Ben showed interest in a woman of no status.

Without a word, the earl splayed his palm against Miss Ramsey's back and led her out of the ballroom.

Ben wanted to go after them; his best friend and his...his...

He cut his glare to Prudence. Her contempt for the poor was proof of her fear of becoming the same. What could Fable ever be in his life with Prudence here? "If you don't wed Sudbury soon, I'll find you a husband to quicken your departure from this house."

Tears gathered at the rims of her eyes but they didn't fall. "You find it easy to be cruel. Ever since that day...we found out…" She paused to gather her strength. "You can be a monster, Benjamin." When he looked away and took a step to leave, she stopped him with a hand on his wrist. "I know how much you suffer. Don't you understand that? I know the reason you hate being here and yet you can't leave. I know what it's doing to you. And I know you need someone to—"

"Pru," he quieted her, softening his tone, "I'm not a child anymore. I'll see to what I need, hmm?"

"Do you think you need a woman who comes from the streets?" she asked, her pretty face marred by a sneer that Ben doubted she was even aware of. "A woman who probably has to beg for every pence she puts in her pocket?"

Ben closed his eyes as if he could see before him what his sister was describing. It made his heart ache. He didn't want Fable to beg for money ever again. It angered him that Prudence could show such callous disregard for others. He opened his eyes and regarded his sister with an incredulous grimace. "Was I not fighting to protect her as well as you when I almost lost my arm?"

"When you fought against the Jacobites?" she asked, looking a little lost.

"Yes. All your lives would have changed if a Stuart took the throne again."

"Benjamin, you fought against the Jacobites for revenge," she pointed out with a short laugh. "How many did you kill? Thousands? More? What does that have to do with someone like Miss Ramsey?"

He stared at her in disbelief then clenched his jaw. "I didn't kill enough."

His words finally produced tears she couldn't hold back. Instead of comforting her, he turned his back to her and faced two women, one young, one older. He blocked their path and their vision from his sister while she composed herself.

"Your Grace," the older woman smiled behind a powdered face and fluttering fan. "It's a pleasure to see you again. You remember my daughter, Lady Clara Bishop—" Ben barely flicked a glance Lady Clara's way when her mother began listing all her attributes as if she were a prized cow for sale. Ben was sure neither Lady Clara nor her mother noted the clenching of his jaw, his bare shred of tolerance as he pretended to care about either of them.

"Lady Chelmsford!" Prudence finally stepped around his broad shoulders, smiling. "Of course my brother remembers your lovely daughter, Lady Clara."

Ben didn't care if Lady Clara's father was the Earl of Chelmsford or the king. He made no movement to agree or disagree with his sister, though Lady Clara was smiling brightly. He didn't find her unattractive or unsuitable to be a wife. Her hair was dark sable brown pinned into curls over her ears. Her eyes were wide and filled with willingness.

Ben knew what was expected of him at a marriage ball. He was to meet the ladies, dance with those he liked, and by the end of the night choose one to wed. If he chose no one…his thoughts wandered back to Miss Ramsey. She knew that her leaving meant he couldn't choose her.

He already knew he wouldn't choose anyone else. But he'd promised Prudence he would meet the hopefuls.

The first was Lady Clara, who didn't seem to mind his aloof, curt treatment. He thought if he had to dance with her, he'd throw himself on his sword first. Next came the opposite in Lady Elizabeth Drake, who literally trembled like a terrified dog if he happened to glance in her direction—so he didn't. He barely held back his mournful sighs and low, threatening growls through conversations with Ladies Loretta Cornel and Margaret Somner. The more time he spent with his sister's idea of suitable wives, the more desperate he became to escape them and hurry to Miss Ramsey.

"I can speak six languages," boasted Lady Joan D'Artane. "I can embroider the most detailed designs, and prepare thirty-two dishes."

Ben looked over her shoulder at the open doors leading to the garden. Prudence was out there with Sudbury, who had returned. It was clear they were arguing.

"I'm also well versed in poetry and I can play several instruments," Lady Joan went on.

Ben exhaled.

"I understand you were the king's personal guard." She paused in listing her attributes to mention his. "A highly decorated captain in his army."

Ben guzzled down the remainder of the wine in his cup and nodded, then looked around for the next lady on the list. He caught Sudbury coming into the ballroom and storming back out through the main exit.

Prudence returned from the garden and looked around. When she saw Lady Joan's mother, she smiled brightly as if she hadn't just come from fighting with the man she cared for.

Ben turned away then ground his jaw when he saw Lady Isabel Talbert and her mother coming for him. He wasn't sure which of the two looked him over as if he was the last morsel of meat more, the mother or daughter.

Before they reached him, he turned and hurried out of the ballroom. That was it! He'd had enough!

When he reached the bottom of the stairs, he looked up hoping to see Miss Ramsey there at the top. She wasn't there. She'd called it a game. But it wasn't. This marriage ball made him think about what he needed to do. Either marry or return to his duty and fight. He didn't want to marry anyone his sister…or his father chose. He didn't want to marry Fable either and leave her a widow. He had to write to His Majesty soon.

He wouldn't go to her, though he longed to see her. It was better this way. If he saw her, he likely wouldn't be able to walk away. He had to stop lying to himself. He cared for her. He didn't know how or when it began, but he anticipated and remembered every moment spent with her. And he had to put an end to it. Now. Tonight. He wouldn't send her away, but he wouldn't let himself feel anything more than fondness for her. To do so was hurting her and would hurt her even more later. Even if she somehow defeated and replaced his anger and drive for revenge and could fill his days with happiness and peace, he would have to deny her love so that he didn't deny his father's wishes.

It broke his heart and as he turned away from the stairs, it made him angry with his father for the first time. He didn't care where Fable came from, who her family or what her status was. She stirred him. He couldn't set his eyes on her without being stirred. Deep within, deeper than even he could have imagined, she broke through layer after layer. If he let her...but there was still enough of a defense to keep her at bay.

He stayed awake practicing his swordplay alone, until Sudbury finally joined him beneath the stars.

Ben's arm was strong, his aim sure, when he swung his heavy blade at his friend. Sudbury didn't hold back either, but parried and jabbed with the grace of an elegant bird. Ben had to block after almost every strike, but the speed and weight of Ben's assault finally wore his opponent down. Sudbury dropped to his knees and held up his arms.

Ben lowered his sword and bent over to catch his breath while his friend did the same.

"Do that before the king and he'll snatch you right back up," Sudbury remarked earnestly. "You're ready."

Ben thought he'd be happier to hear those words. He was ready. Three years of hell and he was finally ready. His heart should be light. It was finally time to stand before the king and prove his skill. But he felt an unfamiliar pull.

"What is it?" his friend asked. "I thought you would be happier to hear that."

"I'm happy, but—"

Sudbury waited. "But? By any chance does it have to do with Miss Ramsey, with whom you spend all your time?"

"It can't have to do with her, Simon," Ben told him quietly. "If the king takes me back....it's what I've waited for."

"She waited for you," the earl informed him. "When the ball

was over, she waited but you didn't go to her."

"How do you know she waited?" Ben asked him. "Did you return to her room after your fight with my sister?"

"Yes. I thought it would be the first place you went."

Ben imagined her waiting for him. He felt terrible but not going to her was the right thing to do.

"How…how was she when you left her?" He didn't want to know. He shouldn't want to know, but he seemed to have lost control of his mouth.

"Melancholy," Sudbury told him. "I found it difficult to leave her. Honestly, Colchester," he argued when Ben glared at him. "She pulls at the heartstrings."

"See that she doesn't pull too hard on yours, Sudbury," Ben warned him, then muttered under his breath when his friend laughed.

"Brother," Sudbury grinned at him. "Your father is gone. I believe the war will be over soon. Live how you wish to live."

CHAPTER NINE

BEN WAS DRESSED by two servants Enis and Alger with Stephen overseeing the choices of attire, and finally tying the knot in his cravat.

"By the way," his old war-time friend said in a low voice. "I saw Miss Ramsey sitting in a chair in the hall."

Ben's heart began to involuntarily thump against his bones. "Which hall?"

"The one outside your door and to the right, just beyond the painting of your father's prized hound."

"What is she doing there?" Ben steadied his voice and slowed his breath. Why did the need to hurry and go see her suddenly overwhelm him? "Is she waiting for someone?"

The steward picked up the barely contained anticipation in the duke's voice and gave him a surprised look. "I asked her that very question and she replied that she was waiting for you."

Ben was sure the steward could hear his heartbeat. How should he feel about this? She was bold without a hint of arrogance, beautifully ethereal, beguiling his senses and clouding his good sense.

"I told her she was waiting at the wrong door and showed her where she should go."

"So she's outside my door?"

When Stephen nodded, Ben didn't know if he wanted to thank him or wring his hands around the steward's neck.

"All done," Stephen stepped back to examine him and nodded with a smile.

Ben didn't reply or say a word to him as he left his rooms.

When he pulled open the doors, he was ready to tell her that there was not, nor would there ever be anything between them. But when he saw her waiting for him, every other thought was held captive by the fleeting, reckless desire to kill anyone who tried to take her from his presence. He was doomed.

He hated himself and the day that brought him here. He wanted to be someone else, someone free of the chains that bound him, free to offer his heart to her. But she wasn't his destiny. Feeding the warrior was, ridding the land of Jacobites was.

"What are you doing here?"

"I thought you might want to take a stroll with me, maybe through the garden." A hint of a smile hovered around her lips. "It's a beautiful day."

Did she think he had nothing better to do than stroll around aimlessly? He stared at her. Did she have no one else to ask? He realized when he tried to swallow that he would have been miserable if she went strolling with someone else.

He nodded and swept his hand before him indicating that she should join him.

"I haven't forgotten that you promised to teach me to read," she reminded him, leaning in with a playful smile.

"I will if you can cease fainting for days on end."

She set her hand on her hip and quirked her brow. "I'm not the fainting type," she let him know. "I really don't know what's come over me."

"Starvation? Exhaustion?" he supplied.

"I've been hungry before," she said, "but never on the verge of starvation. I'll admit I was pretty exhausted."

"You should be resting, not strolling," he admonished with his gaze to the ground and a tender threat in his voice. He wasn't angry with her and he didn't want to hurt her by speaking roughly to her.

He wanted to call Sudbury to the yard and have a go at fighting him just to prove to himself that the warrior still lived within him and he hadn't turned into a bucket of sun-warmed honey over this woman.

"Is that why you didn't stop by my rooms last night?"

"Hmm?" He lifted his gaze to her. Poor decision. How was he expected to think straight when she was so pretty, looking up at him with her huge, bold, beguiling eyes. He felt more of his defenses crumbling. How could he think of fighting and battle when he was looking at her, shrouded in the fire of the sun? He had to blink to bring himself back to the present—to what she had asked.

"I didn't come because," he paused, keeping his eyes on hers, "because I don't wish to cause you any sadness."

She smiled softly at him, making his heart ache for something unfamiliar, yet haunting.

Happiness.

"How do you know you will?" she asked.

"Because…" Why? Why did he have to tell her? He felt a knot grow in his belly, making him want to double over. "Because I intend…no. I dream of returning to battle." It wasn't the truth anymore. He didn't dream of it. He dreamed of her. "I don't think I can be happy any other way, and even if I do marry, I must do what my father wished."

He didn't wait to see her reaction, but turned to look ahead. When a moment or two passed without any reply for her, he turned to her again.

He was certain he'd never look at another woman the same way. He held his breath when she took a little breath and opened her mouth to speak.

"Look, Your Grace, I honestly don't understand your allegiance to your father. I've never felt it. I never even knew it existed until now. None of the people my mother or me knew felt any kind of loyalty to anyone, beginning with their parents. But I know you were young when you lost him. You never had a chance to show him the man you'd grow to be. I'm sure that stings."

He swallowed and nodded so slightly he wasn't sure if she saw it.

"But he's gone," she continued. "He isn't looking down, watching to see whether or not you obey his last wishes. Where exactly would he be looking from? Not Heaven if he's more interested in being honored by his son than he is in enjoying Paradise, and do you think he would really want you to join him so early in your life?" She waited a moment for him to answer, then bowed her head repentantly. "I'm sorry. I got carried away."

She got carried away over him. He liked how it made him feel and then cursed himself for it.

"Are you angry…with me?" she asked, sounding as if she worried about his answer.

"No," he answered without hesitation.

"That's good." She smiled at him but there was only sadness in her eyes.

"Fable—" he began, regretting and unsure about his decision, but she cut him off.

"Because I think we should skip the stroll. It won't do either of us any good. I'll be going." Before she drew her next breath, she turned back and marched the other way.

Calling forth every last shred of strength he possessed he didn't go after her.

He was sorry he let this go on for as long as it did. They'd called it a game, but it had become so much more to him. It troubled him because this was a battlefield he'd never been on. His opponent had the power to render him weak and pitiful at any point in time. It scared the hell out of him.

But there was another part of him that watched after her, aching to stop her, haul her in his arms, and kiss her until they were both senseless. And then take her to his bed.

Instead, he spent the day mostly alone, with her on his mind.

He had a game of chess with Sudbury, which, incredibly, he lost. After that he practiced his sword fighting with the earl, and won.

By the time the sun went down, it felt as if fifty days had passed. It was better this way, he told himself. Stay away from her. But he wasn't sure he could do it again tomorrow. Madly, he missed her more than he'd ever had missed anyone before. Her sweet face enchanted him. It astounded him how such a fairy looking woman had found a way through his iron defenses. Had she? He wanted to scoff at the way the memory of her beguiling smile made his heart race until he felt light-headed. The way her wide, aqua eyes pulled him into their depths and tempted him to give up everything for her, mainly his revenge. He wouldn't take her for a wife, defying his father and his sister, and end up leaving to slaughter or be slaughtered, making her a widow.

It drove him mad and he couldn't lay his head down on his pillow. If she felt anything for him, and he believed she did, then his words—his possibly *last* words to her, were hopeless and hurtful. She hadn't wanted to spend another moment with him.

He ran his hands down his face as he paced before his bed.

When she said she was going, did she mean going to her rooms, or leaving the premises? Why hadn't he checked to see if she was in her bed?

And if she wasn't, should he go after her again?

Something shook him from deep inside like an earthquake. For a moment he couldn't move. It felt as if every bone was crumbling, every muscle withering. He closed his eyes, and with his father and his need for revenge gently pushed to the side, he left his bed.

FABLE WASN'T SURE she'd ever get used to being tucked into bed, but she remained still and compliant while Edith pulled up her blanket.

"Is it the duke who took away your smile, dear one?"

Fable shrugged and then nodded and sniffed. "He can't be happy with me."

"Oh, now that's the most foolish thing I've ever heard. Why, he is already happy with you."

"Oh, Edith," Fable scoffed. "His heart belongs to no one. No one alive, at least."

"I do confess that most find him unapproachable and uncompromising," Edith went on. "But he's changed since you arrived. He seems less…angry. We all notice it, Miss."

"That makes it even more tragic, Edith. He'll do what his father wanted. He'll do what he believes he needs to do. Avenge his parents. That's the kind of man he is."

"We'll see," Edith said with a sigh. "His Grace is strong-willed and wise. He will make the right choice. Now to bed with you."

Fable looped her arms around the servant's neck and pulled her in for an embrace. "Goodnight, Edith."

The woman startled for a moment unused to such behavior, then, as her heart warmed, she patted Fable's back. "Sleep well, Dear."

Fable waited while Edith blew out the candles and then left her alone. In the dark, she wondered who she was that another person would tuck her in and blow out the candles besides her mother? But her mother never had. She soon fell asleep to the sound of raindrops against the shutters and memories of the duke's handsome face.

But his face changed as thunder peeled and lightning flashed in the night sky. His smile was grotesque as he reached for what was in her hand. She looked. It was the pocket watch. He grabbed for it but she snatched back her hand and began to run. He chased her through dark, wet alleys, along dimly-lit roads, and through a pitch-black forest. His clutching fingers always felt as if they were a hair away from her, ready to snatch her away. She ran until her lungs burned and her legs ached. But just when she thought she had escaped him, he appeared in front of her and caught her in his arms. *You call for the duke. Do you know him?*

"Let me go!" she cried out, fighting and struggling while he held her in his vise-like embrace.

"It's all right," a soothing male voice said in her ears. "You're safe."

Her eyes shot open as a scream left her lips. "No! Duke?" The instant she recognized him, she wrapped her arms around his neck and held on. How did she get into the hall…into his arms? "Ben. The time traveler was after me."

"You're here with me now. You're safe," he soothed and lifted her off her feet.

She melted against him. How did she end up in his arms? Had she been sleepwalking? "How did I come to be in the hall?" she asked, so glad and thankful that he'd been there.

"I couldn't sleep and I was on my way to check on you and found you dreamwalking."

Suddenly she forgot her dream, but hadn't he rejected her? "Do you check on me at night?"

He stared at her then nodded. "I know you sometimes have night terrors. Like tonight. Come," he said gently, carrying her back to her rooms. "I'll bring you back to bed. Do you want me to call for Edith?"

He spoke so softly to her and with such comfort she could have fallen asleep on the way. She shook her head and held onto him. "I just want you."

He closed his arm around her tighter. "You have me."

Fable shivered. What did that mean, she had him? Did he mean she was a guest in his house and as such she fell under his protection? Or was he speaking of something more personal, more serious? Hadn't he already told her that he had to honor his father's wishes? How long would she have him? She blinked herself out of her reverie. It was dangerous to start depending on someone.

She wanted to tell him to put her down, but her mouth stayed shut. She let him bring her to her bed but releasing him was still humiliatingly difficult. She was afraid the time-traveler would never stop chasing her.

"Maybe," she told the duke while he helped her into bed. "I should meet with him—"

"Absolutely not," he said, his gaze level with hers, his tone, deep and foreboding. "I'll meet with him if he ever dares to show up here."

"Ben?"

"Hmm?" He pulled up a chair to sit close to her by the bed.

"How come you never ask me where the pocket watch is? Don't you believe what I told you?"

"I believe you," he told her softly. She didn't know why he would, but she was happy he did.

"He said if the policemen took his pocket watch, he'd kill them all. And now I have it. I can't give it back. I may need it to return to my time. Besides, I don't have it with me."

"You're truly thinking of leaving?" he asked. His voice was hesitant, laced with regret.

There was nothing here for her. She wouldn't stick around while he was marrying one of those horrible shrews, or gleefully going off to war.

"I'm not so sure I could survive here, Your Grace."

"I'll see that you do," he insisted.

"How? By keeping me as your servant?"

"You were never my servant."

She wouldn't try to figure out his meaning. If he felt something let him tell her, but only if he meant to remain with her.

"He's here and I'm afraid of him," she told him, staying on the important topic. "I don't think he came from the twenty-first century originally. His clothes looked more like he came from here. And he had a sword with blood on it."

The duke left the chair and sat in bed with her. When he opened his arms to her, she sank into them. "Before he brought me here, he asked me if I knew his wife. He said the pocket watch had eaten her up. I don't know what he meant except that she traveled through time with it. First he asked me if I knew her, then he asked me if I knew you. At first, I felt bad for him. Crazy, you know? But when the police came, he held his sword to my throat."

"If he wants to live," Ben growled above her, "he better not show his face near you ever again."

Fable closed her eyes and let herself take comfort in his strong arms and warm promises.

"Ben?" she asked, happy that he hadn't blown out all the candles. When she opened her eyes, she could see him as well as feel him in her arms. "There's something you should know about me. I used to cheat people out of their money in card games, dice—"

"Chess," he added, sounding stern.

She stared at his neck in his untied shirt. "What do you think of me now?"

"Why did you do it?"

"To eat."

He stroked her back and caught her gaze when she raised it to him. "Fable, I think the same thing about you that I thought this morning. You're a wonder to my senses. You're treading where none before you have ever dared go."

She thought of the audacity of herself to attend his sister's ball as an uninvited guest. "I'm sorry for involving myself in your private affairs."

He smiled, staring into her eyes in the dim light. "Miss, you're welcome in every part of my life."

Was she?

"What about your war? What about your father's wishes?"

He took in a deep breath, then let it out. "I was afraid you might have left Colchester after what I told you. Your absence made me certain that I don't want you to leave. Mayhap I should try living my life and give being happy a try. Finally. The only way to be happy is to be with you."

She was sure there were hearts floating from her eyes at his words. She wanted to laugh...and giggle...and cry tears of happiness. Was he real? Were her prayers for a different, safer life finally answered? And not only answered, but added to? "I want to be happy too," she told him softly.

He closed his arms around her and held her tighter, closer. "Let me be the one to make you happy, Fable."

She wanted it to be him. Could it be? "You're the person in my life I didn't know I needed. Or maybe I did know it and that's why it was so tragic. You didn't exist in that time."

"I'm here now."

With her ear pressed to his chest, his voice echoed through her as deep as the shadows.

"What about your sister?" she asked. Prudence West was a force to be reckoned with. She would be against anything they did. "Why does it seem she cares more about money than your happiness?"

"Likely because she believes money makes us happy." He stroked her hair down her back while he spoke, lulling Fable to the brink of utter comfort. "She was thirteen when our parents were killed. She was our father's only daughter, and the apple of his eye. His last wish means everything to her. As for my father, he knew I was a bit sentimental and he worried that I would marry for love and lose the fortune he took years to build. So he added a clause to his will that his last wish was for me to wed into a powerful family. My sister is determined to see his wish fulfilled."

"What about you?" she asked then yawned. "You feel strongly about his last wish, don't you?"

He shook his head. "The last thing I've given any thought to is taking a wife. I never really thought to live past the age of thirty years." He smiled warmly when she gave his arm a slight slap.

"Another reason Prudence has trouble with poverty is because we weren't saved from the full terrible clutches of it," he told her. "Three years after our parents were killed, we were thrown out of Colchester House by His Grace the Duke of

Addinton for debts my father allegedly owed. We were left to live or die on the street."

When Fable heard this, she opened her eyes and lifted her head off his chest. "You were homeless?"

He nodded. "For two years, we stole and begged for scraps of food."

"What?" She rubbed her eyes and opened them even wider. "Why didn't you ever tell me?"

"My sister hates that we were once 'street urchins'. She will be angry if she knows I told you. I'm glad to be telling you now though. I understand some of the hardships of living out there, especially for a girl. I saved my sister from being raped thirteen times, and was stabbed several times for it. But at least she had me. You had no one."

"You felt responsible for someone else," she pointed out. "I was free of that."

She felt him breathing and let it lull her again. "How did you return home?"

"We met Lord Andrew Holt, the Marquess of Cambridge and he took us in. But I was troublesome."

Fable looked up at him again. "*You* were troublesome?"

He ignored her doubtful tone and continued. "I joined the Royal army and three years after that I rode back to Colchester House with proof that my father never owed any debts, killed the Duke of Addinton and his men, and took my house back."

She stared into his doe eyes and tried to imagine him wild with rage and revenge. She quirked her brow at him. He wasn't the enraged, wild type. Captain Ben West was put together, composed, and disciplined. He was the planned out, quiet assault type of guy.

"You're very attractive," she said boldly, and then looked away to blush.

"Why do you say that?" he asked, his voice deep and low with restraint that started out playful.

"I like that you took back what was yours," she told him.

"What about the killing?" he asked her quietly. He didn't look worried by what her answer would be, but the slight shift of his resolute jaw revealed how he felt about it.

"It was a consequence of his vile actions."

He was still for a few seconds. Was he breathing? Fable looked into his eyes and then smiled when he pulled her closer and held her more tightly.

"Ben?" she said after another minute and let her gaze settle on his lips. "I've never been in love before."

He moved his warm palms up and down her back. "Neither have I."

"I've never been with a man before."

"Nor I with a woman." His voice resonated through her blood, her bones.

She felt him move his fingers through her hair, over her chin, then under it. He lifted her face gently and then moved closer to kiss her.

And then his lips were pressing against hers and she couldn't think of anything but the wonderful warmth and safety of his arms, the tender curiosity of his lips, and his kiss that told a thousand stories of a man losing his heart to a woman. As she suspected, his bottom lip was plumper, softer. She tested it instinctively with her teeth. He reacted by pulling her closer into the warm, hard angles of his body. She shivered with desire and the anticipation of fulfilling it. She opened her mouth to his, welcoming his tongue with a fleeting dance of her tongue across it—until he pushed her down gently and deepened his kiss, capturing her tongue and holding it still with his. His mouth was hot, like a brand, sealing her as his. Oh, she shouldn't have come this far. Now, she didn't have the resolve to hold back. Yes, she would be his. She would happily be his. He made her breath come hard and fast. His hungry tongue, like a curious touch over the pulse of her throat made some muscles loosen while others grew tighter. When he scraped his teeth over her chin, her legs opened involuntarily, nestling him close. She felt his body growing tighter, harder as his lips returned to hers. Her heart felt as if it were going to pound right out of her chest.

Finally, he withdrew. He gazed into her eyes. His plump, red lips hovered above hers. "No matter how much I fight it, or how unfamiliar it is to me, I'm almost fully certain that I love you, Miss Ramsey."

Chapter Ten

Prudence West stopped on her way toward the north-west wing, where Lord Sudbury's rooms were and stared at the door to the guest room. It had been an hour now since Miss Ramsey had stumbled out of the room and tumbled into Benjamin's arms. What had her brother been doing making his way to the guest room so late in the night? He'd carried the waif back into the room and there he stayed—fool that he was!

She looked longingly toward Simon's room. She needed his company. She couldn't sleep. Slumber only brought nightmares of sleeping huddled in an alley outside in the dark, afraid, oh, so afraid that she would lose her brother every time he failed to return to her until the morning, beaten up and bleeding but in possession of enough money to pay for their lodgings for another few days. But worse than him not returning to her until morning, was when he was with her, fighting off some miscreant who thought to have his way with her in the alley—of seeing a knife in her brother and blood gushing like a spring from his belly. Ben had no idea how much she had grown to depend on him. She had a wonderful, handsome man who loved her and wanted to take her away but she couldn't leave Ben—and she hated herself for it.

After more than an hour, she gave up waiting for her brother to exit the guest room. She felt the blood rushing to her face as her careless rogue of a brother kept a woman like that for his pleasure. *How could he?* she raged silently. The woman was a pauper! Oh, their poor father! Thank God he wasn't here to see this. Benjamin was sure to lose their father's fortune to some wench. Staying in her room for so long likely meant that he bedded the urchin. What would he do if she turned up pregnant with his child? Oh, the very thought of it made Prudence's bones shake.

She hurried to Simon's door. On the way, she tried to remember any lady who sparked her brother's interest in the past. He was a dark, brooding killer, made all the more dangerous because he walked with the favor of the king. After they were told about the deaths of their parents, Prudence's soft-spoken little brother had retreated into a dark place and became an angry, vengeful young man. Their father's servants helped them survive for three years until Lord Addinton came to Colchester House and threw everyone out, including her and her brother.

Prudence rubbed her palm over her belly and let out a little groan. Those were the worst days…years of her life. She hated remembering the way she begged for food. And she'd only finally done it because she was starving to death. While she begged for scraps, her brother fought in competitions and often won enough for them to eat and sleep for a few days. He fought. That's all Benjamin did. He didn't give himself any time for girls or their wiles. He became one of the fiercest fighters in Colchester, where they barely survived until Lord Cambridge took pity on them and rescued them from the streets.

Oh, she hated remembering. It was Miss Ramsey's fault that she did. What kind of spell had that ragamuffin put on her brother? And how could Prudence break it? She had to, for Lady Alexandra Augustus, the king's own niece, was in love with her brother. Benjamin was too rich, too handsome and powerful to be with just any woman. He could propel the West name to the highest heights if he married right. Prudence worked diligently for years building up the duke in the eyes of the most elite nobles. But truly, all Ben needed to do was show up to melt the powder off ladies' faces. He was unquestionably the most handsome man in the kingdom, after him, of course was Lord Sudbury. Ben had money and it showed mostly in how he dressed. He wore the finest silk and silk velvets, imported cotton, and handmade lace. Other men could wear the same thing, but her brother wore it well. He was tall and elegant with an untouchable air about him. But to his sister, he would always be a young boy crying his heart out for his mother or training alone every day and night for three years, cutting the air with the fierce fury of his sword. Revenge was the source that drove him. His one and only desire was to kill Jacobites and once Prudence had a home with Lord Cambridge, her brother left her to kill for Queen Anne and then for King George. She hardly saw him for nine years, save for when he returned to Colchester House to slaughter everyone in it and then sat in his rightful place, in his father's chair. Once he had established that everything was his, he brought Prudence back to her home, and then he left again to go fight alongside the Duke of Marlborough. He created a name for himself with his heroic deeds at a battle in southern Germany and then again when he saved the king's life multiple times.

He could marry any woman he desired. How could he—after everything—give up his social status for a destitute beggar?

"Lady Prudence."

She stopped and tilted her head up. "Simon, what are you doing in the hall at this late hour?"

"I was hoping to have a word with you. I was on my way to your rooms."

His velvety voice seeped through her, warming her blood. He was Benjamin's childhood friend and fought at her brother's side in every battle he'd been in, including taking back Colchester House. As far back as Prudence could remember, she'd always loved Simon Hamilton. "A word?" Her heart thumped hard, making her feel a little ill. "What about?"

"Come back to Sudbury with me," he blurted.

"What?" A wave of lightheadedness washed over her and she held her hand to her forehead. She laughed a little but he looked to be quite serious. *Not now. Not now.*

"Let's leave in the morning, Pru. After our marriage—"

"Simon," She took a step back, shaking her head. "What is this about? Did Benjamin put you up to this? He wants me to leave. Do you think I would wed you because my brother is forcing you to do so?"

He smiled, but Prudence knew him well enough to recognize that he was anything but happy.

"Forcing me?" he asked. "How long have I been asking, Prudence? You always have a reason to postpone it. I don't want to wait anymore for Ben to take a wife."

"But he needs—"

"No, he doesn't. He's a grown man who can make decisions on his own. He doesn't need you meddling in his affairs."

"Simon." She pulled on his sleeve and opened the door to his rooms, then pulled him inside. "I saw him take Miss Ramsey to the guest room over an hour ago, and he still remains.

"So?" he argued. "He's fought on battlefields! He's not a child."

"But she has nothing! She's a street urchin!"

His strained smile faded. "Instead of worrying over her social status, be glad your brother is finally taking an interest in something other than killing."

She wanted to say more, but he did have a point. But oh, why did the first woman to bend Benjamin's iron resolve have to be someone like Miss Ramsey? It was clear that Simon didn't understand.

"My dear," her beloved softened his tone and pulled her gently into his arms. "I want you to be mine completely. Marry me and come live with me in Sudbury." He lowered his head and kissed her, muddling her thoughts.

No, just this one thing. Let her help her brother find a wife worthy of him and the name West. Oh, for her father's sake, let her help bring pride to their name.

"Simon," she said, pressing her palms to his chest to push him away, "Don't you remember how my father's name was dragged through the dirt as being a debtor and causing his children to be cast out into the street? Well, just as my brother wanted to clear our father's name, I want to elevate it. I want everyone to know the name West and to respect it."

He was quiet and kept his head down.

"Well? Do you have nothing to say? I'm telling you my brother won't be respected if he falls in love with a girl from the street."

He finally looked at her. "Things could turn around for her, as they did for you."

If he were anyone else, she would have slapped his face for making such a comparison, but she loved him too much to put her hand to hurt him. "It's not the same thing, Simon. My prestige was taken from me. All we know of Miss Ramsey is that she came here from Ipswich with nothing. She'll bring everything down."

"Pru, you don't know her. She's doing him good."

What? What was this she was hearing? "Are you defending her?" But it wasn't the first time, was it? He liked the urchin. She fell back into a chair and fanned herself.

"My love," he said as he knelt before her and took her hand, "in your zeal to elevate your father's name, you have become someone I no longer understand."

She pulled her hand away from his and bolted to her feet. She pushed past him and went to the door.

"You can leave now," she said, opening it.

"Prudence, I'm on your side."

"Are you on the side of someone you don't understand?"

"I didn't mean it the way it came out."

"Go," she insisted, too angry to care. Not only was her fool of a brother in love with that woman, but the man Prudence loved most defended her!

"Prudence," Simon said in a sterner tone. "This is my room."

"I don't care. Get out!"

"If you keep this up you're going to lose him. We all might."

"What? What does that mean? How might we all lose him?"

He didn't answer but moved toward the door. She stepped in front of him, blocking the way. He could have easily moved her out of his way, but he didn't.

"My love..."

"Yes?"

"He can't go on much longer with so much darkness in him without fighting."

"But he can't fight—"

"He practices every day without fail," Simon pointed out.

Just as he practiced when he was a boy and became good enough to fight for the queen. Her eyes opened wider as the horrifying truth dawned on her. "He intends to return to the king."

Loyal to who he was, he neither denied nor affirmed it. "I think she can stop him."

The urchin could stop it? "How? By falling in love with her? Tell me, is she that special?"

"Yes. I believe for Ben, she is. His happiness is important to you, isn't it?"

"He can be happy with the king's niece," she insisted.

"No. He has no interest in her, in any of them. You know that."

"You're asking me to stand by and let him wed a beggar."

"If he returns to the king," he countered, "whatever more he can do for your father's name might end for good."

She paled. Returns to the king. Yes, Benjamin would do that, and he could die. Even if he brought shame to their father's name, she didn't want to lose him to some Jacobite blade. She'd lost enough to them already.

"Is he able to fight again, Simon? The truth, please."

"You know how determined he is, Prudence. He can fight. I don't know for how long, but long enough to convince the king that he's ready."

She held her hands to her mouth and swayed for a moment.

Simon was there immediately to hold her up.

These were her choices? Lose her brother to a pauper, or lose him to death. Either way… She wanted to weep, to yank out her hair and wail. How could he even consider returning to the battlefield? Was fighting and killing truly all he cared about?

"I need to think about all of this," she told Simon, sounding defeated.

"Very well then, I'll walk you back to your rooms." He took her hand without another word and led her out.

When they passed the guest room door, she stared at and wished her brother would open the door so she could throw her shoe at his stubborn head.

FABLE SAT AT the hand-carved wooden table in the dining hall. It was the first time she actually sat at the table and ate. As a matter of fact, it was the first time she'd ever sat at *any* table. And she'd never imagined one could look like this one—covered in different dishes of food. That was what Ben had used to lure her here. Food. He'd asked her what she liked to eat for breakfast. She told him scrambled eggs, buttered toast and a cup of coffee.

She smiled now lifting a hunk of bread that looked as if it had been roasted over a flame, to her mouth. He'd had the cook prepare what she liked, and—with Fable's prompting, what he liked; barley cakes, biscuits, over-easy eggs, ham, fresh butter, marmalade, and various fish dishes. There were melons, grapes, berries and different creams. She'd never seen so much food in one place.

He'd had Stephen out since early this morning buying coffee beans, roasting them, grinding and finally boiling them. She brought her cup to her mouth next and sipped the strong, bitter beverage. It made her shiver. She guessed this was what coffee was supposed to taste like. She added some fresh sweet milk then closed her eyes and almost purred like a satisfied cat. When she opened her eyes, she saw that Ben was watching her from across the table, wearing the faintest hint of a smile.

His declaration from the night before resonated in her head. *I'm almost fully certain that I love you, Miss Ramsey.*

He loved her? That's when she knew all this was a dream. She was in a coma somewhere. He loved her? What did it mean? What should she do about it? She knew one thing, she was losing her hardened heart to him.

"Have I thanked you for all this, Your Grace?"

"Yes. A dozen times," he answered, looking as if he didn't mind at all. He rested his hands from eating and looked at them, rather than at her. "Have I told you…" he paused to clear his throat "… how lovely you look?"

"Many times." She let out a little laugh while she ate. She'd *felt* lovely, like a pampered princess, standing still while seamstresses measured her for new gowns, which His Grace had ordered to be fashioned not only for beauty, but for comfort without any whale bones to pinch and prod, or corsets that cut off her air. Just a few hours later two gowns had already been finished. She chose one made of fine, sapphire-colored, silk velvet with silver thread sewn into soft swirls throughout. It was unbelted and hung in flowy waves and pleats from her shoulders to the floor over a matching bodice and soft, cotton petticoats instead of hoops. She had sat impatiently, wanting to see him while two different women washed and dried her hair. She loved all the attention and enjoyed it while they brushed her long locks and pinned them up.

"I have to write some letters this afternoon," he told her while they ate together this morning. "After that I can teach you fencing. I need to practice."

"When will you teach me to read and write?" she asked, spooning some cream onto a chunk of melon and then happily eating it.

"Tonight," he told her, gazing at her. "Over candlelight and wine?"

She smiled, blushed, and nodded. She couldn't help but think about the night she'd spent in his arms. Though he'd kissed her with passion and promises, he hadn't tried to have his way with her. He was as awkward and untried as she was. He'd slept for what was left of the night. She lay awake as the hours passed, listening to him breathing next to her, staring at his beautiful face while he dreamed, hopefully of her. The thought of spending another night with him thrilled her.

"Ah, Miss Ramsey," the villainess snarled as she approached the table on the arm of a man who Fable pitied. "I wasn't told you would be joining us for breakfast." She shot a scornful glare at Ben. "I could have made arrangements for food more to your taste."

Wow. She was an evil villainess, all right. She didn't waste time but struck with a smile on her pretty face.

Ben sipped his coffee and stared at his sister. "Prudence, make arrangements for the next time I don't tell you something because it will happen again. You aren't Mother, and I'm not a child. As for the food, I've arranged it. It's all her favorites."

He looked at Fable and smiled. "You like it, hmm?"

She smiled at him. How could she hide it after all he'd done this morning? "Yes, thank you."

He laughed quietly over her thankfulness while Lady Prudence stared at him. It was because Fable was leaning in that she heard Lord Sudbury's soft voice when he spoke to Ben's sister.

"I haven't seen him this happy since he was ten years old."

Fable couldn't help but glance at Lady Prudence to surprisingly find her big, dark eyes shining with tears while she stared at her brother.

Lady Prudence, the wicked villainess of Fable's tale, was actually very beautiful when she wasn't glaring, snarling, or hurling insults. Her eyes and face were rounder, her nose smaller than her brother's. Otherwise, she resembled him.

Those glassy eyes fell on Fable and hardened looking her over. "New gown?"

"Yes. It was made for me this morning," Fable happily told her. "His Grace took pity on me when I mentioned the bone stays in my last gown stabbing me. This is so soft." She held out her arm. "Do you want to feel it?"

Lady Prudence somehow managed to smile through her icy expression. Fable continued to smile at her, and also at Lord Sudbury.

"No. I do not want to feel it," the lady sneered.

"Oh, Stephen!" Fable held up her index finger to Lady Prudence and then waved to the steward. "The coffee is delicious," she told him. "Pure heaven. Thank you for all your trouble."

"It was no trouble at all, Miss," the steward told her with a kind smile. He was very fatherly looking, Fable decided. He had kind eyes and a patient smile.

"Have you had breakfast?" Fable asked him. "Come and sit and have some of your wonderful coffee with us."

The steward cast Ben an uncertain look.

"It's all right, Stephen," Ben told him. "You may sit with us."

Fable clapped her hands and then hurried to get the steward a cup of coffee.

When she returned, Ben was, as usual, smiling at her. His sister was not.

"Miss Ramsey, we don't serve the servants."

Fable's smile softened. "My lady, I didn't ask you, His Grace, or Lord Sudbury to serve anyone. There's nothing wrong with a servant serving another servant."

"You are no one's servant," the duke corrected.

Fable graced him with a smile, then shifted her gaze back to his sister. "Stephen worked all morning to make the coffee we're all enjoying. Whether one has an abundance—" She looked around at all the food on the table, "or if you have nothing, gratitude is something we should all practice."

"He can drink it in the kitchen," Prudence said unmoved, and pushed her cup away.

Stephen began to rise from his chair.

Fable didn't want him to go. If this was what having money and power did to a person, she wanted no part of it. This wasn't her home. She couldn't tell Lady Prudence that if she didn't like it, leave.

"Stephen, sit down." The duke's rumbling voice warmed her blood and made her want to smile. "Prudence, he's my loyal steward. He'll sit at my table from this day on."

"Sir, I—" Stephen tried.

"Drink your coffee," the duke ordered. The steward obeyed. "It's very good," Ben added, holding up his cup to Stephen. "Thank you."

Sitting near Ben, Lord Sudbury caught Fable's eye and smiled with a slight nod. Beside him, the villainess cast her a stunned look.

Fable didn't want to be her rival, or her enemy in any way. After all, she was falling in love with her brother. Enemies only made one's life miserable, and this life she was living right now was too good to harbor animosity toward anyone. But could a street urchin find warmth in a heart so cold? She remembered winning the heart of cranky Old Ernest Hemmingway from Bleecker St. back in twenty-seventeen. She knew Ernest Hemmingway wasn't his real name, but if that's what he wanted to be called, who was she to argue? One good thing about living on the streets was that you could be whoever you wanted to be.

Old Ernest sold fish behind the piers. Every Tuesday, Fable's mother set off with Fable in tow to the piers. Old Ernest used to save fish for her that was starting to lose its freshness. But after her mother tried to steal two bluefish, he refused to ever speak to her again. Fable and her mother went three months without any seafood—until her mother begged her to go speak to Old Ernest for her. She hadn't gone directly to him, but stayed half-hidden and watched him from where he could see her. Finally, he called her over. She went with her long hair bouncing around her delicate shoulders. She didn't ask him for food, but smiled at all the filets and whole fish over ice. Fable didn't like seafood, but her mother did. By the end of the day, the cantankerous old man smiled at her as if she were his treasured grandchild. She returned to her mother with three bass and a bag of shrimp.

Fable knew how to win affection. She didn't smile now, in case Lady Prudence thought she was gloating over having her way. She looked away and set her gaze on Lord Sudbury.

"My lord," she said, keeping her voice soft, but just loud enough for Lady Prudence to hear. "You spoke the truth when you said the duke's sister was the most beautiful woman in England."

Lady Prudence blushed and then smiled into her hand.

There now, Fable thought, quietly slapping her hands together under the table. That wasn't so difficult.

"Miss Ramsey," the Duke of Colchester said in a quieter voice so that only she and Stephen could hear, a look of pure entertainment on his face. "What other wonders are you hiding?"

Chapter Eleven

Ben sat at the desk in his study, trying to pen a letter of apology to Lord Brambley for not being able to escort his daughter to London. But all Ben could think about was Miss Ramsey's tour of the house with Stephen taking place while the owner of the house sat alone writing letters.

Last month he would have welcomed being alone, which he sought to be most of the time. But not lately. Since he'd met her he always sought the company of Miss Ramsey. He felt a need he couldn't control to see her, hear her voice, hold her, breathe her, watch her while she ate or slept. He felt more familiar with her than anyone else he knew. And he wanted more with her. More—beyond the physical, though, even now, alone in his study, the very thought of being in bed with her in his arms made him remember how badly he'd wanted to kiss her and undress her, and make love to her. He believed she was a virgin—though he knew it was only by the grace of God that she was if the life she described to him was the truth.

He was a virgin too. He knew the basics of what to do from listening to his soldiers while they laughed about their experiences around campfires. Ben didn't think it was a laughing matter, unless the laughing was done by the pair involved.

He wouldn't mind laughing with Fable while—

He pushed out his chair and stood up. He loved her. There was no denying it. He'd already confessed to her. He wanted to go find her. Would he appear the fool? Pathetic? He hated this unfamiliar need in him because he couldn't control it. And he'd become a master at controlling himself when he was off the field. He had to control it all or risk releasing the warrior. Since the injury to his arm, he'd had to leash all the anger, the endless need for revenge, blood, and destruction. Without his arm, he was useless. But in three years, with steadfast dedication, he'd strengthened his muscles and recovered the use of his arm. He'd been planning on writing to the king about meeting with him to return to service. But here he was, hesitating. Hesitating! And why? Because of a woman! A woman without a home, a family, or a pence to her name. Not only that, she claimed to be from another time and that there was a man armed with a sword chasing her. She didn't have a shred of proof to support either claim, save for villagers who had seen a red-haired woman appear out of nowhere. There was no proof it was her. Even the pocket watch wasn't in her possession. And yet, here he was in the hall, ready to go find her. He looked around, swallowed, and then set out to check inside every room. He didn't care if she was out of her mind, he would believe what she told him was real to her.

He thought about losing her and felt sick to his stomach. Missing her would be unbearable. He didn't miss anyone in his life, except his parents. But his heart felt heavy when he wasn't with Fable, burdened with the desire to exact revenge that burned as hot as it first had seventeen years ago. The warrior had become a friend to him, but being caged had become torturous.

But since that first day when she fell into his arms, she made him forget the warrior and eased the pain. She soothed him like a comforting aroma to his soul. She made him laugh again, and she broke his heart. She gave him peace—and now he craved it even more than revenge.

He searched the second-floor, hurrying through the wings, but didn't find her. He laughed at himself as he searched, then shook his head in disgust. Why had he agreed to let her go with his steward?

On the main floor, he spotted Prudence and Sudbury on their way out of the house. Good, the last thing he needed was to explain to his sister why he was searching for Miss Ramsey.

He did his best to avoid anyone who might wish to speak with him. Whatever it was could wait.

After another quarter of an hour, he found her where he'd found her the first time, in the garden. Stephen waited a few feet away while she knelt before the cross on his parents' memorial, praying in silence. Ben went still seeing her and remembering that day…she'd been hiding. He would kill anyone who tried to hurt her.

He looked around, narrowing his eyes on any sound that didn't seem natural.

He didn't want to interrupt her prayers so he stood watch until she was done.

"Oh." Her dulcet voice rang across his ears from behind, "Did you finish writing your letters?"

"I needed fresh air. I'll finish later," he told her, turning to see her.

She smiled and leaned in closer while Stephen made his way toward them. "Were you missing me, Duke?"

He turned around and stared at her, more afraid than he'd ever been on any battlefield. She had a hold on his heart. He didn't need to have loved before to know that what he was feeling now was love. Perhaps it wasn't too late to stop it. Did he want to?

"I still have a letter to write to the king." He looked up from the ground and met Stephen's knowing gaze. His steward was well aware of his plans. "But I don't want you out here with only Stephen to guard you. Until the man chasing you is stopped, you'll only come out with me."

Had her eyes always been so big, so blue-green with shards of gold? Had her skin always been so clear, her lips so pink?

"So then," she teased, "you were worried about me?"

He wished he could control his own damned face. But he

couldn't help but smile at the way she turned his complaining into compliments. He nodded then turned again and began walking back to the house. She followed with Stephen and then picked up her pace so that she was walking beside Ben.

"I was thinking of you," she confessed.

His heart pounded in his ears. What had become of him?

"It doesn't seem fair that when I finally meet someone I can fall for, it's now, here, in a time I don't belong. I feel like when my purpose for coming to the past is complete, I'll be pulled back—I mean, ahead."

"What's your purpose?" he managed.

"I don't know. Maybe something that has to do with you."

Like me falling in love for the first time in my life and not dying on the battlefield? "You said the pocket watch brought you here," he said. "Leave it wherever it is. Never touch it again and then it can't pull you back."

"So—" her smile made him almost trip over his feet—"you don't want me to go?"

He took a few more steps, aware of Stephen passing them and wearing a wide smile on his face.

"No, I don't."

When she laughed merrily and ran to catch up with Stephen, Ben smiled and even let out a slight, short laugh. She was clever and yet, she possessed an innocence that was untarnished by society and its many rules designed mostly to keep women quiet and in their place. Fable grew up forgotten by society and free.

Still laughing, but now at something his suddenly humorous steward said, she spun around to face Ben. Her hair, like splashes of fiery sunshine spread out around her and then settled over her shoulders. "Are you returning to write your letter to the king, or can you teach me to fence now?"

His letter. Yes. His arm was well enough to return to battle. But…he stared at her waiting for his answer…a little more practice would do him good. "Come with me."

She bounced up, clapping and looking quite happy. He realized that watching her bloom in the safety he provided made him happier than he ever felt in his life. It was odd how another person's joy could rub off on the hardest heart. "All right, come, then," he urged curtly, trying not to appear too ridiculously gleeful.

She hurried to him and looped her arm through his. "I enjoyed my tour. Your house is, like, colossal. I've never seen so many rooms and we didn't even finish seeing them all. The halls are enormous. Why, I think you could fit dozens of people in that house! It's very beautiful."

"There are many people taking care of it," he said, taking no credit for its upkeep.

"You have a huge staff. How do you afford it all? How do you make money?"

Ben liked her boldness to ask him such questions. The ladies in the *ton* would never think to be so honest and candid. They hired others to find out anything they wanted to know about his wealth.

"Mostly from farms, orchards, rents on my lands. I've been given a lot of land from the king. But most of it was my father's. Thankfully, Lord Addinton didn't get his hands on it."

"So, you're pretty rich," she concluded.

"Yes."

"What do you do with all that wealth?" she asked softly, glancing at him from beneath her veil of lashes. "Do you help or feed the poor, or, like Lady Prudence, do you consider the poor repulsive and beneath you?"

He flashed her an insulted look. But it was only to mask his guilt of ignoring the people she spoke of. "You're poor, Fable. Do you think you repulse me?"

She smiled and shook her head, pardoning him and trusting him easily on his word.

He liked that it was so easy to make her happy. He liked that she didn't dwell on Prudence's unkind treatment. She seemed to even forget the man chasing her. He hadn't, and hurried her along to the fencing house.

"What do you know about fencing?" he asked on the way.

"I know thin swords are involved and you get to say touché when you win!"

He laughed softly and then wondered how she'd managed to soften his armored heart so thoroughly.

"That's part of it, yes," he said with a nod and then a knowing curl of his lips. "Think of it more like a chess game. It's the same, it's outwitting your opponent. Being a step ahead—up here." He pointed to his head.

"But we're the chess pieces."

His eyes danced across her face. "Yes."

They entered the fencing house and saw that Sudbury and Prudence were already there.

After a brief greeting, Ben took Fable to the changing room and looked through the rows of clean white uniforms hanging neatly in an open wardrobe against the wall. He found the smallest one there, probably used by young John Frenton, his lieutenant's brother.

"Put this on," he said, handing her the uniform. "I'll change around that bend."

He found his uniform and walked off around a corner of the changing room. He began to undress, and the instant he did, she invaded every moment of his thoughts. He wished he were taking off his clothes for another reason. He remembered to breathe while he put on his white breeches and white military-style padded jacket, but she was there—in his head, happy while she ate, grateful while she sipped coffee, shining brightly while she soothed away his every care.

He blew out a deep breath and shook his head to clear it. This was no time to let his thoughts wander. He chose his foil and held his mask under his arm while he waited for her to finish changing.

He felt his iron control tightening his muscles by just being here. Fencing reigned in the warrior and helped him exercise his control as well as his speed. It was different when he practiced with his heavy sword, requiring the warrior to build muscles and stamina.

"Ready," she sang rounding the corner to reach him.

Whatever he was thinking or imagining about her couldn't compare with the vision of her. His eyes reveled in the sight of her in a uniform that hugged her body and showed off all her delicate female form. He felt his heart flip. It made him cough.

"It fits well," he said like a fool.

He helped her choose her mask and a foil that felt comfortable in her small, gloved hand.

When they entered the fencing room, Prudence, who was there to watch Sudbury practice, gasped upon seeing Fable in a uniform. But when he turned to see how Fable was doing on the walk to the floor, he found her quickly looking away from him and blushing at being caught. She hadn't even noticed Prudence and her disapproval. It made Ben smile *again*.

After teaching her how to stand and what some words meant, she was eager to learn some moves. He stood beside her, and much to his sister's indignation, showed her how to lunge and parry.

Being so close to her, holding her arms in the correct positions, feeling the heat of her cheek when he spoke against it, touching his fingers to her thighs to get her to spread her legs wider for a lunge, threatened to snap the iron control he prided himself on. He wiped his sweaty brow and fought to steady his breathing. What was wrong with him? All he could think of was holding her in his arms, kissing her. He rushed through the rest of the instruction and stepped away from her.

"Dip the blunt tip of your foil into that cup of ink," he instructed her. "Everytime you land that tip on me, the point will be marked with an ink spot. Understand?"

She nodded, making her hair shimmer in the sunlight streaming in through the windows and muddling his senses.

As tradition dictated, he saluted her, and had her do the same before they put on their masks. He breathed and then forgot to again when she spoke.

"Be gentle with me."

It didn't take long to discover he couldn't lift his foil to her. He was showing her a riposte; how to counterattack after he blocked her with a parry. But when he tried to lift his arm to tap her, he found it impossible. He wasn't in any pain. His arm didn't disobey because of his wound. He'd been fighting for too long. Offensive maneuvers meant injury or death to his opponent. Lifting his sword against her, even in practice, seemed to be impossible. Every point he described to her, she picked up and used on him. He should have parried or lunged and tapped his foil to her, but no part of him would obey to move when it came time to take the offense. Watching her stretch and move didn't help. Even her sloppy movements managed to catch him.

She won every match and ended up laughing too hard while he stood there covered in ink spots to continue.

Through the corner of his eye he saw Sudbury staring in awe at the fearsome captain's soiled uniform.

"It's a good thing my enemies don't know about you," Ben told her lightly as they removed their face masks. "They would use you to win against me in every battle."

She blinked her wide eyes at him. "That's the nicest thing anyone has ever said to me."

"Miss Ramsey," Prudence said standing near her chair. "Do you truly think what you're doing is decent? The *ton* would never approve of—"

"What's indecent about trying to learn how to protect myself? I won't depend on the duke or anyone to protect me. I'll protect myself."

Prudence laughed at her. "You're a fool."

"What if all the men are off fighting and you're attacked?" Fable asked her. "Don't you want to fight back? I already know some self-defense moves my friend Patrick taught me. I can teach you. A woman should know—"

"Enough!" Prudence commanded, fanning herself. "Benjamin, I implore you to cease your interest in this woman at once! Her outlandish ideas that women can protect themselves will be your ruin!"

"Your Grace," Fable said, turning slightly to him, "would you help me demonstrate 'street defense'?"

"Of course." Was this how easily he would agree to whatever she asked?

"You could get hurt," she added.

Should he smile? Was she being truthful? There was one way to find out. Curiosity made him—

She came close, took hold of his wrist, tucked her shoulder—what? He was going over! He lay on his back staring up at the ceiling. What just happened? Did she flip him over her shoulder as if he weighed nothing at all? Impossible. She was no bigger than an insect!

As he stood up, he saw Sudbury, hands on his head, stricken, once again. His sister stood as if frozen with her hands to her chest, her eyes huge with both terror and astonishment.

"Your Grace," Fable cast her bright beautiful eyes on him again. "Come at me."

"What?"

She motioned with her hands to come forward. "Attack me as if you had a knife."

"No. I—"

She moved closer and took hold of his wrist again.

"Fable, don't—"

She turned her back to him, wrapping his arm around her throat as if he was attacking her. "You follow me into a dark alley. You have a knife so you think you can do what you want to the girl walking alone." As if on cue, she flipped him over her shoulder!

She did it again, he thought, staring at the ceiling.

"But I'm not done," she announced, making him dread her next move. "First thing is to get rid of his weapon." With that, she grabbed his hand and twisted it backward. "His friend wants to help!" She pointed at Sudbury and motioned him forward. He shook his head, refusing. "Then there's nothing left to do but use the knife and kill the one on the ground." She bent to Ben and pretended to hold a knife to his throat. He stared into her eyes.

She was a fighter, this one. He liked it and began to smile at her.

Poor Sudbury thought to take that opportunity, while they stared into each other's eyes, to attack. Coming from behind, his shadow stretched toward the ceiling. Fable saw it, turned, and swept her leg across Sudbury's ankle. He lost his balance, but he was too big to take down with a sweep. While he teetered, she hooked his ankle with her foot and with the strength of her leg behind her, pulled him down to join his friend flat on his back.

Finally, she let go of Ben's hand, untwisting his wrist. Though the pain stopped, he missed the feel of her.

"Who taught you to fight like that?" he asked as he stood up. Sudbury sat up and shook his head in stunned surprise.

"Many people taught me," she told him. "There was always a man to keep away. But for every *one*, there were *two* who wanted to help me."

You follow me into a dark alley. You have a knife so you think you can do what you want to the girl walking alone.

His stomach turned. He wondered how many times it happened to her. "Don't go back there, Fable," he said close to her ear, his voice, as shaky as his hands at his sides. "Stay here."

She looked up at him. His mouth went dry and his pounding heartbeat in his ears made him feel lightheaded. "With me."

Chapter Twelve

STAY HERE WITH him.

Fable had a dozen questions in her head, like; With him, how? As a servant—as she'd agreed to, as a girlfriend, a wife? Her heart thudded in her chest. Did he mean as a wife?

I'm almost fully certain that I love you, Miss Ramsey.

Did he love her? Would he defy his sister? Or try to make Fable his mistress while he took another woman as his wife? She quickly erased that question. She'd rather return to the alleys and shelters of New York City than be his mistress.

He'd invited her to stay with him. Did he intend to protect her from the sword-wielding warrior who was hunting her down, probably at this very moment?

She wanted to ask him, but Lady Prudence had much to say while the men brushed off their breeches.

"Miss Ramsey, I would never believe it, and I saw it with my own eyes. You took them both down. Lord Sudbury..." she took a moment to steady her breath... "a giant of a man, and my brother, a famed warrior, untouched by any heart. You could easily kill them both if you wanted to."

"I don't want to," Fable assured her. "And neither of them came at me with a sword. The self-defense I know does no good if a sword is slashing down upon me." She thought of the time-traveler. He was here in 1718 and he'd followed her to Colchester. She was sure it was his voice she heard that night in the rain.

She couldn't fight him and his sword off.

The duke's sister looked as if she was considering Fable's words. Fable just basically gave up her defense. She had to be close to her attacker to defend herself against him. Now the men knew, so that if she ever had any intentions of hurting them, she'd fail.

Lady Prudence gave the earl and the ink-covered duke one last *amused* look, before she returned her attention to Fable before she left. "We'll speak about this again. Come, Simon."

Fable nodded. That was a good beginning. She turned to share a smile with Ben and Lord Sudbury as he caught up with his lady in three steps of his long legs.

"Fable?"

She turned to the duke when they were alone. She fell captivated by the stark contrast of his black hair and eyes against his pale complexion and white uniform. She shouldn't let herself be swayed by someone's physical frame.

"I'll teach you to defend yourself against a sword."

She sucked in a little gulp of air. How about being swayed by the way his lips looked while he spoke words that broke down her defenses? She wanted to ask him what about after that? How long did he intend to let her stay?

She closed her eyes. Nothing ever lasted. She moved to leave him and change into her gown. He reached for her hand to stop her.

"Lady, you put me on my back twice and now you make me risk a third time when I reach for you?"

She smiled. She loved this open, caring side of him. She turned to face him. "So, what is it, Duke? Do you love me?"

When he lowered his chin to his chest and laughed, she wanted to step into his arms and kiss him for all time, no matter what the future held, if this was all temporary—she wanted to kiss him and hear him tell her that it was forever—even if it was a lie.

"Yes," he told her and nodded. "I love you."

His voice…no, no, his words…she didn't know. It all made her blood warm and her bones tremble. Should she tell him she loved him? What did she know of love?

"Ben—"

He pulled her against him and dipped his mouth to hers. His lips and tongue gently coaxed her lips open. His arms closed tighter, pressing her against him. She could feel his breath, hear him breathing her in. His strength covered her, consumed her. Nothing in her life ever made her feel so safe. She fit into the hollows and hills of his lean body as if she was born to be there. And, oh, but he smelled good, like dew covered grass and a hint of sandalwood. He filled her senses and tempted her to give up her defenses and go all in with him.

But wouldn't it be worse to have it all with him and then lose it?

Could she step away from the delectable cushion of his lips while they caressed her and molded to her? Could she stop the tremor he caused along her spine, the promises she wanted to cry out? She would never leave him or cause him harm.

I love you, Ben. I love you. I'll always love you.

Even if she lost it all later, she wanted this with him—whatever it was—now.

She ran her fingers through his raven hair and traced her fingertips down his jaw, exploring him, knowing him. Was he real? Oh, please, God, please, let him be real.

He slid his hand down her back and ran his palm over the curve of her backside. "Did I tell you how pleasing you look in this uniform?"

Having never been held and kissed so passionately before, she wasn't really sure what else to do…so she followed his lead, noting that his ass was almost as hard as the rest of him.

"You look pleasing too."

He tilted back his head and laughed, then zeroed in his gaze on hers. "You're bold and scandalous," he accused with a curious arch of his brow. "Will you do whatever I do?"

When she laughed merrily, still in his arms, he leaned down and kissed her again.

When he withdrew, his gaze as hooded as hers, she leaned up on the tips of her toes, curled her arms around his neck, tilted her head, and kissed him.

Finally, with a deep little growl, he released her. "Go, change into your gown," he ground out. "I'll wait here and change when you're done."

What happened? Was something wrong? "Ben—"

"Fable, my…protective cup is beginning to pain me."

She threw her hands to her mouth, stared at him for a second, and then burst into laughter. A second after that, they were laughing together.

Fable didn't think anything of the duke's odd behavior. To her, there was nothing odd about him. He was a stern captain at times, but he was also compassionate and lighthearted at other times. Like everyone else, he wasn't the same all the time. Nothing odd about that. His Grace the Duke of Colchester was perfect.

But the two guardsmen entering the fencing room to practice—soldiers who had fought under the captain of the King's Royal Army and knew him well, were quite stunned to see their captain laughing.

"SHALL I COMPARE thee to a summer's day?"

Though he kept his tone low from where he was sitting opposite of her on the floor of his study, the duke's strong voice reverberated through Fable's blood.

"You try." He held the book of poems by William Shakespeare and pointed to the words. "Shhhhh-ahh-lll."

She nodded, remembering the next, one-lettered word. "Shall I…"

"Very good," he whispered through a smile and pointed to the next word. "Cc-omm-ppp—"

She couldn't help but smile at the way his lips pursed to pronounce the p sound. She wanted to kiss again.

—"aa-rrrre. Compare."

She repeated the word then fixed her gaze on his face in the soft light of the hearthfire and the dozen or so candles lit inside his study. There was furniture; a desk and chair, two larger, mahogany chairs with carved legs and arms, and upholstered in velvet, and an uncomfortable looking sofa. She liked sitting on the floor with him. He was slouchy and flexible, and incredibly sensual. Twice, she had to stop herself from climbing into his lap and kissing him.

"Good," he encouraged. "So, shall I compare thee—" his Adam's Apple jumped up and down and his meaningful gaze poured into her—"to a summer's day?"

She blushed, suddenly feeling like he was no longer reading.

"Thou art more lovely and more temperate," he continued and slid closer to her.

She smiled at him, emboldening him closer still. She thought…hoped he was moving in to kiss her, but though, at one point, he was teasingly close enough to do it, he only skirted around her to sit behind her, his back against the wall, his breath against her nape. He sat close, his long legs spread out on either side of her, and held the open book before her.

"Rough winds do shake the darling buds of May," he recited against her ear. "And summer's lease hath all too short a date."

"Too short a date," she repeated. "That's very sad. Summer is only here for a short time."

He put the book down and closed his arms around her from behind. "But it returns," he pointed out, resting his chin on her shoulder.

She smiled, liking his optimistic outlook. She didn't remind him that one must get through the winter to welcome summer again. She leaned her back against his chest and felt his heart beating against her ribs. She sighed, sounding more like Desdemona when she purred in the sun. "Let's enjoy the summer while it's here."

He was quiet for a little while, just sitting with her, holding her. What was he thinking about? Was he as happy and content as she? She covered his hands that were folded on her belly.

"Fable."

She closed her eyes and drank in the way her name sounded on his lips. "Hmm?"

"Do you intend on returning to your century?"

She opened her eyes. Is this what had made him quiet? He didn't let her go when she turned to face him. "I don't intend on it. No." Looking into his eyes while they searched around in the darkness of—as they say—the windows of his soul, she knew she would be happy to stay with him until her last breath. She hoped he saw it burning like a blazing fire within her. When his features relaxed into a warm smile, she knew he did.

"How come you never ask me about the future…or the man chasing me?"

"You were homeless. The future sounds no different than today. As for the man chasing you, the thought of him enrages me. But I haven't forgotten him. After years of patrolling, my men know the people of the city, as well as some of the surrounding countryside of Colchester. They are searching for a stranger traveling alone, fitting the description you gave me. The people of the city are also reporting anyone suspicious to my men. Is there anything else you want to tell me about him? You said he appeared out of nowhere? Tell me about that."

She had to shake her head a little to clear it from the spell he'd put her under with the lull of his deep, soft voice, his lips pouting around some words and dancing over others. His tongue teased, peeking out from in between his pearly teeth and shapely lips. He knew it lured and tempted, and he liked it. She could see it in his eyes. She could see everything in his eyes.

"I…" She pulled herself together and began again. "I had been trying to get some sleep and the street started shaking like an earthquake was happening. Everything looked wavy for a second or two, and then he was there. Just like that."

"You were trying to sleep on the street?"

"What? Yes, that's where I slept every night, Ben. Though I believed one day I'd get my own place."

"A place with fifty-seven rooms," he said and traced his finger over her temple to her jaw.

"Fifty-seven?" she asked with a quiet laugh. "I didn't see them all on Stephen's tour. But besides that, I didn't mean this house."

His smile faded. "Why not?"

"What do you mean 'why not?' This isn't my house."

"If you live here, is it not your house?"

She laughed again and half-turned so that she leaned more into the crook of his left shoulder than against his chest. She did this because she couldn't think straight while looking at him when he spoke. She wasn't used to this kind of attention from this kind of man.

"Whether I'm here as a guest or a servant," she said, snuggling against him, "it doesn't make this my house."

"Living here as my wife would."

Her heart flipped into her throat. She tilted her head and looked at him. "Ben, marriage is pretty serious. We've known each other for such a short time—"

"What do I care about time?" He pulled her in to face him again. "You make me forget who I was and question who I want to be. I only know that while I find out, I want you with me, at my side. You've awakened me, Fable. I've never felt for anyone what I feel for you. I'll never feel it toward anyone else. My heart is lost to you, so what do I care how long I've known you? I want to keep knowing you for the rest of my life."

She didn't know how to react to those kinds of words. Her eyes burned and she did nothing to stop her tears from forming. "Do you mean that?"

He nodded, staring into her eyes.

"It's hard for me to believe someone's words," she told him. "No matter how nice they are to hear."

"I know." He tightened his tender hold and lowered his face to hers. "Believe this." It was almost a plea as his eyes dipped to her mouth and his lips parted. His kiss was tender, curious, and meaningful enough to make her tears fall. He withdrew, hovering over her and spread his thumbs under her eyes to wipe her tears. He waited until she wrapped her arms around his neck and then he returned to kissing her. The more his lips molded to her, caressed her, the more steamy her thoughts were becoming. Her body responded. Her breasts felt full. Her nipples were tightening, and something burned below her navel and made her want to move her legs.

Her position between his thighs made it easy to feel him getting hard. Her first instinct was to get up and run! She knew about sex and what it entailed. Many nights, as she lay awake in the park with her mother, she heard others doing 'it'. 'It' usually included a drunken guy in a minute round of humping the woman beneath him before he came and it was over. She'd often heard her mother's girlfriends talking about it. Would it be like that with her duke?

If his long, slow and sensual kisses were any indication, the answer was a resounding no. When he bent over her, arching her back so he could kiss her throat, she was tempted to spread her legs and climb on him. What would he think of her if she did it?

He kept kissing her, getting harder beneath her. She was glad she'd only worn her nightdress and chemise to bed and moved up over him, fitting him against her warm niche. The instant he felt it, he turned his body over hers, pinning her to the floor. His mouth had grown hungry—or had it always been hungry and he'd contained it, having no time for such trivial things as love?

She smiled against his teeth, knowing by the tender heat in his gaze and the passion in his kiss what he felt for her.

She couldn't help but rub herself over him. It felt instinctual, and primal, irresistibly good. She thought she might lose herself just from touching him. His fingers left an indelible brand everywhere they traveled over her, undressing her. When she lay beneath him in nothing but her thin chemise, she wondered with trembling bones if she was really going to do this with him.

She helped him pull his night shirt over his head, then ran her palms down the sinewy muscles in his arms. He was offering himself to her, and she was doing the same, so grateful for so many past decisions not to use her body to get what she needed.

As she had guessed, he moved and kissed, and touched with slow, deliberate ease. She could have stopped him at any time, but she didn't want to stop. She wanted to devour him—be devoured by him.

She raked her fingernails softly across his flat abdomen and felt him respond between her legs. He tugged on the laces of his night breeches and yanked them down. His cock sprang forth like a trumpet announcing this was indeed a man.

Fable closed her eyes and waited for him to stick it in her. When nothing happened, she opened her eyes. He was watching her. "Am I rushing you? If you're not ready—"

"I'm ready." She coiled her arms around his neck and pulled him down to kiss him.

He splayed his palm on the ground then worked her chemise up over her bare belly with his free hand. He paused for an instant and traced his fingertips over her belly before pushing the chemise up further, over the twin mounds of her breasts, her head, her hands. Freeing her, he leaned down and tasted her nipple with a few licks first, then gently kneaded her and sucked until she cried out.

She knew she wanted him inside her. It was almost too shocking for her to consider. Sex. Finally, after twenty-six years of holding on to the only thing that was hers, she offered it up to him.

"Don't doubt me, Fable," he commanded in a husky voice. "I'm going to marry you."

So many twenty-first century men would think nothing of

saying that if it meant they'd get sex. But she believed Ben was saying it to reassure her. He wouldn't leave her when they were done. She meant something to him. What they were about to do meant something to him.

"I don't doubt you," she vowed. His eyes drank in every inch of her face then came to rest on her gaze as he lowered his head to kiss her. No longer was his kiss patient, curious. Now he was hungry, and the hunger wanted to be satisfied. He nibbled her bottom lip and drank her in as if she were an elixir he needed to live.

His deft, broad fingers moved between them and unlaced her drawers. She yanked them off the rest of the way and kicked them aside.

His naked body covered her like a blanket. "Do you want to move to the bed?"

She shook her head. Something about being on the floor felt feral, like his kiss, his teeth, his tongue. He licked a trail down her chin to her throat and kissed the curve of her jaw, the small hollow between her neck and chest. Every touch set more of her on fire. She tunneled her fingers through his hair, over the width of his shoulders. The heat of his mouth made her legs spread wider.

Nestled between her legs, he moved with sensuous steadiness, rubbing the length of his desire over her, using the heat and heaviness of it to coax her to open further.

"Lady," he whispered against her ear, "have I told you that I love you?

She smiled, gazing into his eyes. She hoped he saw all that she felt for him. "Your eyes tell me everytime you look at me, Your Grace."

"Then I shall always look at you," he promised and used his knees to spread her wide. He kept his promise as he gently pushed his way into her. But then when the searing pain waxed and she broke their gaze and cried out into his shoulder, she felt him sink into her. Not just inside her, but everywhere. Had he fallen asleep? "Ben?"

When he lifted himself up on his elbows, he looked like something completely different than a doe-eyed duke with the elegance of a prince. His eyes appeared darker, glassy, as if he—

"Are you crying?"

"Not anymore," he said, looking down at her. He moved himself deeper into her.

She ran her hands down his back and fought through the pain. "Tell me why you were crying. Don't hide anything from me."

He stared into her eyes and she understood what he was telling her.

"I was overcome with feelings for you," he confessed tenderly while he broke through completely. He stopped moving, giving her time to relax. She was thankful for it.

"Have I told you that I love you?" she asked softly and began moving under him.

He closed his eyes and bit his lip then opened them with a smile on her. "Your kiss has told me."

She laughed softly and then found herself shockingly smiling at how he was making her feel. When he stretched upward above her and he panted like some wounded beast, Fable watched him release himself full-force into her.

For an instant, pure, unadulterated delight swept through her, and her eyes opened wider and the blood drained from her face.

"What is it?" he asked, falling onto his back.

"What if I get pregnant?"

"So?" he chuckled. "It won't be the last time."

"Ben." She gave him a little pinch in the side. "I'm serious."

"So am I."

"I don't know how to be a mother. I had a terrible role model. I don't know anything about babies."

"I think you and I were meant to learn to do things together," he let her know, leaning over to give her a reassuring kiss.

She smiled. That was a nice way to look at it. But—"What about your sister?"

"She'll come around," he told her. "Let's not speak of this now, hmm?" He silenced her with a kiss that sizzled her nerve-endings.

"Let's not speak of anything at all," she purred and straddled him. She giggled at her own boldness, then leaned down and kissed the lips that were waiting for her.

CHAPTER THIRTEEN

"WHO IS SHE?" Lady Witham cast Benjamin's guest a slanted glare while she sipped her tea in the dining hall.

"My Elizabeth heard she comes from Belstead," the Duchess of Braintree said in a low, secretive voice.

The ladies at the table turned to the Marquess of Ipswich's wife, who shook her head. "No one in Belstead has heard of her."

"The duke certainly seems smitten with her," Margaret Somner's mother, the Duchess of Halstead remarked.

"If anyone knows anything about her, it's you, Lady Prudence." The Duchess of Nottingham, Lady Charlotte's mother, set her resentful gaze on Prudence.

Her pride was still wounded since Benjamin had Lady Charlotte removed from Colchester House. But it hadn't stopped her from accepting Prudence's invitation for tea.

"I know only this; my brother is smitten indeed," Prudence told them, looking up from her cup and setting her gaze on Miss Ramsey sitting across the room with Stephen and Edith and two other servants.

Soon, she'd have all the servants sitting at the tables with them!

"You don't like her," Lady Witham said snidely.

"What I think of her doesn't matter." But truthfully, Prudence didn't hate her. She was homeless, as Prudence had once been. But that was where her empathy ended. Benjamin needed to keep their father's name well respected.

She let her gaze slip to her brother speaking to these women's husbands. Prudence knew him well enough to see by his fidgeting that he wanted to finish up with them and get back to Miss Ramsey.

She'd wondered what it was about her brother's guest that attracted him so much, but after watching Miss Ramsey flip her brother twice and knock Lord Sudbury off his feet, Prudence could see how such an unconventional woman would pique Benjamin's interest. Was that all it was? Curiosity? Would he grow tired of her? Watching him flick his gaze to where Miss Ramsey sat laughing with the help made Prudence doubt that it was trivial. She couldn't remember a time in Benjamin's life when he was interested in a girl. What girl would have shown him any interest back then when he was always covered in bruises? She realized her brother was considered very handsome now, but when he had a black eye and a fat lip he was less adorable.

Goodness, but did he smile every time he met Miss Ramsey's gaze? The fact that he smiled at all…Simon had been correct. Her little brother looked happy. She had to admit, it was nice to witness.

It took her a moment to realize there was a server standing beside her about to set down a tray of cinnamon scones on the table. "What's this?"

The server didn't answer but moved aside to make room for Miss Ramsey.

"I hope you don't mind, Lady Prudence. I asked Lord Sudbury what you enjoyed at the table and he told me you liked cinnamon scones, so I asked the baker to prepare them for you."

Prudence sat there stunned for a moment. What was she to say to that? The scones smelled delicious. She looked over to where Simon sat and smiled at him. Then she turned her gaze on Miss Ramsey.

"Thank you."

"Does the baker take orders from you, then?" the Duchess of Braintree asked.

"I didn't order him to do anything," Miss Ramsey told her. "He did it because it was for Lady Prudence—" Miss Ramsey smiled at her—"As anyone here would do."

Prudence knew the baker didn't do it for her. None of the servants cared for her. She was unkind to them. The baker did it for Miss Ramsey. "Until someone takes my place," Prudence brought up with a short laugh.

"No one can take your place," her brother's *guest* assured her. "Most of these people have known you since you were a little girl. They loved you then and they love you still."

Prudence cleared her throat and took a moment before she spoke. She found her brother, coming toward them. He was still smiling. Simon was smiling, as well, but then, that was nothing new for him.

"What's this?" her brother asked when he reached them and saw the tray of cinnamon scones.

"They are a gift from Miss Ramsey," Prudence told him. So then, he wasn't a part of this?

He set his gaze on Miss Ramsey and Prudence swore she hadn't seen her brother's eyes go so warm in almost twenty years. Something in her heart thumped watching him. Did this woman make him happy? Prudence had to ask herself, what was more important, her father's name, or her brother's happiness?

"That was very thoughtful of you," he told his guest with the most tender inflection in his voice his sister had ever heard. He turned to Prudence. "Wasn't it."

"Yes, very," Prudence agreed. "Why don't you both have one?"

Her brother accepted, but Miss Ramsey refused the offering. "The baker wouldn't allow a single scone to leave the kitchen if it wasn't perfect. I ate two of them already." Her smile widened into a grin that Prudence hated to admit, was quite endearing.

Her brother thought so too. Staring at her, he let out a little laugh.

Prudence looked at Simon leaving his seat and heading their way. She knew what these looks and dreamy smiles meant, for she shared them with Simon since she was a child.

"What else is the baker holding back in the kitchen?" Benjamin's voice dragged Prudence's attention back to him and Miss Ramsey. "Come, show me."

"Yes, Your Grace," Miss Ramsey replied with a secretive smile, then sweetened it up when she turned to Prudence. "Good day, my lady."

Prudence watched them walk away. Simon was stopped by the Earl of Chelmsford. She was happy the nobles who'd come for her ball were leaving in a few days. Benjamin had refused to open the guest rooms to most of them, so their lodgings were elsewhere. Still, they came for tea and to hopefully find out who among their daughters her brother was thinking of choosing for his wife.

"She has her hooks in him and now she's trying to dig them into Lady Pru," snarled Lady Rayleigh, mother of the well-educated Joan D'Artane.

"He'd never choose her as a wife, would he?

"She's like a red witch with that hair of hers falling all around her. Why isn't it tied up?" Lady Witham complained.

"Why doesn't she powder her face? She almost looks indecent!" Lady Rayleigh added indignantly.

"Poor duke. He's helpless toward her," Lady Ipswich lamented. Everyone knew her daughter was in love with Benjamin.

Prudence wanted to hold her hands over her ears to block out their clucking voices. Yesterday she would have sat here agreeing with them. But today…she thought of her brother's happy face. She looked at the scones.

"We should help him," the Duchess of Braintree suggested.

"She just showed up here one day," said the Duchess of Nottingham slyly. "She could disappear just as easily."

Prudence closed her eyes. How had it come this far? What

were they saying?

"With her out of the picture, the duke would have to choose one of our daughters," Lady Ipswich pointed out.

"What do you suggest we do?" asked Lady Chelmsford, biting into a scone.

"Bringing her harm isn't the answer," Prudence told them. "Besides, I doubt anyone could lay a hand on her without ending up flat on their back."

"Have you been so easily bought with a tray of cinnamon scones?" the Duchess of Nottingham asked her. "You should have tossed them in her face.

Prudence had enough. She turned her clenched jaw on the duchess. "Are you now telling me what to do in my own house, Duchess?"

"Good afternoon, Ladies," Prudence's handsome beloved saved her from saying more, like; get out and stay out! No, the Duke of Nottingham's eldest son had fought alongside Benjamin. She almost sighed thinking how that fact hadn't mattered to her brother when he threw Charlotte out.

"Lady Prudence, may I speak with you?"

She blinked to clear her thoughts and smiled at him. He still made her heart race. "Of course."

"Let's go for a walk in the garden," he suggested, taking her hand as she hurried to him.

She heard the other women swooning and sighing over Simon. She wasn't jealous. They were old, powdered, married ladies. No one had ever made her jealous. Except Miss Ramsey that day in the hall while they shared laughter over a kitten. But her brother had vanquished every doubt about to whom Miss Ramsey was losing her heart. She may be poor and she may have come here to take Benjamin's money, but she looked at him the way Prudence looked at Simon.

He led her to the garden outside and turned to her. She looked up at him knowing and loving every inch of his face, every curve of his lips and how they felt against hers.

He pulled something from his coat and took her hand. "Prudence, marry me today." He held a small box open before her. In it was a ring—

"I'll extend my leave," he vowed, handing her the ring. "We'll go home to Sudbury and you can make it our home until I come back to you. It's time, my love."

It was time. Benjamin must have told him something—that he no longer needed her.

"More than anything I want to be your wife. Let me just get Ben—

He shook his head. "Ben has fallen in love with Miss Ramsey, Prudence. Can't you see it?"

"Yes, but that will wear off."

"Has it worn off for you?" he asked.

She stopped arguing lest he believe it had. "No, my love. It never will."

"Then trust the man with whom you share blood."

"But, Simon, what if he loses everything?"

"If that happens, be grateful he's with a woman who knows how to live with nothing. But he'll never have nothing. Not as long as I live."

She looked up into his eyes and then threw herself into his arms.

While he held her and then placed the ring on her finger, she thought about what the ladies meant about Miss Ramsey disappearing. Should she tell Simon? Her brother? Or maybe this was the answer to her prayers. Miss Ramsey would no longer be a concern and Prudence would have had nothing to do with it.

BEN WATCHED HER move toward the kitchen, then hurried forward and grabbed her wrist to stop her just before she entered.

"I thought you were hungry?" she asked.

He smiled and dipped his gaze to her throat like a wolf that hadn't eaten in a week.

She squeaked with surprise and excitement when he swooped down on her. Narrowly escaping, she took off running. Ben grinned watching her departure. He drew his bottom lip between his teeth and then gave chase.

He couldn't stop the thought of his thrilling victory with her alone in the vacant east wing—where she was heading. All day, while he was stuck entertaining boring noblemen, his thoughts were with Fable and the night they spent together on the floor in his study and then in his bed. She was bold and playful, innocent and yet purposefully alluring and unashamed. She thrilled him. He couldn't get enough of her and after talking through the night and making love in between, he wasn't done.

He almost caught her twice and basked in the sound of her laughter. He could have outrun her, but what fun would that be? They passed a few servants, who stopped what they were doing to watch them in stunned silence.

When Ben saw a large set of wooden double doors, he sped up, took Fable's hand and led her the rest of the way. He pushed open the doors and pulled her inside and into her arms.

"Where are we?" She giggled into his mouth when he kissed her.

"It's a guest room that probably hasn't been occupied since the house was built for my father." He looked around, trying to see into the shadows the shuttered windows created. "I think it's used for storage now."

"Are there candles?" she asked into his chest. "I want to know for certain that no one is watching us."

He checked around and found some candles and lit two then inspected every corner. When he came to the last wall, he turned to toss her a reassuring smile. They were alone. There were paintings resting against the wall. His candles fell on a painting of a face that still haunted his dreams. He went still. His father. How long had this been here? He would have it brought to his rooms tomorrow. For now, he turned it around to face the wall, and not him…or her.

He turned to smile at her.

"What is it?"

"A painting. Come, through there." He pointed to another door. "So I can have my way with you." His eyes darkened on her and he laughed and led her forward.

The next room was a parlor with cushioned chairs and a sofa upholstered in crimson linen.

"Are you trying to win over Prudence?" he asked her while she stepped around the sofa to open the shutters of a window.

"Yes. Should I not?"

He went to her and closed his arms around her. "I think it's an excellent idea. I know Prudence can be difficult. Thank you for trying." He bent his head to kiss her mouth.

He felt as if he were living in a dream. He was happy. He had truly forgotten what it felt like. Seventeen years of plotting revenge, training in order to carry out that revenge. He'd killed hundreds of them before and after he returned from Germany. How many more before his heart was satisfied?

But he didn't think about revenge or fighting when he was with her. She made him care about living. While he branded her mouth with his, a fleeting thought crossed his mind about what he was willing to give up for her. Today he cared less about fighting than he did yesterday, and less yesterday than the day before that. He only wanted to kiss her, breathe her, hold her—

And now they were finally alone.

He kissed her wildly, passionately while he pulled her out of her clothes, and she pulled him out of his. He stopped now and then to have a look at her, to gather her in, and reassure himself that she was his. When he set her naked body down on the sofa, she spread her legs to receive him. His heart thundered like a war drum in his ears. He loved her for wanting him. He'd make certain she always wanted him.

He moved over her then rested his chest against hers. "Do

you feel my heart beating?"

She nodded and smiled. "Is that because of me?"

"Yes," he told her softly while he pressed his lips to her chin and her neck. He stopped and looked at her as he sank into her. "You make me feel like I'm being reborn."

He couldn't look at her without almost falling off the edge of control. He didn't want this to be over so quickly, so he closed his eyes. He lowered his head to drink from the breasts she offered him. His muscles trembled at her hold on him, closing tight around the length of him until he almost cried out.

He lifted her to him when he hovered over her and thrust deep into her over and over, slowing his pace, and then quickening it again. He kissed her and whispered things over her skin about how very beautiful she was to him, and how much she meant to him. Every promise to love and protect and honor her—and anything else she added—was sealed with a kiss.

When they almost slipped off the sofa in each other's arms, they laughed and kissed some more. He let her turn over so that he was sitting up under her, his back slouching against the cushioned back, his erection pointing straight up.

She wasn't afraid to climb right on him. He smiled and held her hips while she moved up and down, tossing her head back like some wild forest faerie sent to steal his heart and his virginity. He smiled and sucked in his bottom lip. He'd gladly give up both.

He watched her as she deepened her movements and clenched him tighter as he swelled inside her. They released their passion together, and when it was over, she fell over him.

He took his time catching his breath, though with all his practice on the field, it didn't take long. He took her face in his hands and smiled into her eyes. "I love you."

"I love you, too," she replied in turn.

"I told Sudbury so that he could prepare himself," Ben told her, "for when I tell Prudence that you and I are to be married."

"Married?" Fable asked in surprise.

"Yes, Stephen has sent for the priest."

"You're really going to marry me, Ben? I'm poor."

"Not for long." He smirked smugly.

When she laughed behind her hand, he pulled her down for a kiss, then pushed her down on her belly and rose up above her. He smiled and bit his lower lip, then swooped down on her.

Chapter Fourteen

Fable woke alone in her bed, where Ben had carried her last night when she was just too exhausted to walk another step. She'd wanted him to stay with her but he told her their bodies needed rest, and if he stayed there wouldn't be any rest to be had.

Did she dream that the austere duke, so still and stoic at court, was truly a pot of boiling passions spilled out for her? She shifted under her blanket and felt the sting of reality between her legs. Her lips felt puffy from all his kisses. Oh, but she didn't mind. She loved him.

She smiled. He wanted to defy everything and marry her. Captain Benjamin West, His Grace the Duke of Colchester was in love with her. She let out a squeal of joy and disbelief.

She was still smiling in bed when Edith pushed open the door and stepped inside. "Oh, my lady, it's good to see you smiling again."

Fable sat up and stretched. "I was just thinking of His Grace." She leaned forward, closer to the servant and still wearing her gleeful smile, spoke in a low voice.

"Have you seen him this morning?"

The older woman nodded and took her hand. "He rode to Harwich with the Earl of Sudbury earlier for a meeting of high ranking noblemen or some such thing. It's been planned for a month and His Grace couldn't get out of going. He grumbled about it but he promised to return and eat with you."

Fable smiled and sighed then dropped back upon her pillow and closed her eyes. If he wasn't here then she'd dream of him all day.

Edith left her alone after she drew the curtains back and filled the room with sunlight.

Fable didn't get a chance to think about her beloved before there came a rapping on the door.

"Come in," she called out from the bed. When no one entered, she slipped out of bed and padded to the door. She opened it. No one was there. She was about to close the door when she spotted an envelope on the floor. She bent to take it and looked up and down the hall.

Closing the door again, she went back to her bed and sat in it, then opened the envelope. Was it a love letter from Ben? No, he knew she couldn't read, and besides he didn't seem the type to write love letters.

The handwriting was light and pretty and the paper even smelled nice. But she had no idea what it said.

Someone knocked at the door again. Before Fable could call out though, the door opened and Ben's sister, the villainess of her adventure, entered the front room, and then the bedroom.

"Miss Ramsey," she said standing at the foot of the bed, "if you can rouse yourself, I would like a word with you."

Fable didn't know why Lady Prudence's snappish retorts made her want to giggle. She kept her chin to her chest to hide the smile threatening to appear and got out of bed.

"Um, since you're here, did you write this?" Fable held up the note.

"What is it?" Lady Prudence took it from her.

"Someone left it by my door a few minutes ago. If you didn't write it, can you read it to me?"

Lady Prudence stared at her for a moment as it dawned on her why Fable couldn't read it herself. She looked a bit ill, then opened the envelope.

"Dear Miss Ramsey,

We are writing to request your presence at our afternoon tea. We believe His Grace the Duke will likely take you as his wife. Being so influential, we would, of course, covet your friendship. If you would accept our invitation, we will be completely open and honest with you, as we are now.

The tea will be held at the house of Lady Witham at two. Just tell any one of the carriagemen outside Colchester House where you want to go. He will take you.

You will no doubt notice that Lady Prudence will not be in attendance." At this, Ben's sister paused and clenched her jaw before continuing. "That is because we decided not to invite her. We would like to get to know you without her hateful prejudice against you overshadowing our time together. It is best not to tell her about this. She hates you. But, of course, you understand why. Still, we hold nothing against you and would like to take you into our fold.

We do hope to see you,
The Ladies Tea Club."

Lady Prudence crumpled the note into a ball and threw it toward the fire. "Do you believe a word of that?" she sneered. "They want to take you into their fold? It's more like they want to laugh at you. I know them, and their fold is poison. Don't meet them. They mean you nothing but harm."

"And yet," Fable said softly as she went to retrieve a robe one of the servants had given her, "you would push for your brother to be bound until he dies to one of them."

Lady Prudence didn't answer with words, but her face grew deep red. She turned and went to sit in the front room. Fable followed her.

"My brother is quite taken with you. In fact, he's decided to take you as his wife."

Fable didn't really know what she should say. She knew how to try to put people at ease. It was an important trait to learn on the streets, where the same laws didn't apply and fights broke out over nothing.

"I can see why he's fond of you. You're an enchanting little being when more closely observed."

Fable blinked. Did the villainess say she understood why her brother was taken with her? Was she calling her enchanting?

"But Miss Ramsey, my father's wish must be fulfilled. Benjamin loved him as much as I did. He has lived almost his entire life avenging him and our mother. Don't think for one moment that not granting his father's one wish won't eat away at Benjamin."

"Are…are you telling me to stop seeing him?"

"It's not even that you come from an average family. You have nothing! Absolutely. Nothing. You are not the best for my brother. I think when your enchantment wears off, he'll resent you for taking him from fulfilling our father's last wish."

Fable's eyes filled with tears at each word that felt like a hammer to her bones. She stepped back, into a chair but she didn't let herself fall back or sit. Was his sister right? Would Ben grow to resent or even hate Fable because of his father? It was true, she had nothing, at least nothing his sister or apparently their father would see of value in her. She swiped a tear from her eyes and straightened her spine. "I love him, my lady. I've never loved anyone before-not even my mother. I won't give him up. I can't. Please, don't ask it of me."

Lady Prudence's eyes glistened with tears, but her lips grew tight against her teeth. "You're selfish."

Fable didn't care if she was selfish. "I'm sorry."

Lady Prudence pivoted on her heel and left, slamming the door shut on her way out.

Fable didn't return to bed but dressed herself and then left her rooms. She didn't believe the women who stuck their noses up at her really wanted to get to know her. She imagined them laughing at her, as Lady Prudence said. She remembered other, "normal" kids laughing at her from their schoolyards as she and her mother passed them with their shopping cart of possessions. It had stopped bothering her years ago—and she'd never been to an English tea before. It seemed like an afternoon of pretend fun. So, why not?

She went directly to the ornate wooden front doors of Colchester House, pulled one open and stepped outside.

Thanks to the villainess, Fable needed something to help her forget the lady's words. *She wasn't best for Ben. He was merely enchanted, and when that wore off he would resent her.* She closed her eyes to stop her tears. That was another thing she hated since being here. She never cried before. Well, to be honest, she hadn't cried since she was eight and her mother tried to sell her for a night of food and a bed. Fable had had no intention of paying her mother's bill with her body so when the thug tried to put his hands on her, she stabbed him twice with a knife she'd swiped from her mother's belongings. She'd run away, her hands covered in his blood. She hid in a dark alley and cried until her heart dried out and there was never another tear to shed until now. Ben stirred her heart and made her cry.

She walked out into the courtyard and looked toward a carriage waiting to drive anyone from the house anywhere they wanted to go. She went to it and climbed inside. "The house of Lady Witham, please," she called up to the driver.

She closed her eyes and was immediately soaked in memories of his face, a face that had become more expressive over the last few days. Nowadays he smiled at her with tenderness she hadn't seen him offer anyone else. His gaze warmed on her like coals heated by an inner blaze. Images of his puckered lips and dark, dipped brow swept through her. Was this her punishment for possibly murdering that man when she was eight? To fall in love with a duke and take him from the power and safety of the arms of the king's niece? Yes, The Ladies Club was right, she did understand why Ben's sister hated her. Lady Prudence called her selfish, and she was, she admitted to herself while the carriage took the path north. It seemed more remote, Fable noted, unlatching the window and peering out. They rode over brush and bramble for about twenty minutes, in Fable's estimation, and finally the carriage stopped. She heard the driver leave his perch and jump down, feet on the ground. What was going on?

The door opened and without haste, the driver grabbed her by the collar and pulled her out of the carriage. She fought him with everything she knew and every ounce of strength she had, kicking, elbowing, stomping into his shin, head-butting him, splitting his flesh and sending her reeling.

Despite her best efforts, he dragged her away and pulled something out of his pocket. Fable heard a man shouting her name. Ben! But even as she opened her mouth to scream for him, whatever her captor had pulled from his pocket began to glow with blue light.

"No!" she begged, but it was already too late. The earth shook, the air waxed and waned. "No no no no. She struggled one last time against her captor's tight hold and saw Ben thundering toward her on his horse—and then the glare of street lights almost blinded her.

"Nooooo! Oh, please Lord, no!" She couldn't believe it. She couldn't be back. Please, don't let her be back. She imagined herself wailing her mournful disbelief until they found her dead on the street somewhere.

She turned her tearful gaze on the grimy scum hauling her along. Her heart raced. She hoped it would beat until the moment she killed this man. After that, she didn't want to live without Ben. She didn't have to open her eyes to know where she was. *When* she was. In a place in time where Ben no longer existed. Just like that. No! She wanted to scream, pull her hair from her head and fall to her knees. Nooooo! She couldn't leave Ben. She opened her eyes and glared at the man holding her by her wrist, the time-traveler who took Ben away from her. "What did you do?" she screamed at him. "Why did you take me and bring me back here?"

"Calm yourself, woman," his throaty voice reverberated through her.

"If you say that again, after what you've done, I will *calmly* cut your throat with your own knife first chance I get."

He stopped pulling her and turned to face her with a surprised look on his face. "You are a curious little hellcat."

She didn't wait for him to take his next breath but kneed him in the groin. He went down, but didn't let her go. She lifted her foot to kick him in the face but he grabbed it and yanked her the rest of the way down. She landed on her backside. Pain shot up her spine and momentarily blinded her, but the instant it ebbed, she scrambled to get back on her feet.

"I thought you would be grateful to me for bringing you back to your home," he huffed, shackling her ankle in his steel fingers.

She looked around quickly. Were there no people on the street in New York City? It was night. What time? The street looked familiar. She didn't want anything to look familiar.

"My home is back there," she cried out, pointing her thumb over her shoulder. She tried to kick him in the teeth with her free foot, and missed. He glared at her and sprang to his feet, as agile as any twenty year old. He yanked her up with him and dragged her into the nearest alley. The alley where she had been trying to sleep the night she first ran into this thorn in her side. She couldn't help the well of tears that overtook her. This was what she'd feared—being taken from Ben in an instant and being brought back here to the loneliness, the darkness, the constant caution every second of her life. Never being safe. She looked around through her tears. They were on 46th and 9th. "Send me back!" she begged the time-traveler. "What do you even want with me? Wait." She wrinkled her brow. "How did you get the pocket watch?"

He stared at her and chewed the inside of his cheek. "Very well, I'll answer your questions. I cannot send you back until I find my wife. I don't want anything from you. Just do as I say and help me. Lastly, the watch will keep returning to me as long as

Dorothea and I are separated."

What? You mean she didn't have to hide it and run all the way to Colchester to keep the watch safe from him? She glared at him, but then her expression darkened.

"What do you mean you can't send me back until you find your wife? I have nothing to do with her. Do you think I can find her because I come from here? You're nuts! Nuts! Send me back this instant!"

"You are part of this now," he told her, ignoring her panicked screech and pulling her forward.

"Part of what? Where are you bringing me? Take me back, Mister. Please."

"We traveled together across time to the past," he explained calmly while she struggled against his vise-like hold. "Our DNA was imprinted as one. I can no longer get to this time without you, and you can no longer return to that time without me."

She stared at him while he tugged her along. It couldn't be true. Oh, she was going to throw up. "Look," she managed, "like I said, you're a nutjob. I'm going to the cops first chance I get. I'll tell them you kidnapped me and—

He finally stopped and turned to look straight at her. "Do you not understand? You will never get back without me."

She stopped speaking and looked around. She would never get back...please God no! She didn't want to be here without Ben. Tears welled up in her eyes and she dragged her feet. Was what this man saying true? She didn't care. She felt as if she were dying, minute by minute fading into nothingness. Just as she was before...before him. She wanted to stop the traveler and beg him until her throat was raw and his ears burned to please, please send her back. She would die here.

"Mister, please," she sobbed but he said nothing and he didn't slow his steps. He pulled her along toward the east side, claiming that he had a dream telling him his Dorethea was there. Fable didn't question him. Stranger things had happened. She didn't care how she looked in her eighteenth century dress. New

Yorkers weren't concerned with such trivial things anyway.

New Yorkers. She was back. Her heart would never stop breaking. She should have known life with Ben was too good to be true. She cried most of the day. When her first night with the gruff time-traveler came, he followed her over a wall and into Central Park where some homeless people slept under a small bridge, and pointed to a clear spot on the ground.

"I think it's better if we sleep apart from others," the gray haired traveler suggested.

"Why?" she asked him, sniffling. It was a wonder to her how she had a drop of moisture left in her body.

"Because then one of us will not have to take watch while the other sleeps."

He meant him and her in that order. She thought about it and rubbed her eyes dry. She'd like to rob him of his sleep, but it would just slow them up. "Look, Mister," she said, glaring at him. "I don't know you. You could be trying to lure me away from humanity so you can what, rape me? I'll tell you right now, I'll fight you tooth and nail. Do you understand?"

He smirked and then chuckled, and nodded. "You are a hell-cat indeed. I'm surprised you found a place back there. As for me, I don't want to rape you. I want to go home, just as you do. I have searched and waited seventeen years and finally I have found the right century. Nothing will stop me, Miss. Do *you* understand?"

She remembered the blood on his sword and swallowed hard and nodded. But after an instant, she thought of life without Ben. "I don't care what you do. I'm going to sleep. Goodnight."

She heard him grumbling while he sat and then she stopped thinking of her captor and thought about the best person in her life. What if she never got back to him? What if she had to wait seventeen years to see Ben again? She couldn't do it. Finally, she opened her eyes to see the Georgian-looking traveler sitting with his back against the wall and his legs stretched out before him. His eyes were opened.

"You can go to sleep, Mister. It's eluding me. I'm wide awake." She sat up and pulled her blanket around her shoulders.

When he didn't move or respond, Fable figured he must be asleep. She'd heard that some people slept with their eyes open. She should kick dirt in his face for snatching her and bringing her back here, but she felt sorry for him.

When he spoke suddenly, she startled almost out of her skin. "I'm not the one who needs a bodyguard, Miss."

He was kind of right. She would get attacked before he would. "We all need a bodyguard in this world. Take a rest and tonight I'll keep watch."

He dipped his brow at her and was quiet for a moment or two. "What can you do?"

"I can wake you up."

She didn't mean to make him laugh and she wanted him to know it, so she huffed at him.

"Were you a servant?"

"What?" She set her wide eyes on him. Who was he? How did he know where she'd been? Had he asked around about her? Was he in cahoots with the women of The Ladies Club? How else would he have known that she would be needing a carriage when she did?

"In Colchester House, were you a servant?"

Fable shook her head. She felt a well rising to her throat, making it difficult to speak. "I was something else."

"Oh? What?"

"I was his beloved."

The traveler studied her for a moment then said in a low whisper. "Who's beloved?"

"Ben's. Benjamin West, His Grace the Duke of Colchester."

Her unwanted companion was silent after that. He said little more until morning while she rambled on tearfully about Ben's attributes. "He is nearly unbeatable at chess. I say nearly because he lost to me a few times." Yes, she was proud of it. It compelled her to stiffen her lower lip. "It proved all my years of practice with Old Hank the Shark were not in vain."

The traveler stared at her and seemed to be at a loss for words. He did manage to repeat Old Hank's name.

"He's very fair and patient with his sister," Fable went on, forgetting again, everything but Ben.

"Old Hank?"

"No. Ben," she cleared up. "Lady Prudence is Ben's sister. She apparently hates me because I'm a 'street urchin.' But you know what? I don't care. I've been hated before. I can withstand it all with him by my side."

"And he returns your sentiments?"

She nodded and then turned away when her eyes filled with tears again. She wept silently—though the time traveler would argue that her whimpers and sniffles kept him up until morning.

When the sun rose, he pulled her away from the sleeping area and followed her to a coffee-shop that was close by. She eyed him. "I don't suppose you have any money." When he shook his head, she shrugged, asked him to step back, and held up her finger. It didn't take her long to make enough money for breakfast.

"You're a beggar," the traveler said with traces of judgment in his tone.

"Yes," she told him, though she had stopped being one for a little while. "If it means not starving to death, I'll beg."

"You must learn how to hunt."

"There are no hunting grounds in the city. If you hunt in the parks, you go to jail."

They entered the coffee shop and Fable sat at the counter while he washed up in the restroom. She wasn't hungry even though they hadn't eaten dinner last night, but she knew he must be. She was right. He ordered a three egg vegetable omelet with bacon and home fries. They were both served coffee.

"So, what's the plan?" she asked him while he ate. "Where are we going? And tell me again why I had to be with you? Why did you take me away from…?"

His fork paused on the way to his mouth. When he saw her tears hovering over the rims of her eyes, he sighed.

"Yes, well my tears are your fault," she huffed and wiped her eyes.

"All these tears are because I took you from him?"

She nodded and blew her nose into the thick paper napkin near his plate.

He remained silent while he studied her. Then, "I don't know yet where she is. My dreams were busy in 1718 with where to find *you.*"

"Your dreams?" she asked, ready to abandon this nutjob. But he had the pocket watch. And she didn't know how to use it. What if she zapped herself to when she was a baby? She'd have to live her life over again. Oh, no.

"Yes, my dreams give me direction," he informed her, interrupting her thoughts.

"That's how you knew where to find me."

"Correct. Now, I just have to wait until I dream."

She remembered the previous night. "Mister, you need to sleep in order to dream."

He nodded. "It's difficult to sleep in different places every night."

"I rarely slept in the same place."

"Where did you rest your young head?" he asked, and continued eating.

"Anywhere I could. I was trying to sleep in that alley the night you first came here."

He looked at her and put down his fork. "You have no home here?"

"No."

"I see."

Fable narrowed her eyes on him. "It sounds as if you're judging me by what I have, not who I am. Just like Ben's sister." He didn't deny it but kept eating. It angered her. "What business is it of yours if I was homeless or not?"

He mouthed the word *was,* and stopped eating again. "You plan on living at Colchester House."

When she nodded he looked away.

"Snob," she murmured with distaste.

"Pardon me?"

She decided to no longer speak to him about her life. "Why did you need me to come back?" she asked instead.

"It's the rule of the watch."

"What rule of the watch?"

He removed the pocket watch from inside his coat and held it up to her.

When she shook her head, unable to read the inscription, he read it aloud. "Go forward alone or go back together."

"I traveled to this century with her the first time but I didn't know she was here. It took me four days to find her, after I began to have my dreams. But when I tried to return us home and wound the crown, the watch began to glow. It took me, alone, to the fifteenth century, the eleventh, eighth, eighteenth, and so on, leaving my wife here. It took me seventeen years to figure out how the watch works."

She shivered inside at the thought. A wave of pity washed over her. Imagine trying to find Ben for seventeen years? Would she remain as steadfast and devoted to Ben? Yes. She didn't hesitate.

"Where did the watch come from?" she asked.

"My wife found it in the garden. We think it was dug up when we had the roses planted. It shone from within without flaw, as if it had been cut from a single sapphire. When she brought it to me, it wasn't working. We believed it was broken. I tried to wind it and took hold of the crown. I began to turn it clockwise. The air blurred. I heard Dorothea call out to me and rush forward, and as I looked upon my wife, she faded like an apparition before my eyes. An instant later I was here in 2024, alone. Dorothea had traveled back two days before me—which proves how dangerous the watch is if one tries to use it and doesn't know what they're doing. As I said, I found her and then lost her again. I ended up at the mercy of the watch for almost seventeen years, until I began having dreams that Dorothea was still in this time, and also how to return here."

Fable still didn't like him for taking her from Ben but she wanted to help him. "That had to be very difficult for you."

"It continues."

"We'll find her," she vowed.

He gave her the hint of a smile. "I'd be in your debt."

She finished her coffee and pushed the cup away. "Tell me, have you killed people with your sword?"

"Of course. I served in the Royal Army. I've killed many."

"Oh," Her eyes opened wider. "Ben was…is a captain in the army. He saved the king three times!"

"Yes, you mentioned that among his many attributes. His father must be very proud—"

"His father was killed by Jacobites when he was a boy."

"I see." He picked up his cup. "How has he fared these many years?"

"Not well," she let him know. "He has a lot of anger and not much happiness in him." His handsome face appeared in her mind. He was smiling at her. She remembered what her friend, Edith had told her. *But he's changed since you arrived. He seems less…angry. We all notice it, Miss.* "Though I think," she said in a soft, quiet voice and tears sparkling in her eyes, "he has cheered up some."

"Because of you?" he asked just as quietly.

"That's what I'm told." She wiped her eyes and slapped her hands on her thighs. "Let's go find your wife so I can go back to him and make him happy."

He nodded, then waited while she paid, and followed her out.

"Where are we going anyway?"

"Is there such a place called 96th and Madison?" he asked as innocently as a lamb.

"Yes. There's a great diner there. How do you know it?"

"I dreamed of it."

Fable wondered what kind of sixth sense he possessed that he could dream such things. And was it a coincidence that he dreamed of the area where her angel, Bernadette worked?

She looked at him while they walked. Something about his profile and strong, straight nose reminded her of Ben. Is that why she was helping him? She had to believe he was telling the truth and the sooner he found his wife, the sooner Fable could return to Ben.

"Wait," she said, stopping. "You can't meet the woman you love and haven't seen in seventeen years looking like *that*."

He lifted a hesitant hand to his hair.

"Let's just get you fixed up a little. Look," she pointed across the street, "there's a barbershop. I also need some new clothes. There are cheap places close-by. It won't take me long to find something."

It took her ten minutes to make twenty-seven dollars. He needed a shave as well as a haircut, so she panhandled for another quarter of an hour asking people politely if they could spare some change and made another thirty.

"Now, come on, let's make you presentable."

The barber had to stop four times when he tried to turn on the electric razor to shave the traveler's nape, and the warrior nearly jumped out of his seat.

Fable almost couldn't believe her eyes when she saw the traveler cleaned and pruned. His hair was closely cropped in back and a bit longer in front. Instead of giving him a clean shave, the barber trimmed his mustache and beard and made him look like a nobleman.

When she saw him, Fable couldn't help but smile at his awkward discomfort at her appraisal.

"Wow! That's a huge difference."

"I hope she remembers me," he said quietly.

"Of course she will."

She meant to encourage him—though she owed him nothing

and if he tried to double-cross her and leave before he returned her, she'd kill him.

When he tilted his head to look at her from a certain angle, she stopped breathing for an instant. Without all the fur, he looked very much like…Ben.

"Come," he said, pulling her along again, "Let's get you new clothes and find my wife."

She nodded and followed him out then hurried to a nearby thrift store. Thankfully, there was a dressing room that was more of a curtained closet. She tried on three pairs of jeans with shirts in different colors to go with them and had to step out from behind the curtains to look at herself in the mirror. While she took a moment to think about it, the traveler cleared his throat. She looked at him through the mirror. He stood tall beside a rack of clothes appraising her.

"You look most appealing in the second showing—"

Showing? Fable had the urge to laugh and blush.

—"though I do not know why I should tell you."

She wasn't sure why he would withhold a compliment from her and shrugged as she disappeared behind the curtain again. "Mister?" she called out, pricked by his cryptic response. "Why shouldn't you tell me?"

"You wish to appear appealing to the man you care for—even though you must know that a beggar does not belong with a man of his status. Therefore I should not aid you in your quest."

Fable's blood fired through her, scalding her temper. What? She was the one helping him! Why, that—

"However," he continued, "I would have you know that if we were in my time I would make certain you had something fine to wear."

She popped her head through the slit in the curtain and stared at him. Should she thank him? Smile? She thought she saw him smile as she closed the curtain again. Hmm, maybe the wicked time traveler wasn't so wicked.

"How do you know you can trust a dream?" Fable asked him

after she paid for the clothes. She bought the first outfit. It was the cheapest.

"Because I don't know what these streets are called, but they are in my thoughts. They are real."

When they reached 96th and Madison, Fable almost felt sorry for the man getting ready to see the woman he'd been searching for for almost two decades. His hands shook, he was breathing harder than if he'd just finished running up a hill. They looked around at the four corners. On the western side were apartment buildings. On the north-east corner stood a parking lot and on the south-east, the diner where Bernadette waited tables.

"We should go to the diner," she told him. She wasn't sure why she suggested they check the diner first except that she didn't believe in coincidences. She wondered about Richard and Dorothea's story. How had he held onto the hope of finding his wife? Did his Dorethea feel the same way?

He looked toward the diner and started toward it without another word. Entering behind him, Fable stayed close in case he thought to grab his wife and leave Fable and the twenty-first century behind.

They stepped inside. There were six booths, five were occupied. No one present was his long lost wife, nor were the two waitresses, one of whom was Bernadette. When he made his way to her, Fable followed close behind.

"Welcome to Tess' Diner. How many?" She looked up from her notepad in her hand and when she saw Fable, she looked about to give her a happy greeting.

"We are not here to dine," the traveler interrupted. "I'm looking for someone."

Bernadette glanced down at the hilt of his sword sticking out of the long, steel scabbard hanging from his belt. He was going to have to put that thing away somewhere.

Bernadette looked over her shoulder at the door to the restroom. "Is one of those medieval fairs going on in the park?"

"Yes," Fable answered before the traveler had a chance to.

"Near Belvedere Castle."

"How are you, dear one?" Bernadette said to Fable. "I haven't seen you at your normal places."

"I know. I've been…um.." she had no idea what to give the waitress as an excuse as to where she'd been.

"Dorothea West. Is she employed here?" he rudely interrupted.

Fable fastened her wide gaze at him. West? What did it mean? Nothing.

"I'm her husband," he went on, "Richard West, Lieutenant-colonel Richard West."

Everything. It meant everything.

CHAPTER FIFTEEN

BEN GROANED AND opened his eyes, then rubbed his head. Night had fallen. How long had he been out? Fable. He remembered her in the clutches of a man fitting the description of the man who was chasing her. The culprit had found her. He'd taken her. Ben's belly twisted and doubled him over where he lay crumpled against a boulder behind a stand of trees. He'd been away from her, just as he'd been away from his mother.

"Fable," he groaned out. She was gone. Into the future where he could not go. He closed his eyes, unable or unwilling to rise to his feet, feeling the weight of an entire life without her. But wait—

He pulled himself to a sitting position. Where was his horse? What force had flung him out of his saddle and into a boulder? What were those lights beyond the darkened treetops?

Rising to his feet, he squinted into the darkness of the forest. But…it wasn't so dark. He could see high poles stuck into the ground. On top of each pole was a lantern. There was no flame, he realized as he walked under one. Where was he? He didn't recognize the trees. These appeared in the dim light as though they had been planted intentionally in certain groups and in rows along a neatly paved road.

He wasn't in a forest.

The tree line ended too abruptly just there, beyond another pole with a round lantern at the top.

He heard the blare of some kind of horn somewhere ahead. He moved toward it and came to a short stone wall almost hidden by the thick bushes and tree trunks blocking it. He jumped over it and landed on the other side on both feet.

Then backed up and fell on his arse when he looked around him. It was chaos. Mayhem. Horseless carriages filled the streets in two rows. One going one way and the other going the opposite way. They looked more like giant, armored beetles with eyes that lit up the street. Lights like the ones atop the poles. There were colored lights built into metal encasements and suspended in the middle of the streets. Green lights, yellow and then red lights. Red caused the metal beetles to slow their speeding and stop.

He watched while the opposite rows increased their speed when the lights turned green. It was fascinating, mesmerizing. The carriages moved with no outside help.

He finally tore his gaze away and looked up at the high structures taking every foot of the other side of the wide street. He tilted his head to see the tops of the buildings. They reached the heavens…and there were even taller fortresses in the distance. His blood raced through his veins when he realized where he was. The future. *Her* future. She was here! He'd followed her and made it through with her! Hope wasn't lost! But where was she? How would he ever find her in the checkerboard rush of the future population?

"Fable," he said softly. "Which way should I go?" He looked at the other side of the street, and then looked back toward the small forest. He glanced up and saw a sign high up on the same pole that housed the light. 110th Street/Central Park North. North. He remembered what Fable had told him about where she'd been before being taken back to the past. *46th Street and 9th*. If this was 110th Street, then he needed to go south. South was back through *Central Park*.

Wasting no time, he leaped over the short wall once again, this time, to enter the park, not leave it. He ran away from the wall and the mayhem and went deeper into the woods. While he ran, he wondered why the time-traveler brought Fable forward. How did he pull her back without the pocket watch? What did he want with her? Ben prayed it was nothing nefarious. But as the moments passed, he grew more anxious. When he found them, and he would—he was going to kill the time-traveler. He didn't worry about getting back. He wouldn't even think of home until he found Fable.

He hurried past gated enclosures of what appeared to be places to play for children, with swings and colorful climbing structures. He kept going. Thankfully, there were signs in the park that told him he was going in the right direction.105th Street. 103rd, 102nd…he kept going. She might not be at 46th Street and 9th, but it was all he had to go on in a completely different world.

He broke through the park on 60th Street and 5th and kept going. There were very few people around to stare at him while he ran. He finally reached 49th Street when the sun began its ascent, casting the city in a golden-purple hue. But when Ben stopped, it was to stare at the maze of streets with tall buildings on every side. He'd passed a cathedral with tall, jagged steeples, a building with hundreds of flags on poles jutting out of it. It seemed a bit quieter here, with clear glass windows, clearer than he'd ever seen, without a hint of green.

He shook his head at himself, refusing to get caught up in the fascination of this place. He had to get to 9th. He turned in the direction of what he hoped was west, and hurried toward the wide road. Were these the streets on which Fable had slept her whole life? He wondered how she got any sleep at all with all the lights. The sky was starless but the city was bright like the day. He'd seen giant words strung up in lights and flat, moving images of people tall as the buildings.

He felt a new wave of pity for her at having grown up here, right here on the noisy, bright, dangerous streets. But when he found her, he wouldn't let her know about his pity, lest she scold him. He smiled at the thought of her.

Which way? Which way?

He stepped off the little edge, in a hurry to find her. The blaring of a horn rang through his ears. He turned and was blinded by a pair of lights. He didn't remember the carriage hitting him or anything else for three days while he lay in a hospital bed with a concussion and two broken ribs. He learned dozens of new words, medical and non-medical, from the people who cared for him. If the urgency to find Fable wasn't driving him, he would have stayed around his hospital room marveling at all the different wonders of the twenty-first century, though his physicians and nurses told him it was his hard head that saved him when it hit the pavement. His caregivers wanted him to stay to perform more tests, especially after he told them his name and date of birth.

But he had to leave the wondrous hospital and find Fable. How? Even if she'd gone to her previous "home" on 46th and 9th, it didn't mean she was still there. Chances were, she wasn't.

He left the hospital, dejected and more than a little lost. It had been night when last he walked in Fable's future. But now, the sun shone down on a sea of people walking to and fro with their faces bent to small, hand-held devices. He'd never seen so many people—and none of them saw him despite his attire being a bit…outdated, and his face and form being a bit outstanding compared to the other men around him. He'd been walking aimlessly and was surprised when he looked up to find that he'd gone the wrong way, taking a wrong turn somewhere and found himself on Madison Ave. Madison. Madison where? His left side hurt and made walking more strenuous. He removed his coat while he walked and wiped his brow with his sleeve. He stopped when he came to a crossing and looked out at all the—what had the physicians called them? *Cars.* He had to wait, along with a dozen other people, for the cars to stop before he could walk.

He looked up. 97th and Madison Ave. He watched the image of a red human in a circle with a line through it flash from a small box affixed to a pole. For the briefest of moments, he wondered how the people of this time shaped light in the image of a person. His heart thumped. Don't walk. Was he going the right way? He wanted to call out. How many people were in this city? *Fable!*

The light changed to a green human walking.

He stepped into the crossroads with the others. Why was he moving this way? Was he simply following his feet? He looked into the distance. He could see the next sign. 96th Street. South-toward 46th. Right.

When he saw the small tavern-type of establishment on the corner of the street, he thought about having something to eat. At the thought of something nourishing, his insides grumbled. He wondered how a person paid for a meal here. He checked the pockets sewn into his coat tossed over his arm. He had a few coins, two guineas in gold, and some bank notes. He doubted any of it was of use here. Maybe the gold had some value. Could he get a meal for a little gold?

He made his way to the establishment and stepped inside. Opening the door, a little chime sounded when he hit it with his head.

"Welcome to Tess' Diner. How many?

Ben stared blankly at the woman who greeted him. "How many what?"

She tossed him a well-practiced smile. "How many in your party?"

He thought about it for a moment then blinked. "One."

"Right this way." Her tone softened, along with her gaze when she turned to have another look at him. "Are you visiting the States or do you live here?"

He remembered Fable telling him about the country where she came from and the physicians confirming that the States was where they were. "I'm visiting."

She led him to a table near a window and handed him a certificate of sorts with lists of the foods they served.

He smiled at some of the descriptions and then remembered the only way he could pay.

"My lady," he said, "I'm afraid all I have to pay for my meal is this." He produced a guinea and held it up to her. "It's gold."

"What's it worth?" she asked, holding it up to examine it.

"More than a meal, I suspect."

She shrugged and handed it back to him. "Today's meal is on me. Take this to Able's Best Jewelry on 84th and Madison and tell him Bernie sent you. He'll tell you what it's worth. He'll even buy it from you. He's very fair."

"I can't accept your gracious offer. I will repay you for today's meal."

"Fine," she grinned at him. "Have a look at the menu. I'll be back in five to take your order."

He looked over the booklet, marveling over the colorful images. Golden pancakes served with his choice of meat. Something called Challah French Toast that looked especially appetizing in the image of it. He touched it half-expecting to touch the food displayed. There were a variety of eggs served with dozens of different side dishes. Tea and coffee. He was still looking everything over when she returned.

He told her what he chose; a three egg vegetable omelet.

"Would you like home fries or French fries with that?"

Ben gave her a curious look. "Since I've never heard of either, I'll have both."

Her expression didn't change while she wrote in a small pad with a quill-less quill. He waited a moment. She looked up and smiled at him. "Hash, bacon, sausage, plant-based?"

He looked at her the same way the physicians and nurses had looked at him when he told them how he traveled here from the past. "Plant-based…meat?"

She nodded but said nothing.

"I have never heard of hash or plant-based meat. Is it any good?"

She nodded. "I'll bring you sausage. Hmm?"

He nodded his head. "Oh, and could you direct me to your restroom?" He was thankful for his brief hospital stay and for learning some twenty-first century words from the staff.

She pointed to a door to his right and then smiled when he rose to go to it. He disappeared into the restroom as the chimes sounded over the front door.

⋙⋘

BERNADETTE'S SMILE FADED as she turned away and delivered the order to the chef. She looked toward the patrons who had just entered the diner.

"Welcome to Tess' Diner. How many?"

"We are not here to dine," said a man with a British accent. Bernadette took in the sight of him in the same antique style of dress as the man in the bathroom. He was older but just as handsome.

But it was the girl that captured Bernadette's attention. Fable Ramsey, what was she doing here with the Lt. Colonel? Were they connected? Gran had told her a little about Fable. Not why she was important, but that she needed to survive and that Bernadette should feed her when she could. Bernadette found it to be a pleasure. Fable was grateful for everything. Bernadette liked her. She looked around the diner now with the barest amount of interest. She wanted to be somewhere else. Her loose hair was painted in orange and red, splashed with bronze and traces of gold. It fell all around her shoulders, drawing every eye to her.

"I'm looking for someone," the man said.

Bernadette looked over her shoulder at the door to the restroom.

"Is the Renaissance Fair going on in the park?" another customer asked the medieval-looking man after coming close and checking out his attire.

"Yes," Fable, who was dressed in modern clothes, answered. "Near Belvedere Castle."

Bernadette was finally able to greet Fable when the man interrupted them again.

"Dorothea West," he said, looking rather tortured. "Is she employed here?" When Bernadette began to shake her head, he continued quickly. "I'm her husband, Richard West. Lieutenant-colonel Richard West."

At his introduction, Fable Ramsey went still as death. In fact, Bernadette asked her if she was all right. The girl nodded but her stunned expression hadn't changed.

"No, sorry," Bernadette said, turning back to the man. "Your wife isn't here."

He went pale and gave her a stricken look. "Are you certain?"

When Bernadette nodded, he turned to the girl. But she was no help, staring into his eyes with tears in hers.

"Why didn't you tell me?" she asked him in a soft voice.

Tell her what? Bernadette wondered. What was it about her that was drawing the woman who was more than a waitress closer to her? Something—Bernadette wasn't sure what it was, laid buried deep in Fable's consciousness.

"Miss!" the patron at table six called impatiently.

Bernadette nodded to him then turned back to the couple. "Don't go away," she said before hurrying to the customer at table six was waving his hand at her.

After she handed him his bill she returned to the renaissance man and the redhead, but they were gone.

To her right, the handsome patron who ordered the three egg omelet left the restroom and returned to his table.

Bernadette gave the front door a regretful sigh then looked around as if she expected someone to appear. She lowered her voice. "What's this all about? I expected the Lieutenant Colonel, but why was Fable with him?" Her gaze settled on the patron who'd just taken his seat again. She considered his clothes, his British accent… "Does he have something to do with the man who just left?"

She hurried to bring his coffee and set it down before him.

"You look a bit pale," he noted. "Are you unwell?"

"There was a guy in here a minute ago with clothes like yours," Bernadette answered. Were they connected? And why hadn't her gran filled her in on the extra details? "He had a sword—

"A sword?" he asked, suddenly very interested. "Was he alone?"

Bernadette shook her head. "He was with Fable. A girl I know. He was asking me about—

The patron sprang to his feet, almost knocking over his table. Yes. There was definitely a connection between them. "Where did they go?"

"They left, Please sit!" she called out as he took off, leaving the chimes ringing. She wanted to ask him if he knew Dorothea West. "There is something I need to tell you."

"WHY DIDN'T YOU tell me the truth?" Fable demanded again while she hurried to keep up with the traveler's steps. Oh, he couldn't be Ben's father, she lamented. Ben's father was killed—seventeen years ago.

"Now you know it," he replied impassively.

"But how?" she asked, following him into a building on the other side of the street.

"I told you how. The pocket watch brought us to the future—to this time. Our disappearance, according to what you told me, was believed to have been caused by the Jacobites."

"So you didn't die," she said, following him into the lobby.

"We did not die," he agreed.

Fable thought she must be going mad. Was any of this even real? No one ever proved to her that it was. No one but Ben by making her fall in love with him. Love was the proof.

And if it was all real, then this was the man who had written his last wish into his will. A wish Ben might have granted out of his deep love for his father.

"Your alleged deaths put your son on a death-defying path. He lives his life with regrets and guilt no little eleven-year-old boy should have experienced. I think he misses your wife as much as you do." She sniffed and wiped her tears from her cheeks. She didn't realize that he stopped moving and turned to stare at her. "I can't imagine the joy you'll bring him when he sees you and his mother alive."

"You seem to know much about him. Did he tell you these things?"

She nodded. "He told me what you wrote in your will. Don't be so terribly disappointed, Your Grace. You'll be happy to know that your daughter is desperately trying to see that your will is done and making your son miserable in the process. But your son loves you and without me there, he won't deny your last wish."

His gaze on her grew warm for an instant. "Since I live, that is no longer my last wish."

He turned away from her before she could ask him what he meant. He walked up to the concierge and paused. Fable hurried forward and grabbed his sleeve, stopping them from probably getting arrested.

"I wonder if you can help us," she said quickly, turning to the stern-faced, sixtyish-looking man behind the desk. "Do you know the people who live here?"

"Of course," the concierge replied.

"Can you tell me if Dorothea West lives here? She may…" Fable let go of Ben's father and moved closer to the concierge "…go by another last name."

The concierge typed something into his computer, waited a moment spent staring at Fable, then read. He shook his head. "No one here with that name or any other variation."

His smile lingered on Fable until she cringed in her skin and turned away.

The lieutenant followed her out and to the other buildings in the four corners, checking everywhere for Dorothea. No one knew of her. When night came, Fable made enough for a cheap dinner from a nearby fast food place. They walked to the park and sat on a bench to eat.

She picked at her fries and remained quiet while he scarfed down two burgers. How could she eat when this man, this kidnapper, was Ben's father? She almost laughed and turned away to cough into her hand instead. Could it really be possible that his parents had traveled through time and have been lost ever since?

"Are you crying for him again?" Lt. Colonel West asked with a sigh.

"I'm crying for you," she told him truthfully, "striving to find her must have been very hard all these years. But look, you did it. She doesn't live on the corner or work at that diner. That doesn't mean she won't visit there. That is where you were led, Lt.. I think we should stay around there and wait."

"Very well," he answered without hesitation, and dug into his burger again.

Fable knew he had no other choice really. His dreams hadn't told him what to do if his wife wasn't found immediately.

"But I'll have you shed no more tears over me, do you understand?"

"I'll cry for whom I please."

"You are quite a belligerent little thing."

"If your wife has spent seventeen years here, you better prepare for belligerence by the handful."

Despite the sunset's deep golden light, she caught his smile as he looked away.

Like a blanket of gloom covering her, she remembered this man's wish for his son. Now that he was alive, he would, no doubt, enforce it. She shouldn't help him, but he was the only way back to Ben. Her stomach dropped. Why would he bring her back to his son when he didn't approve of her? She had begged for money in front of him, she'd shopped for thrift shop clothes, she slept with other homeless people without fear. She didn't want to know what he thought of her.

"Eat." He handed her half of his burger. "You must keep up your strength."

She took his offering when he shoved it at her. He watched, waiting for her to eat.

She took a small bite and then another.

There. She was sure of it. He smiled at her with the fading sunlight in her eyes.

"What are you called, little one?"

"Fable." She decided not to tell him her last name since Lady Prudence had thought her a Jacobite because of it.

The lieutenant-colonel studied her with his smile deepening with amusement. "Fable, I can see why my son has been enchanted by you."

Funny, his daughter had said the same thing to her. Was that all it was? Ben was charmed by her? It would fade. Love lasted. It lasted seventeen years without a shred of evidence that Dorothea West even lived.

She could give up, jump over the wall and disappear inside the park. Let the Lt. Colonel and his wife return to Ben without her. But she didn't believe she was no good for Ben. She didn't believe he'd be happy if she left him and stayed here. Alone. To die alone.

Giving up was not an option.

Chapter Sixteen

Ben didn't sleep. He walked as night and semi darkness fell over Manhattan. He walked the perimeter of Central Park and wove through Fifth and Madison Avenues. He tried to cover as much ground as he could, but how big was the city? He didn't check inside the park. Fable had told him she slept in alleyways and on the streets. She hadn't mentioned the park. He guessed the park was more dangerous at night. He checked every alley, every alcove. He thought of what the server at the diner had told him. The man she described had to be the one who'd been chasing Fable and pulled her back to the future. The redhead had to be Fable. She'd been close. So close. Why was she still with the traveler? Was she his captive? He should have asked Bernadette if Fable seemed nervous, afraid. Was there anything else? Bernadette had said the man was asking something. Ben hadn't stayed around to hear the rest.

He pulled at his hair as he hurried through the streets, looking, searching. He wouldn't give up. She was here, somewhere. He was grateful that he'd reached her in time and traveled through time with her—else she would have been lost to him forever, and terrified that her captor would harm her before he could find her.

As morning drew near without finding her, he called out her name, but to no avail. He walked until he came to 84th and Madison. Able's Best Jewelry wasn't open yet so he sat on the ground. He'd sell his gold for twenty-first century money and get some breakfast at Tess' Diner. He wanted another chance to speak with Bernadette.

He was surprised and thankful when Able finally appeared and opened his store. When he saw Ben's mint, gold guineas he brought Ben upstairs to his private office and offered him fifteen hundred dollars in cash for both. According to Able, he had enough for breakfast, dinner, and a bed for one night or more, depending on where he stayed.

Ben would eat breakfast and save dinner and the bed for Fable. He intended on finding her before then.

He walked to 96th Street and was glad to see the diner open for business. He looked to the street light and was about to hurry over to the other side when a flash of burnt orange and glistening gold caught his eye.

His heart thumped hard in his chest and tears blurred his vision. He swiped his hands across his eyes and took a better look. "Fable," he barely breathed out.

She was walking with the culprit, heading his way.

He took a step forward, and then ran to her, past people rushing to and fro. He never took his eyes off her.

"Fable!"

She saw him and covered her mouth, then took off toward him.

When they reached each other, they didn't slow, but crashed into each other's arms. Ben held her, afraid to ever let her go again. "Fable. Fable, my love, are you hurt?" He held her at arm's length to examine her better. He ran his hands down her cheeks while his eyes roved over her.

"Ben. Ben, how—"

He looked up at the man bold enough to step toward them. The bastard who had chased her and dragged her back here. "You!" Ben leaped for him and grabbed him by the collar.

Fable screamed out his name. "Don't hurt him!"

Ben wanted to kill him but—but he took a better look into

the culprit's eyes. For a moment, all he could hear was his own breath. His heart was still as the culprit's face grew more familiar. Was it the face of …his father?

Ben released him and stepped backwards. "What is this? You—you—who are you?"

"You don't recognize me?"

Ben shook his head, hoping to clear it. "You cannot be the one I recognize. He's dead."

"Benjamin—" the man said gently.

Ben ignored him and turned to Fable. He didn't know if he could trust his eyes or his ears. But he could trust her. "Is this real?"

"It's real," she told him. "The pocket watch transported them here—

"Them? My mother's here?" he asked on a stilled breath. He returned his attention to the man. He didn't realize tears were streaming down his face. When he did, he did nothing to stop them.

"Yes," the man he'd meant to kill let him know. He spoke slowly, softly, as if he feared anything more would chase Ben away. "She is here. Somewhere."

It couldn't be true. Could it? Ben didn't know what he was thinking. Was this a dream? His parents weren't dead? What? He was afraid to doubt it, to move, to breathe.

"Benjamin," he said in a sorrowful voice. He didn't move to go to Ben, but remained in his spot, "it's me, your father. I'm real and I'm so very, very sorry, Son"

Son, the word echoed through Ben's blood and shook his bones. He thought he would never hear either of his parents call him son again. Slowly, he took a tentative step toward him to have a closer look. Was it possible that this was his father? Ben resembled him—his seventeen-year older father.

Then his father reached out and wiped Ben's tears with his thumbs. "My Benjamin."

At the sound of his father saying his name, the floodgates

opened. Ben wept and the two of them threw their arms around each other.

Did he truly have his father back? Was it possible? "Father," he whispered, then repeated again and again as years of revenge and hatred faded into the four winds. But Ben's turmoil and shattered past weren't healed so easily. "What happened? Why did you never return to us?"

"I could not return on my own. I must return with the one who traveled with me, and that is your mother, otherwise the pocket watch brings me where it wants. I learned that the hard way. I had meant to use Fable to keep the lawmen away that night, instead she brought me home. I wanted to go to you and your sister…" While he spoke, tears streamed down his face. … "But I had to return here to get your mother. I was home. Just feet from Colchester House, but I couldn't leave your mother. I had to return here, but the only way to do that was to bring back the original one who had left."

Ben looked at Fable. She'd come into his life for a reason. He knew it, but he thought it was only for him. To bring happiness into his life. She'd already done that, but to reunite him with his father and mother was something he couldn't truly comprehend yet.

"Maybe we should go someplace more private to sit and talk," Fable suggested, looking around at the people slowing their place to watch the two men embracing and weeping.

They went to Tess' Diner and as they stepped inside Ben took Fable's hand and brought it to his lips for a kiss. "I feared I lost you."

"I feared the same."

"She shed buckets of tears for you," his father added, listening.

When he saw her, Ben smiled at Bernadette and introduced her to his father. "And this is Fable Ramsey, my beloved."

"Your beloved?" the waitress asked, staring with curiosity lifting her dark brows.

Fable gave him a nervous smile and then slipped it to his father. Ben suspected what was troubling her. But he was happy his father met Fable. He seemed fond of her, smiling at Ben when he told him how she'd wept for him. Who wouldn't be fond of her? She had even broken through Pru's armor.

He sat with her opposite his father and held her hand. She tried to separate her hand from his or pull their entwined fingers under the table. But he wouldn't let her. He was beyond thankful that he had been given another chance to make his father proud of him because of the woman he chose to wed.

And she was not one of the ladies on his sister's list.

They agreed with Bernadette when she remarked how close they had come to reuniting yesterday.

When they ordered breakfast Ben and his father's order made them smile that they ordered the same thing.

"How is Prudence?"

"Haughty." There were a dozen more things Ben wanted to say. Things like; obnoxious, selfish, overbearing and more, but why upset his father? "Somehow she has managed to sink her claws into my friend—do you remember young Sudbury?"

"Of course, his father was a close friend."

"Yes. Well, he will bravely wed Prudence within the year."

This news seemed to make his father happy. "I hope to find your mother before then so that we may attend our daughter's marriage day."

"Tell me what happened to you and Mother," Ben asked, wanting to hear it all.

"I have spent these many years trying to find her." He told Ben everything he knew about the pocket watch and how he believed it worked. He listened when his father told him about his dreams.

His father was correct, they had to find her. Ben had to find her. This time he would save her. "I agree with Fable. She could walk through those doors at any moment. We should wait here for her. But we should also do something."

"I'll try to panhandle for a few dollars so we can take out a small *in search of* ad," Fable told them.

"What is panhandle?" Ben asked her.

"Asking for money from people on the streets."

Ben felt himself stiffen up. His gaze slipped to his father. Had the proud 1st Duke of Colchester seen her begging on the streets?

"She made quite a bit, Ben," his father let him know. "She made me presentable to meet your mother with a haircut and a nice shave, kept us fed, and more by doing this panhandle."

"The key is not to lie to people. If I'm hungry, I ask for something to eat. If I need clothes, I ask them for help in getting me something to wear. It's about honesty."

Ben quirked his mouth looking at her. "It also helps that you're beautiful."

She blushed and pushed him away slightly with her shoulder.

"I have money, Fable," he let her know earnestly. "You have no need to panhandle."

He told them about selling his gold guineas and what he'd gotten for them and smiled when Fable clapped her hands.

"You did well, Ben—Your Grace," she corrected with a wary glance at his father.

"Ben," Ben corrected.

"Young woman," his father said, "why do you struggle to deny what's between you? You wept for days on end when I separated you from him. You spoke so highly of him, you made me proud to be his father, and when I asked you what you were to him, you told me you were his beloved. Now, oddly, you seem to want to convince me that you are nothing more than his friend? Should I wonder if you misled me?"

"Abso—" she began to protest. But Ben was quicker.

"She did not mislead you," he assured his father. "She *is* my beloved." When she squirmed in her seat, he looked across the table at his father. "She knows how you feel about me marrying below my status."

"Yes, she and I have discussed it. Though not at length."

Ben blinked at him and then back to her. "What did you discuss?"

Bernadette delivered their food and Ben didn't get an answer to his question. Both men smiled at their vegetable omelet with home fries and toast.

"How do they expect a slight being like yourself to consume all of that?" his father chuckled looking at Fable's plate piled with pancakes and butter. They watched her pour syrup on top and on her bacon.

"You laugh," Ben said, "but on her first day at the house she ate a braised duck, two roasted chickens, six hard-boiled eggs and three cooked fish."

"I needed protein," she reminded him. He still had no idea what protein was. He wasn't sure his father knew either when he mouthed the word.

"How did you meet each other?"

"I found her in my garden praying for protection from you, I assume."

"Yes," his father agreed and cast her a repentant look Ben had never seen his father wear before, "I'm afraid I terrified her."

"She ran from you for four days and ended up in my garden, where she fainted in my arms."

A hint of a smile hovered around his father's lips and he nodded, but he said nothing. It appeared Fable and his father had become friends. He spoke very casually to her, calling her Fable instead of Miss Ramsey. Of course his father liked her, Ben thought watching her lift her fork to her open mouth. She closed her eyes as if she missed pancakes slathered in butter and sweet syrup more than she missed anything else. She opened her eyes and plucked a slice of bacon from her plate then shoved it into her already full mouth. Cheeks bulging, she looked up to find him staring at her with warm amusement in his smile.

He laughed softly and took a bite of his omelet.

"You seem happy, Son."

Ben looked across the table and set his fork down. "I'm happier than I've been since you left. I grew up without you. Your death shaped me. Before Fable came into my life—even after, all I wanted to do was fight. Almost dying on the battlefield helped me live. But my lust for Jacobite blood grew like a dark disease within me. Happiness was not something I sought." He set his gaze on her nibbling on more bacon. "And then light burst through the darkness and I lived again." She looked up from her food. His heart sounded in his ears. "When I first awoke in Central Park, I thought I was still home and that I'd lost you forever. Dying would be less painful. I will not lose you again, Fable." He wanted her to know it and he wanted his father to know as well.

"Ben," she said his name softly, meaningfully. "Try this." She held out her cup to him. It was covered with a lid, and in the lid an X was cut to fit a thin tube from which to suck.

"What is it?"

"Cola."

He would have drank no matter what was in the cup. She had but to ask. He didn't care if he'd fallen for her without any hope of return. He didn't want to be anywhere without her.

He bent his head and put his lips to the tube and sucked. At the same time, she inclined her mouth to his ear. "I love you."

His head was reeling, either from the sweet, fizzy, refreshing drink, or from her warm breath against his temple, her words settling on his scarred heart.

He let go of the tube and smiled at her, then turned to his father. "I'm happy now."

"Son, I would have you know there was nothing I could have done. I had to follow your mother. Even if it meant leaving you and your sister. I knew you would both be well cared for."

A cold, dreary day in December drifted through Ben's memory, when he and Prudence were thrown out of their home by Lord Addington.

"I understand," he told his father, and he did understand. He'd followed Fable into her future, and he would do it over again. Fortunately he was able to find her—and get his father back also. He wasn't about to waste more time being angry or resentful over something he, himself, had done.

"Let's put all effort into finding her, Father."

His father stopped eating and wiped a tear before it fell onto his plate.

"What is it?" Ben asked him.

"There were days I wasn't certain I would ever hear you or your sister call me that again."

Ben nodded, understanding, and wiped his own eyes. His heart swelled with affection for Fable when he felt her hand along his back. She sought to comfort him. The gesture was so unfamiliar Ben didn't know how to react besides to gaze at her as if she was the answer to his prayers dropped from the heavens at his feet.

He smiled yet again, and then returned his attention to his father. "We will find Mum and then go home to Prudence. I think she may never leave Colchester House once you're home."

His father agreed with a chuckle, then "I will remain here while you two do whatever else you feel would help us find her."

"No, I'm not leaving you when I just found you after seventeen years."

Fable agreed not to separate, and went back to eating. When they were done, Bernadette suggested they have some coffee. Ben remembered Stephen buying coffee beans and making Fable coffee at his request. He remembered how she had invited the steward to sit and drink his coffee with her at the duke's table. He smiled now recalling how stunned and angry Prudence had been...and how easily Fable had won her over with a simple compliment. Had she done the same to his father?

"Fable," Bernadette said, handing Fable two little yellow paper packets. "Try these instead of having more sugar in your coffee. I hope you don't mind me saying, but try not to consume any more sweets today. He's a nice guy," she said, pointing to Ben, "and I'd hate to see him lose you again."

"All right," Fable agreed, "but what's wrong with sweets?"

Bernadette stared at her and then blinked. "Diabetes? Didn't your mother ever warn you against so much sugar?"

Fable shook her head. "As you know we had no money for food, and when we did, we didn't waste it on food that had no value. This was a treat."

Ben found that he couldn't swallow with his heart in his throat. Of course, he felt pity for Fable, but what he felt more now that he'd come to know her, was how little she pitied herself. She spoke to Bernadette with a soft, satisfied smile. She had lacked everything and yet, she lacked nothing. Contentment shaped her mouth and gratefulness sparked her eyes with life. She made him want to live and not die on the battlefield. She was balm to his weary soul.

A few moments later, when Bernadette overheard them about their search for Dorothea West, she offered them her phone to search her name. None of them knew what to do with the apparatus. Fable was able to make a set of numbers appear on what she called the screen. But then handed it back to Bernadette. "I don't know anyone to call."

Bernadette sat with them and wrote his mother's name with the alphabet scrambled on tiny buttons. Ben and his father stared at the device in awe and surprise that such a thing existed. It could call someone, tell you who someone was, where they were, and how much they owed. It spoke, and even had a name. But it had no information on his mother. When Bernadette went on her break, she invited Fable to sit with her at the counter while she searched her *phone*.

Ben sat alone with his father and listened while the Lt. Colonel told him about his life for the last seventeen years. His search and persistence were admirable. Ben told him bits about his life, mostly about his battles and the life-altering wound to his arm.

"The lady told me how you were willing to fight me for her, without knowing who I was."

"Yes," Ben said, turning to look at her where she stood with

Bernadette. "I would fight anyone for her."

His father didn't answer but watched them both for a moment and then looked into his cup.

His silence did not go unnoticed by Ben. "Father," he began, then laughed softly and shook his head in disbelief. "I look at you and I feel as if I'm dreaming."

"I must admit," his father confessed, "On the day I brought her back here, I went to the house and saw you when you left on your horse with another tall man. You had grown from a boy to a man, but I recognized you. I would have recognized you at any age. If she had never told me that you saved the king more than once, or how you fought eighteen men and found victory without help, or especially how endlessly patient you are with your sister, I would have been proud of you the instant I saw you and how you carried yourself in the saddle."

Ben smiled and lowered his eyes. "I feel as if my life has always been about making you proud. I was robbed of that. To hear you say it now..." He wiped his eyes and laughed at his tears, but his father had many of his own.

They talked over coffee until Fable returned and slipped into the seat next to Ben's. Bernadette's break was over and she had to return to work but she left Fable the phone. "We didn't find anything."

"You are clever," Ben's father remarked. "Have you figured out how to use the device?"

"A little. I can ask Siri whatever I want and it'll send me the information I want...if it's on the web. "I was wondering if there was a name she might have gone by back then, when your life was normal?"

Ben's father thought about it for a moment. "Thea! It's short for Dorothea. It was the name by which I called her when we were alone. Thea!"

Fable immediately spoke into the device asking it for information on Thea West. When the screen changed, she handed the phone to Ben to read the results.

"There are three. One is in her eighties, one is in her twenties, and one…hmm, she's the correct age."

"Hold that pointer over her name and tap it—"

"Tap it?"

She helped him, then waited with him.

When the screen changed he looked it over. "There's no image of her. It says she's a social worker and won the National Social Worker Award in twenty-fourteen. "Ms. Thea W. Halstead received the—"

"That's her!" Fable and his father both blurted at the same time.

"She was born in Halstead, Essex," Ben's father informed them. "The W obviously stands for West." He turned to Fable and cast her a curious look to match Ben's. "How do you know her?"

"I don't," she told them. "I was supposed to meet her the day after you brought me into the past. She's my social worker."

CHAPTER SEVENTEEN

WITH BERNADETTE'S PERMISSION, Fable used the waitress's phone to call the social worker's office. They were all disappointed to hear Ms. Halstead was upstate in meetings with HR and would not be back in the office until tomorrow. No, the receptionist could not give Fable Ms. Halstead's cell number, even if it was an emergency. They would have to wait until tomorrow.

When they told Bernadette about it, she noted that it was especially clever of Fable to search other names her husband would know. Once he found 'Thea' he would recognize Halstead, and as he had said, the W obviously stood for West. "Your wife is also clever. You could have found twenty Dorothea Wests and spent more time trying to find the right one. This way, with just one Thea W. Halstead, it guarantees that when you find her, you will have found the right woman."

"Without you," Ben turned to Fable with a look that bound her to him for a lifetime and beyond, "we might not have found her."

"We haven't found her just yet."

"Tomorrow," he said confidently and smiled at her and then at his father. "Let's go find a place to sleep tonight and plan what we need to do and where we need to go tomorrow."

They promised Bernadette they would see her for dinner and when Ben rose up to pay the bill, Fable rose with him and stood on her toes to whisper in his ear that it was customary to leave a tip.

He gave Bernadette a hundred dollars, and took Fable's hand to leave.

"Go to Liz's B&B." The waitress paused to write the address on a check. "Tell her that Bernadette sent you." She tore it from the pad and handed it to him.

Fable watched him smile at the pretty waitress, and she was thankful that her boyfriend was learning how to get along with people, even people socially beneath him.

Fable let go of Ben's hand when his father came to walk beside them. She took a step back while they continued toward the door and looked at Bernadette.

"Thank you for helping him." She smiled and lowered her head. "His parents are very important to him."

"And he is very important to you?" Bernadette asked her with a knowing smile.

"Yes," Fable admitted.

The waitress nodded as if she knew something no one else knew. "We all have a purpose."

Fable's smile faded. "What?"

Bernadette gave a sisterly smile over to Fable and turned to get back to work.

"Bernadette?" She called out softly as the door began to open to allow Ben reentry. "Do you always speak so cryptically?"

Bernadette turned to her again and for a moment she simply stared at Fable. She didn't say anything. She looked as if she wished she didn't have to. Then, with a great sigh, she proceeded. "I was told you should let him go before it's too late. The people he will gain from this won't accept you. Your many attributes will go unnoticed by them. I'm sorry. You don't belong with him in his time."

"What?" Fable asked stunned and hurt that Bernadette could say something so mean and damaging to her.

"Bernadette." It was Ben coming toward them, casting Fable

a compassionate glance before returning his dark glare to the waitress. "How dare you speak such an evil thing to her? Who do you think you are to say how my family will feel about her once they know her?" He glanced at his father, who said nothing, but nodded his head.

Moving a step closer to her, Ben stared into her eyes. "You are incorrect if you think for a moment that I would allow *anyone's* opinion of her to change how I feel. As for her belonging with me, she is obviously meant to be in my time, since she traveled three hundred years and over seventeen miles to reach me. She most assuredly belongs in my life because she has rescued me from a pit I never wish to return to. Take a look at all the colors of fire and water that paint her, and tell me how was I to resist her light? She saved me, and countless other young, fighting men who would have died by my sword if not for her pulling me back to humanity." He reached for Fable's hand and entwined his fingers through hers.

Never in Fable's life had anyone stood up for her like this. When Bernadette had first spoken what sounded like a curse—what else could it be if it kept her from his side—Fable didn't know what to say. She bit her lip to keep her tears back. She knew how to do it. Surely she'd done it a million times before. She didn't usually believe in such things as curses, so she didn't know why it affected her so. But then Ben appeared at her side to defy Bernadette's words with bold confidence. Was he declaring these things about her? Had she really rescued him from the dank dungeon where his heart lay hidden?

"Who are you, Bernadette? You've been particularly friendly toward us. What do you want?"

By now Ben's father returned and moved closer to hear what was going on.

"I'll tell you who I am, Your Grace," Bernadette said, staring Ben in the eye. "My family finds relics that can manipulate time and we destroy them and set things right."

Fable paled. Ben hardly appeared fazed when he turned to

look at her.

"What are you talking about?" he demanded quietly.

"The pocket watch in your father's pocket."

The Lt. Colonel moved to draw his sword.

Ben's hand on his arm stayed him. When his father lowered his hand away from his hilt, Ben continued speaking to Bernadette.

"Why do you think we carry the watch?"

"There's only one way back, Ben," she told him. "And Richard West has it, so don't lose him because you *have* to go back."

"Are you going to tell us who you are?" Ben's father asked her.

"My name is Bernadette Black. I'm here to put things back to the way they should be. None of you belong in this time. It's taken years to get this all right. Lt. Colonel, you need to find your wife and return with your son to 1718." She turned to Fable. "I'm not sure where you need to be or why you were sent back to that particular time."

Fable didn't like the sound of that. Her heart began to thump harder. "You're a part of all this? How? Why? I need to be with Ben."

"Well, I'm not certain that's poss—"

"Miss Black," Ben said in a warning voice. "I do not know what you're trying to do here, but you ought to end it before there are consequences for you."

Bernadette stared at him for a minute then a smile crept over her face. "My, but you are indeed fearsome and convincing."

"Good, then I will not have to make myself any clearer," Ben told her, his eyes like steel.

Bernadette looked at Fable, her expression clearly going soft, then she nodded. "I'll see what I can do, otherwise, the watch may transport them without you."

Ben took a step closer to the waitress. "Who are you that you will 'see what you can do'? You seem to know much. How? You latched onto me the instant I stepped through that door yesterday. You must have known there was a connection between me and my father yesterday when he came in. But you said nothing."

"I didn't know," she assured him. "And even if I did, I'm not permitted to help you find one another."

"Yet you helped us find my mother."

She shook her head. "Fable did that. I could have sat at that stool for the next two days searching on my phone, but I wouldn't have found Thea W. Halstead."

"Who won't permit you?" Fable asked her.

"I can't say. I believe it's God but I can't prove it. I don't hear a voice. I just know I'm not permitted." She shrugged. "My family has been given gifts in some areas, yet we lack in others."

"What do you know about the pocket watch?" the Lt. Colonel asked her. "Are you the one who left it in my garden?"

"No. But it was left there for a purpose."

"What purpose?" the older warrior asked, reaching for his hilt.

Bernadette smiled cooly at him. "There are hawks in this city. Eagles too. Put your weapon to me and the birds will flock here and pluck your eyes from your head the instant you step outside."

"You're a witch," Ben's father accused in stunned disbelief of her words.

"No, the power to communicate with animals is in my blood on my maternal side, of course—and you're all going to have to sit again if you plan on staying," she told them, looking over Fable's shoulder. "My manager is watching."

She led them back to their table, brought them more coffee, then sat with them, no longer concerned with what her manager thought.

"You seem to know much about this. Tell us, what was the purpose of separating my family?" Ben lamented. "This has brought only sorrow and years of hatred and rage to my life. My sister and I had to eat garbage from the street. I listened to her cries every night, and I vowed to pay everyone back. I lived with hatred that held my heart captive for almost twenty years—

because of this. It almost destroyed my life. It robbed my parents and my sister, and everyone in Colchester of seventeen years." He looked up. Fable wanted to slip her arms around him, but his lamenting was over. Now, he slammed his fist on the table, drawing the attention of the other customers. "Why was the pocket watch left in our garden?"

"We don't know why the pocket watch ended up in your mother's possession. We believe it was one of the items created to destroy the Ashmores. When my grandmother and Aunt Tess found out that it was found and used, they set out to make things right."

Ashmore. Fable's blood felt as if it had just been set on fire. Her belly knotted up and her heart drummed an erratic litany in her chest. Ashmore.

The name spread a mist over her memory, exposing holes…summer sunshine lit the private garden where two two-year-old girls sat in the grass. Around them, plucking worms from the ground, or seeds from the swaying grass, birds enjoyed the day with them…along with a few rabbits, and a brown squirrel. The little girls had the same red hair. One child's eyes were the color of the sea, while the others were the color of the earth. A man dressed in fine clothes with dark hair and sparkling, blue-green eyes and a kind smile came near and knelt beside them in the grass. "Do you like Papa's garden?"

Fable blinked her eyes, returning to the present. Tears spilled down her cheeks. She wiped them, not knowing why they were there. When she looked up it was to find Bernadette's eyes on her.

"Who are the Ashmores?" Ben demanded. "What do they have to do with us?"

Bernadette's attention shifted to him. "In this case, it has to do with Captain Thoren Ashmore, and right now it's what he has to do with *you*, Captain West," she corrected. "He's the only male born to my ancestors for a millennium. We don't know the extent of his pow—gifts. On November 10th—in just two months—he will be falsely accused of being a pirate. On

November 18 he will be hanged. You're the only one who can save him. You're friends with the king. You must go back and convince him that Captain Ashmore is innocent."

"So," Ben's father said through clenched teeth, "you did this to my family to save one person from your family."

"It was done to save your family, as well, and Thoren is first-born male to—"

"I do not care about that!" the Lt. Colonel said through clenched teeth.

Ben ran his hands down his face. "I don't care about the Ashmores or anyone else. Either Fable returns with me or I don't go back."

"You have to return—"

"I will not."

"The watch will pull you back with or without her," Bernadette told him. "That's how it works."

"Then I'll go to the king and make certain Thoren Ashmore is hanged. If you don't want that to happen, then you better make certain I don't leave without her."

Bernadette was quiet. Everyone at the table was quiet.

Fable stared at him. He was bluffing, of course. He'd just gotten his father back, and was about to find his mother. He would never leave them now. Would he? No! She wouldn't let him stay behind when they returned home. But that meant she would have to say goodbye to him and watch him leave her. How could she?

She quickly swiped a falling tear or two from her cheeks and looked away to slow her thrashing heart, missing the tender way Ben and Bernadette gazed at her.

"Do something," Ben said to the waitress. "Help us. Send her back with me and I will do everything I can to save Captain Ashmore. You have my word."

"I'll do my best to help." Bernadette turned to Fable and expelled a sigh. "I don't know all the details, but you're here for a purpose. I get why you went back—it was to save this man…and my relative. You've changed this hardened warrior and if Thoren lives, it will be because of you. I'll remind my Aunt Tess of that."

She was here for a purpose. Her. A homeless, illiterate beggar. She was important and not only to Ben but for another man who came to life in her mind, her heart raced at the sound of his name. *Thoren Ashmore.* Fable had the feeling that Bernadette knew more and wasn't saying. Did Bernadette know who the two red-haired girls were? But instead of questioning the waitress further, Fable smiled at her. "Can you really communicate with animals?"

Bernadette nodded. "Not as well as my grandmother. I'm kind of new at this."

"Witchcraft!" Ben's father blurted out angrily.

"It is not!" Bernadette defended. "Men like you were responsible for the deaths of many women believed to be witches because they were able to do what you couldn't."

"Killing the likes of you is better than falling under the whims of witches," he countered. "Just look at my family for proof. Look at the life of this poor soul." He touched his finger to Fable's arm. "You or your kind obviously dragged her into this. Did any of you think about her feelings…or Benjamin's?"

Bernadette said nothing but stared at the table. Finally, she said in a small, soft voice, "If you meet Lizzie tonight, put all your questions to her." And with that, she rose and went to another table to take an order.

Ben had had enough and took Fable's hand to lead her out. "Let's go find this Lizzie."

His father agreed and the three left the diner without another word to Bernadette.

Before they stepped outside, Fable turned to look over her shoulder. Bernadette's gaze found hers. Fable wasn't angry with her, or suspicious of some malicious plot. No, rather she felt a comforting closeness with the waitress and an unexplained familiarity with a dead stranger named Thoren Ashmore. She smiled at Bernadette and then followed Ben out.

Lizzie's B&B wasn't far from the diner. Fable led her two

companions onward, stopping now and then to say hello to a dog someone was walking.

She didn't feel the need to hurry up and meet Lizzie and find out things she didn't think she was prepared to hear. But they did finally arrive at the quaint townhouse that served as a B&B. Thankfully, Lizzie wasn't there. After a call to Bernadette, the girl who introduced herself as Harper and checked them in didn't charge them for either of their rooms, one for Ben to share with his father and one for Fable. They had nothing to unpack and after washing up they met in the hall and headed out to do a little sightseeing. The Lt. Colonel wasn't up for the walk and hoped they would forgive him for staying behind to rest.

Assuring him that they would, they left the B&B happily with Ben's arm around the back of Fable's waist. They walked back to the east side and she answered Ben's endless questions about electricity, colored lights, video billboards, quietly flushing toilets, and a dozen other things.

He also seemed especially interested in where the nearest church was. When they came to one, he pulled her toward the entrance. "Fable." He smiled at the sound of her name coming from his lips and drew her into his arms. "I want to be with you for the rest of our lives."

She thought of what Bernadette had said about her possibly not being sent back. "But, Ben—"

He stopped her by gently pressing his index finger to her lips. "I will not be separated from you. I will not leave without you, Fable. Trust me."

Yes, she would. He hadn't let her down yet. He even followed and found her in the future. She looked into his eyes. She'd known from the day she woke up in his kitchen and looked into his eyes that he had a kind heart entrapped by cool detachment. Each day in his care proved her first opinion of him was correct. He'd protected her from his sister, let her beat him at fencing, read with her by candle light on the rose-strewn floor of his bedroom—where she bound herself to him.

"Let's go inside and speak our vows of marriage before the Lord God's eyes."

She nodded at his smile and let him lead her into the church.

They didn't speak before a priest, but before God they vowed to love each other until they died—with Ben assuring her they would live long, happy lives.

When they left the church, Fable's heart leapt within her every time she thought of being his wife. And it broke for the same reason. She remembered Bernadette's prophetic words. But Fable didn't need a woman with whatever powers she possessed to tell her she'd never be accepted by Ben's family. She was friends with his father, but the Lt. Colonel knew how she felt when it came to his son. He hadn't offered her his blessing to marry Ben. Marrying Ben meant being married to people who looked down on her too much to let them be happy.

She straightened her spine as they walked. His arm tightened around her waist. He smiled at her. "What is it, my love?" he asked.

She would do anything for him, give anything for him, but she wouldn't let him leave the beloved parents he'd just found, and was about to find. He'd be stuck here with her for the rest of their days. He'd never see his family again.

"Loving you sometimes overwhelms me," she confessed.

He leaned down toward her face and ran his fingers over a tear rolling down her cheek. "I'll carry you if that's what you need, Fable."

She shook her head. "I like walking with you." She curled her arms through his and kept her pace even with his. "What will you tell your father?"

"The truth. I think he will be happy for us," he told her with a reassuring smile. "No more worrying over my family. I'm all you need."

She burst into laughter. "You're all I need."

"What is so humorous about that?"

"Nothing," she corrected when she realized he was insulted.

"Nothing at all." He was correct after all, he was all she needed. "Ben?"

"Hmm?"

She could tell him anything, couldn't she? He wouldn't call her a witch the way his father had called Bernadette, would he? "I feel as if I should know Thoren Ashmore's name. As if I should know *him*."

Chapter Eighteen

When they returned to the B&B, they found Ben's father in a heated discussion with an older woman. To Ben, the woman appeared to be about eighty, or even older, but she argued with fire in her cloudy, blue eyes.

"I tell you, your son *must* return to save Thoren or he will lose the girl."

Listening from the foyer, Ben's blood singed his veins. He slid his hand to Fable's hand and took it, then stepped into the front room. "Lizzie, I presume. How—"

The old woman wasn't listening. She wasn't even looking at him, but her stare found Fable and locked onto her.

"You," she whispered cryptically.

"What about her?" Ben demanded.

Lizzie still didn't take her gaze from Fable. "You look just like him."

"Lady," Ben said in a warning tone. "What is going on? Bernadette said you had answers. So start talking. Begin with who you think Fable is?"

"She's the girl who saved you and many others, including my nephew." She finally angled her head and looked at him. Ben suddenly felt bare and fully exposed before her. He reached for the hilt of his sword. "Whatever you are doing to me, stop now or I'll kill you."

She didn't look away but her piercing gaze changed into

amusement. "You had better begin showing me why you were worth saving."

Ben remembered what she had said to his father. "Who else could save your precious Thoren?"

Her smile faded and she nodded. "No one."

"What's so special about him?" Fable asked, stepping around Ben's shielding arm.

"Oh, but there are so many things special about him. There hasn't been a male born to the Ashmores or to the Blagdens in centuries. We believe he has more power than any before him—including me or my sister. The problem is he doesn't know it. And even if he somehow discovers it, he has no idea how to use or harness it. He must return to me so I can teach him the good and proper way to wield his power. It's been entrusted to us. We must use it for good. He came to this century once with the use of the pocket watch. I think he hid it in the Colchester garden with the intention of returning for it, but he was taken captive and will be tried as a pirate and hanged if you," she turned to Ben again, "don't do something. Once he's safe, you are to give him the pocket watch so he can return."

"What will you do if I do as you ask?" Ben asked her.

"I'll abide by her wishes," the old woman answered with narrowed eyes fixed on Fable.

"My wish is to stay at Ben's side."

Lizzie Black's lips curled upward. "Are you so certain, child?"

"Yes," Fable didn't hesitate to tell her. "No matter whose feet come through those twenty-first century doors, it will still be Ben I'll choose."

The old woman's smile sharpened on her. "You say this as though you know whose feet they might be."

Ben remembered Fable telling him that she felt like she should know Thoren Ashmore's name. He stepped forward. "Enough riddles. Who is Thoren Ashmore to her?"

Finally Lizzie pulled her gaze from Fable's to look at him—but only for an instant. "He is her father."

FABLE WALKED TO her room with Ben and his father behind her. She listened to their low voices as Ben told his father that he planned on marrying her—in fact, he already had. The Lt. Colonel sounded more forgiving than she had anticipated. Still, there was no joy in his approval.

The blow was less painful for Fable because of the shock of Lizzie's words. Thoren Ashmore was her father. She would have called the seer a fruitcake if she hadn't been assailed by the sudden visions—memories?—of a man and his two twin, red haired daughters, Magnolia and Fable.

According to Lizzie, Fable and her sister were originally born in 1682 to Lady Patrice Pruit, who died during childbirth, not Kittie Ramsey who found the two-year-old and kept her, and the Earl of Dorset, Lord Thoren Ashmore, first and only son of Lord Josiah Ashmore, Earl of Winterborne, and his wife, Mercy Blagden.

Was it possible? She and her sister, Magnolia ended up in the twenty-first century when their father used the pocket watch's magic without knowing how to control it. He was brought here with his daughters and like Ben's parents, they were separated, but Thoren was never able to find them. In his desperation to return to the time before he'd used the watch, he mistakenly sent himself to Ben's time.

Fable remembered what Lizzie had told her. Her alleged father lived every waking moment in search of his daughters.

It would be his feet coming through the future's doors.

It was still too difficult for her to imagine she had a father, and such a devoted one as that, living somewhere, a prisoner in the past. And Ben was the only one who could save him. What about her 'twin sister', Magnolia?

Crazily enough, according to Lizzie, Magnolia had the ability to see and hear spirits of the departed. The spirit of Lord

Ashmore, their father had already found her and had taken care of her as Thomas Black, an old gentleman who took her off the streets. Magnolia had seen him as he wished to be seen by her—as an old man. She never knew the good Samaritan Mr. Black was the spirit of her father, who by 2024 had been long dead.

Did Fable care about any of it really? They were her sister and her father in name only. She didn't know them. She didn't love them. Not the way she loved Ben.

When she reached the door to her room, she stopped and closed her eyes, while she listened to Ben and his father.

"We will speak more in the morning," the Lt. Colonel told his son. Then, "Good night, Fable."

She turned, cringing a little, to look at him. She almost backed into the door when he came closer and took her by the shoulders. "Sweet dreams, daughter."

Daughter? Did he accept her then? Did they have his blessing? She looked at Ben and smiled, then smiled at his father.

When Ben didn't follow him to the room, Fable felt her cheeks go up in flames. She hurried to put the key in the door before the Lt. Colonel realized what was going on and demanded that Ben follow him.

Once she was inside, she flipped on the lights. Ben recoiled, then laughed softly at himself. "That's hard to get used to."

She laughed with him and then grew silent and went to him. "Ben?" she asked, disappearing in the circle of his arms. "There is so much to get used to. I never had a father. The thought of meeting him is overwhelming."

"I will not leave your side until you wish it," he whispered into her ear, not letting her go.

"A girl can know a thousand people and not one has ever given her what her heart needs." She looked up into his devoted gaze when he stepped back to see her while she spoke. "She can live her entire life and die without ever meeting such a person." She shook her head. "It's a pity. But not for me. I found that person who fulfills my heart's every desire. It's you, Ben."

He gave her a surprised look, then his playful smile warmed with affection. "Fable, I hope you know how I adore you?"

She hoped the tears filling her eyes and staining them red, along with the tip of her nose, convinced him that she knew.

"My heart was dead," he told her softly. "The things I lived for had destroyed me. But while I was perishing, you, illuminated in your fiery light, slipped through the gates of my misery. You swayed my thoughts from cares I thought were bigger, more important to thoughts of love and devotion."

Her smile widened remembering telling him there were no concerns stronger than love and devotion.

When he ran his knuckles over her jaw and tilted his head to kiss her, she closed her eyes. Her pounding heart grew louder. How would she live without him if she had to?

His lips were soft and pliable as he pressed them to hers. Every thought fled at the passion he ignited in her. Curling her arms around his neck, she deepened their kiss and sighed dreamily into his mouth when his arms coiled around her waist and he lifted her off her feet. He carried her to their bed, kissing her and pausing to smile at her.

"I love you," she whispered, pressing short, soft kisses on his lips and cheeks. "I'll never love anyone but you."

She gazed into his eyes when he laid her down on the bed. "Why are you crying, Ben?"

He shook his head. "I sometimes feel as if you will disappear in my arms—just as you appeared there."

She laughed softly. "I didn't appear. I arrived."

He smiled, but Fable could tell he was afraid of losing her.

"Let's leave tomorrow's concerns for tomorrow," she suggested, not letting him go, but pulling her down, closer to the heat of her body.

He nodded and smiled as he moved over her and lay beside her on the bed. His kisses were hungry but polite, reigned in but eager enough to snap the tethers of his self-control.

Or did he owe his resistance to a stubborn thread of apathy

that had never completely healed? Could she reach the deepest, darkest parts of him? Yes, she thought, helping him out of his shirt and kissing him while she did it. She'd reach him and stroke him, and tame him just enough to cherish her—as she cherished him. Control? Even a hardened warrior's control was nothing compared to an inviting smile from someone much loved. She would prove it. To herself, at least. She could make him lose control.

She bit his bottom lip and ran her palm down the back of his thigh. He pulled himself over her once again and settled halfway atop her. She reached for the clasps of his pants.

He calmed her shaking hands and brought her trembling fingers to his lips. He unclasped his pants and moved out of them.

Fable wasn't nervous about being intimate with him. They'd made love before. But they knew each other so much more now. Ben knew all her secrets. Their bond was even more intimate now. Now, she loved him and would never love anyone but him.

He undressed her as if he were unpacking a treasured gift, his gaze basking in every inch he exposed, kissing trails to here and there and snatching her breath. He took his time, cherishing every moment.

Finally, when her pinkie brushed against his, the control he held onto so tightly, frayed and snapped. He didn't tear her clothes, but pulled and yanked her out of them.

She smiled victoriously.

As if he knew what caused her unusual rush of pride, he laughed. His deep, low pitch filled her and seared her blood. She let herself fall deep into his loving gaze as he slipped his naked body over hers, and then closed her eyes reluctantly when he dipped his face to kiss her.

His tongue filled the darkest recesses of her mouth, slowly, with the skill of a master, though he swore he hadn't kissed many. His full, succulent lips molded to hers and compelled her legs to open wider beneath him.

She knew by the urgency in his kisses, his short, deep breaths, that he wanted her. Desperately. That he would never let her go. He would lose his whole family for her.

"Ben…" she whispered as he pushed his heaviness against her.

He stared into her eyes. "I love you," he told her then covered her mouth with his. He pushed his way inside of her, pausing once to let his passion wane. She held onto him, running her fingers through his hair, her palms down his back. She relished every muscle as it trembled at her touch.

He loved her. He was the first person in her life to ever say it and mean it. Despite the way his sister and many others felt about her, he had never hidden his affection for her, whether he was protecting her from hissing tongues, or spending all his time with her. Even when he tried to run away from what he was feeling for her, he'd returned to stand for her in front of a pack of wolves. Even Edith knew how the duke felt about her. But if Fable ever doubted it, all she had to do was look at him when he saw her.

Oh no! Were those tears burning her eyes? No! Not now! He'll think…

He moved his face closer to hers and kissed her eyelids. It made her want to cry more. All the things she lived without—like a real mother, someone she could trust, someone who loved her the way she should have been loved, a safe home, a hot meal every day without a single fret of where she would eat tomorrow. She'd endured it all. And then he came along and gently offered her everything she ever wanted, everything she didn't know she needed.

"What is it, my love," he asked. "What brings these tears to your eyes?"

"I'm unworthy," she sobbed softly, hating herself for losing it while they made love.

"Unworthy?" He leaned up and cast her a dark look. "Did my father offend you? Wh—"

"Ben—"

"I'm the one who is unworthy of *you*, my love. You have a

grateful and kind heart. You, who have been pelted with things the vile-natured had the audacity to throw at you. You have survived the fear and the loneliness of the night and learned how to flip a man and then have your way with him."

She smiled remembering how she'd flipped him and his friend, Sudbury.

"You have an enchanting nature, but the most dangerous thing you do with all your charms is swindle a man out of his money and his senses. You have remained somehow innocent and grateful though the world flung you about. That is a special sort of strength, Wife. I seek to emulate you."

She smiled gazing up at him, then her lips curled with a playful pout. "You're never going to get over that I beat you at chess."

"I was unprepared for your skill. That is swindling, my dearest."

She pushed him away when he would have swooped down on her. "I've beaten you many times since then, Benjamin. Admit it!"

"You have beaten me many times," he gave in quickly. "On the board and off it." When her smile returned, he leaned in and kissed her.

She felt him trying to break through her wall. She spread her legs wider and lifted them over his hips. She felt every thoughtful thrust, every inch of him. When she dripped around him, he unleashed his passionate heart, probably the same passionate heart revealed on the battlefield, making him a decorated soldier.

She let him have his way with her—after a swift chase. He would never hurt her. Not even if his life depended on it. She trusted him. That's why she giggled and acted irresistibly to him. She hadn't known him for long, but she felt things instinctually for him. She had never been known for acting coy—but she acted that way now and laughed with him, then panted with him again when he held her from behind.

She felt like an empress when he withdrew and then turned her around to face him. With a slight movement, he lifted her against him and then set her down on his heavy erection. She coiled her legs around him and moved with him while he carried her to a cushioned chair in the corner of the room. He fell into it holding her against him. He let her go and spread himself out beneath her.

She needed no further persuasion but straddled him and stroked him with her body. She smiled with a satisfied purr and told him how good he felt so deep inside her, bringing him to a quick end.

"Thank you, Fable," he said softly when they were finished.

"You don't need to thank me for that," she protested mildly.

"Why not? Is this intimacy something you share only with me?"

"Of course."

He smiled and closed his arms around her securely. "I'm thankful that you chose me, my love. This time with you is precious. It always will be. I will always be thankful for it."

"In that case," she whispered, "thank you as well."

He looked as if there was more he would say. He kept silent, save for the chuckle expelling from his lips.

"My father," he began a moment later, "said you told him things that made him proud to be my father. Thank you for that too. It was something I always wanted—to make him proud."

Fable didn't want to ask him if his father still felt the same way knowing they were married. She didn't want to know.

They slept for a few hours in a tangle of arms and legs.

It didn't take long once their eyes opened to smile at each other and kiss, and move like a sensual cloud with Fable gliding over him and then rising up.

She would give up her father and sister, whom she only knew in name, to spend her life with Ben.

He grasped her by the hips and pushed her down the length of him. She arched her back and pulled herself up, languishing in how pleasurable he felt. He yanked her down again. This time, he closed his arms around her and pulled her to him to kiss her, swelling her heart with an overflow of maddening, needful, all-fulfilling love. When he broke their kiss to look at her, his eyes told her what he felt for her in his heart. When he moved beneath her again, she surrendered to all he desired, matching his fervor then slowing again to enjoy their climax together.

As she rested again in Ben's arms, she doubted the pocket watch was powerful enough to move her. If time truly screwed up and she was Thoren Ashmore's daughter, who knew what she was capable of?

If the watch tried to separate them, she would smash it to pieces.

ELIZABETH BLACK, KNOWN to many as Old Lizzie, sat in a wooden chair by an open window in the dark dining room of the B&B. She was staring out, breathing in the softly scented night breeze. Hyacinth and car exhaust. She didn't like being in the city. She much preferred being close to nature and its animal life.

Lizzie possessed 'gifts' that granted her communication with animals, time-travel, teleportation, and seer abilities. She wasn't as gifted as her sister. Tess had been given possession of the keys to time after her fight against the demon lord Raxxix, saving thousands from the ruby dagger, as well as Josiah Ashmore, beloved of her granddaughter Mercy Blagden. For Mercy, Tess would give anything. When Thoren was born, Lizzie remembered one of the house cats called Fiona telling her that the babe possessed many gifts, that he would die young like the rest of the Ashmore men, save Josiah, and that there would be no more males born to the Ashmore line. Out of all Josiah's six brothers, none of them had a son.

Lizzie had reported everything the animals told her to Tess, but she had a feeling her sister already knew. Thoren must therefore live. Everything had been going well, but even when

Thoren married, he had no sons. And then he used that troublesome pocket watch and messed everything up.

Lizzie suddenly angled her head, as if she could hear what no one else could. She froze and then took a moment to breathe before rising from the chair.

Fable, one of the twins upstairs, just became aware that she might have inherited her father's power. Power she would use against Lizzie and Tess if she felt the need. The girl's devotion to Captain West was deeper than anything Lizzie or Tess could have imagined.

Chapter Nineteen

FABLE WAITED IN the hall with Ben for the Lt. Colonel. Her belly grumbled. She lifted it in her palm to it and blushed.

"I'm fine," she hurried to assure Ben, but it did no good.

She watched him with a frown as he hurried toward his father's door and disappeared behind it.

"Niece."

Fable turned and smiled at Lizzie. "Pardon?"

"You're the daughter of my nephew—"

Fable's smile didn't fade or falter. Lizzie was correct. "By how many generations?"

Lizzie looked her over and smiled. "Many."

Alright, Fable thought, that was all the old woman would say. Fable didn't need to know more. It explained why the waitress, Bernadette, who was also the old seer's niece, had fed her when she was living on the street. Fable eyed Lizzie with caution and boldness. She had one more question.

"Where were you all my life?"

This seemed to affect the old woman, who had been like a stone before. "I was not given the gift of finding anyone. No one I know is permitted to find anyone. And even if we could do it, you wouldn't be the person you are today."

Fable shook her head emphatically, causing the spirals of her hair to catch the light. "No. You're wrong. I would have been me no matter what life I led."

"Life shapes you, Child," Lizzie corrected. Then, "The woman who found you removed any trace of you. Even your father couldn't find you for almost twenty years. Do you mean to punish us for it?"

Fable stepped back. "No, of course not."

She stopped and followed Lizzie's pale gaze over her shoulder. Fable turned to see Ben coming toward her, his gaze, curious.

"Good morning, old woman. What brings you to our door?"

"Fable's well-being brought me," she let him know. Her voice held firm against the mistrust in his hard gaze.

"Is your duty truly to Fable?"

Lizzie nodded. "She's an Ashmore."

He dipped his gaze to Fable and nodded. "I welcome your aid, then. But understand this-I love her. Nothing will stop me from loving her. Nothing will cause my heart to doubt what I know. If you try to stop us from being together, I'll stand at her side when we fight for our love."

Lizzie bent her head and laughed. "Oh, Sir, you're melodramatic!. I can almost hear violins—"

"Lizzie." Fable didn't shout. In fact, she whispered *"Please."*

The old woman receded and smiled first at Ben, and then at Fable. "As you both wish. Let me just say, Your Grace, that if you let Thoren die, you will be sentencing her to a future without ever having a father—and despite what she says to the contrary, now that she has one, she might not be so forgiving with you for letting him die. Just a few words from you is all that is needed to save him and give her the life she deserves."

"Am I to simply trust your word?" Ben asked, his voice deep and unyielding. "How will I return to her once I go?"

"You cannot return. You don't belong here," Lizzie told him. "But she can go to you if she wishes. I did promise that, after all."

"And if I fail to save Captain Ashmore?"

Lizzie sighed as if she was tired of dealing with a lower life form. "If you try and fail, my promise will stand, of course."

He was quiet while Fable breathed. Once…twice…she turned to him…three times. Then, "Of course I will do everything I can to save her father."

"Why can't I go with him?" Fable asked without taking her eyes off him. She didn't want to be separated from him for a moment. "If I can join him later, then why—"

"Because your father must come here to set things right. Should he be denied even more years of finding his daughter because she cared more for her own joy than his and went back to the time he just left?"

"Okay. I get it." Fable held up her palms. "I'll stay for a little while and meet him, and my sister too."

They all agreed, though somewhat hesitantly, that she would stay with her father for two weeks. Captain West, his wife, and their son would be returned to their time in the eighteenth century right after they found Dorothea West.

"How terrible a son am I for hoping we don't find my mother today?" Ben asked Fable, leaning in close so only she could hear when they left the B&B.

"I was having that same thought," Fable whispered back. "But she's been lost for a long time. It's about time she's found."

He smiled at her and her toes curled in her sandals. Their night together was what dreams were made of. Fable's dreams at least. When would she be with him like that again?

"Don't take long saving Lord Ashmore, my love," she said, staying close to his ear. "The sooner you get him here…"

He nodded, understanding.

"Daughter," Ben's father stepped nearer to address her. "It would seem that you are not an orphan but the child of a nobleman. It will quiet the wagging tongues of many."

Fable set her gaze on him and smiled. She believed Ben's father was fond of her. He knew the worst about her. He'd *seen* her panhandling, and he was still kind to her. She thought living seventeen years of his life in turmoil for a love he couldn't find might have changed his ways of thinking when it came to love over money and power.

"What fun would it be if a tongue or two didn't wag?" she asked with a playful arch of her brow.

The Lt. Colonel tossed his son a chuckle and then shook his head as if to say, "you have your hands full."

They took a bus to Ms. Halstead's office, which they found after an hour of searching, on the basement level, behind the office of the garage.

Fable looked around at the three women sitting at their desks. One chair was empty. Around the vacant desk were different plants of various sizes. Pictures of children were tacked to the wall to the right.

"We're here to see Ms. Halstead," Fable let the three women know. Two of them were too young to be Dorothea West. The third was about the right age, but neither she nor the Lt. Colonel made any show of recognition at the sight of the other.

"She just stepped out," one of the younger women let them know. "You can have a seat."

Fable thought she could hear one of the men's hearts beating. Ben's? About to see the woman whose death shaped him with rage and violence. Richard West's? About to finally see his beloved Dorothea again? Maybe it was Fable's heart beating furiously in her ears excited for them all, and anxious of being without Ben.

Another door opened and a woman of about forty-five to fifty entered the office. She wore flip-flop style leather sandals, a summery dress in a floral pattern. She wore her long chestnut hair in a braid dangling down her back.

She smiled at Fable on her way back to her desk, and Fable was thinking how much she resembled Prudence, when the social worker spotted the Lt. Colonel. Her eyes widened and filled to the brim with tears. Just before they fell like a waterfall down her face, she shifted her gaze to Ben's.

Recognizing her son, she drew her shaking hands to her mouth and then ran to him. "Ben? Benjamin?"

He nodded, unable, it appeared, to speak as his tears flowed.

"Oh, my baby! Oh, Richard, you brought our boy to me!" She wept in her son and husband's arms for a long time.

Fable watched a bit, then swiped her tears away and went over to stand near the other three desks.

"So, how are your days going?" she asked the women.

"Not as good as theirs," one of them replied.

Fable grinned looking over at the reunited family still hugging. "Right?"

"Fable," Ben looked up from his mother's neck and called out to her. "Come, meet my mother."

Dorothea West stepped back to look at her. "Fable Ramsey? Weren't you supposed to come in about a job? How do you know my family?"

"Mother," Ben's deep, soft voice sounded before Fable could answer, "Fable is my wife."

His mother definitely turned a shade paler. She swallowed then looked about to be sick. She caught herself and smiled. "This is news! Well," she turned back into Ben's embrace. "It was only a matter of time until you took a wife. It's just that the last time I saw you, you were an eleven year old boy—and now you're married!" She laughed and both men laughed with her.

Fable smiled, but she didn't mean it. Thea West wasn't just anyone. She was Ben's mother. What if she persuaded Ben not to save Thoren Ashmore? No, Ben wouldn't change on her.

"Richard, how did you find me?"

"I never stopped searching," he confessed softly, his eyes soaking in every feature of her face.

When she threw herself into her husband's arms, her three coworkers gasped.

"We have so much to talk about" Lady Colchester said, fitting into her role as if she'd never left it.

"I'm taking the afternoon off," she called out to the girls at their desks. "Maybe longer."

"It will definitely be longer," her husband mumbled, shooing her out the door.

"Ben," Fable said, grabbing his shirtsleeve. "You'll be going back soon."

"I'll save your father, Fable. You can count on me."

"I know. Thank you, Ben." She rose up on the tips of her toes and kissed his mouth, then pushed him toward the door. "Don't linger anywhere."

He smiled, letting her push him along. "I wonder if the watch can send us straight to London. It will save much time."

"The watch might not," Lizzie said, standing in the hall outside the door, "but I can."

Fable startled upon seeing her where Fable was sure she wasn't a moment ago. "What are you doing here? Are you bringing him back now?"

Lizzie nodded and stepped in front of Fable, blocking her path to Ben as he reached his parents. The old seer didn't do anything specific but maybe moved her lips around a few words. The air waved as if Fable were looking at Ben in the heat of a desert plain. Her instinct was to run to him, but she didn't move. They were there and gone in an instant.

Tears slipped down her cheeks. She wiped them. This wasn't the end of her and Ben. She was gaining a family—something she never had before. Something she rarely missed. What would it be like having a father?

"How are we getting back to the B&B?" Fable asked, turning to Lizzie.

"I'm teleporting. I don't know about you, dear."

Fable cast her an icy look. "Fine. I'll see you later then."

Lizzie was already gone.

Fable looked around and wondered if she could teleport. She was her father's daughter, an heir to his powers. She closed her eyes and thought about being at the B&B. Then opened them almost immediately. What if she zapped herself into some other century? She shouldn't play around with things she knew nothing about. She was thankful she couldn't see ghosts like her sister.

She left the building on her own two feet, still wondering what she was capable of. Maybe the gifts had skipped her.

"The seer sees."

"What?" Fable spun around. People came and went. None of them paid any attention to her. She looked around.

"The seer sees."

Her gaze rose to where the sound was coming from. A streetlamp. More specifically, a pigeon perched on the streetlamp.

Fable's mouth fell open and she caught her breath as her vision from earlier returned. She was a babe and animals, bumble bees and butterflies hovered around her. She could…communicate with animals like Lizzie and Bernadette. How? "Is Lizzie watching me?"

The pigeon bristled and puffed up on its metal perch.

Fable frowned and looked around, narrowing her eyes. "Why are you spying on me, Lizzie?"

"Seer comes."

Fable looked up at the pigeon and then around her. Lizzie was coming. How did she know that's what the pigeon meant? Heavens! She could understand animals. When Lizzie appeared walking across the street to meet Fable where she stood, Fable sighed waiting for her.

"How did you know I was watching?"

"A pigeon told me," Fable told her candidly and with a touch of sarcasm at the seer who hadn't seen that coming. "Why did you bother leaving the building instead of staying with me if you were just going to spy? Where do you think I'll go?"

"I don't want to mistrust you, child, but you grew up without loyalties."

"That doesn't mean I can't be loyal," Fable corrected in a quiet voice. "I know that it means staying true to a person or a cause without wavering. I'm capable of it. There just haven't been any people around me who earned my loyalty."

"And Benjamin West has earned it?"

"Yes, it is his. I want to trust you, but if you couldn't find me, how did Lieutenant Colonel West find me?"

"He didn't. Tess used the pocket watch to find you, otherwise you would have probably died on the streets. You met Ben and captured his heart and filled the empty places in his heart. We knew that once it began beating again, he would be willing to save your father. And see? It is as I said."

"Lizzie," Fable said calmly as they walked down 53rd street, "you used me as a pawn."

"To save your father and set things right."

To what?...set what things straight? She asked Lizzie what she meant.

"Child," Lizzie said, flustered. "You and your sister had lives you weren't supposed to live. We can send your father back to the time he desires, before he used the watch and separated the three of you. Your life will be different—"

The hairs on the back of Fable's neck stood on end. She knew what Lizzie meant. Fable would grow up with a father, a family. She would be the daughter of an earl, so she wouldn't lack for anything. It would change her. But...she didn't want to change. She wasn't a bad person. Her memory of Ben would probably be wiped clean—no! No, no, no!

She wanted to scream for Ben across time. If he saved her father, she would forget him, what he meant to her. What she meant to him. She would lose what she had never had before, what she didn't know she needed—to be cherished.

She wanted to call him back...somehow. But to do so would be killing her father. She squeezed her eyes shut, as if doing so would chase away the terrible truth. When she opened them again, her tears fell as her gaze fastened on Lizzie's. "Please..."

"Child—"

"If my father chooses to destroy the one beautiful thing I had in my life, and force me back in time so he can fix his mistake, he will prove to me that our only bond is by blood and nothing else. I don't care about blood bonds, since I never had a single one. I will openly reject him, the Ashmores and the Blagdens! I'll find my own way back to Ben."

"Fable, listen to me."

"How can I? You're a liar. You told Ben you would give me the choice of returning to him or not. But I won't be given a choice. If my father must set things right, that means I will never have lived this life that has led me to Ben—and I'm not giving that up."

She turned away from the old seer and kept walking. Lizzie didn't follow her. Fable wasn't surprised. Her veins felt cold from the blood flowing slowly through them. It chilled her and she shivered while she walked. "Ben," she murmured, as if he could somehow hear her, "Ben, tell my father about us. Tell him how happy you make me and tell him not to send me back to my original time. Tell him, Ben. He has to know so he can save us.

Chapter Twenty

Ben looked around at the ornately carved wood paneled walls, upon which hung colorful paintings of fox hunts, and landscapes, along with portraits, framed in rich walnut and mahogany. He recognized the royal study from his last visit here, after he'd saved the king's life and almost lost his arm.

Lizzie was precise. He almost smiled, but caught his mother's eye. She smiled and wiped her eyes. Ben took her hand and brought it to his chest. He never dreamed of seeing her again. Even dreaming of it was too painful, so he didn't. Yet, here she was real and alive.

His head was still spinning from it all when his mother covered his hand in both of hers. "I thought of nothing but seeing my children and my husband again. Let us go home so I can see my daughter."

Ben's smile faded. "We will go home right after I get Ashmore's neck out of the noose."

"We don't owe anyone anything, Benjamin," she told him softly. "Let's forget the past and start a new future together as a family."

Ben stared at her. What was she saying? "Mother, the only way to be reunited with my wife is to save her father."

She gazed up at him and smiled. "My darling son, I have no right to ask anything of you. But even though I haven't been in your life for almost twenty years, I never for one instant stopped being your mother. So, please hear me. In all those years, rather than marry a twenty-first century man who I didn't love, I took classes and worked hard to provide for myself and became a social worker. I help the homeless find a home. Fable Ramsey is one of my clients!"

Ben felt ill. His mother disapproving of Fable because of who she wasn't and what she didn't have was oddly like his sister. For some reason he never believed his mother would be so judgmental. It had been his father's wish that he wed someone of importance, wasn't it?

"Do you mean to keep her as your wife? What can she offer you?"

Ben closed his eyes rather than look into the ones he'd missed for so long and see what he was seeing.

"Thea," Ben's father interrupted. "The woman our son has married is the daughter of the Earl of Dorset, the man our son must save."

"Richard," his mother began.

But Ben stopped her. "Mother, you asked what she can offer me. I will tell you. She offers me peace and solace where there has only been unease and violence. She offers me a reason to smile and to hope that I am capable of being everything she needs to be happy. She's the reason I still breathe, the reason I am still alive. I would be a fool to let her go."

His mother held back whatever else she wanted to say and sighed with a nod instead then disappeared under her husband's beefy arm.

Ben smiled at them then turned to the heavy wooden door as it creaked open. A man stepped into the study and bowed slightly. "His Majesty, the king will see Captain West alone."

Ben followed the servant out of the study. This was happening quickly. Ben was about to see the king without knowing what to say. How was he going to defend a man against piracy when he knew nothing about Thoren Ashmore?

The servant led him through another set of double doors into a large airy chamber with six windows. In the center, surrounded by two high-backed chairs, and various chests, was a carved desk with an upholstered chair, in which sat a slender man with a wig-free head of salt and pepper hair.

He looked up from a parchment he was reading. "Colchester!" He sat the parchment down and rose to come around his desk. "What brings you, Captain? Are you ready to return to duty?"

Words Ben had longed to hear for almost three years. He would have answered with a resounding yes! Before Fable. Now he shook his head. "Your Majesty, I'm here to ask you to allow me to speak to one of your prisoners."

"Oh? Who?"

Ben told him Ashmore's name. "He's been accused of piracy."

"Ah, yes," King George remembered. "He's due to hang today. In fact—"

"Your Majesty!" Ben nearly swallowed his heart. No! Please, do not let him be too late. "Please, order the hanging to stop! Please, Sire! Is it too late?" He spun around and looked at the servant as if he might know when the king didn't.

King George hurried to the door, opened it and shouted that all sentencing was to be stopped. He didn't leave it at that, but stormed down the stairs and rushed out the doors and then hurried to the outer bailey.

Ben made it ahead of him, knowing where the executions took place and racing there. When he reached the courtyard, he stopped when he saw the three men standing on the planked platform with ropes around their necks. One of them had to be Thoren Ashmore.

"Wait!" Ben shouted, running fast enough to reach the platform. "King George is coming as we speak!" he panted. "Wait for him before these sentences are carried out!"

He realized soon enough who the man he was sent there to save was. Thoren Ashmore, the man on the far right, had chestnut hair with streaks of gray and tints of deep crimson falling to his shoulders. His eyes, when his gaze locked on to Ben's were the color of the sea…the color of Fable's eyes. His lips slanted just a bit, but enough for Ben to see a spark of hope in his eyes.

Did he know Ben was here for him? The buzz in the courtyard died down when the king arrived, running on his own two feet. People who were there to see the executions, witnessed instead, the king rushing to save the criminals. Mouths hung open, but not a word was spoken while the king ordered the criminals to be taken back to their cells until tomorrow.

"Now that we have postponed the executions," the king said to Ben in a soft voice threaded with warning. "Have a word with me in private."

Ben bowed and followed the king back to his private study and took one of the two seats by the window.

After a servant appeared and poured their drinks, The monarch set his gaze on Ben. "Tell me now, who exactly did I hurry to save and why did I save him?"

"My king, I would ask that you trust me," Ben said.

"I thought I just proved that I trusted you," England's first German king said. "You are the one person I *can* trust. If you were anyone else, those three would be dead."

Ben had forgotten how much he liked and admired King George. He had shared drinks with his men on the battlefield and fought alongside them. The king had had many obstacles and even more to prove, when he had taken the throne of a foreign country. Ben, a seasoned soldier at the time, had helped him prove his worth.

"He is Lord Thoren Ashmore, Earl of Dorset—"

George narrowed his flinty gaze on Ben. "I happen to know the earl. His name is not Thoren Ashmore."

Ben closed his eyes for a moment then opened them again. "It was in 1682."

The king sipped his drink, let it go down, then tightened his jaw beneath his graying beard at the burn of the whisky. "What are you saying?"

"I am saying he's not a pirate. He's a father trying to find his daughters."

The king stared at him as the moments passed. Then, "You know this for certain?"

"I do."

With a great sigh, the king relaxed in his chair, stretching his legs out before him. "Very well, take him with you when you leave tomorrow."

Ben breathed. Thoren Ashmore was safe. Now to his next dilemma. His parents were a few rooms away. How would Ben explain to the king that he'd found them after so long? There would just be too many questions and there wasn't enough time. "I will be leaving immediately, Sire. My beloved is unwell and I must return to her."

George's expression fell, but he nodded. "Very well, my servant Nathan will bring Ashmore to you but you must promise to bring this beloved of yours to court so I can meet her."

Ben promised happily and then left with Nathan. He descended the stairs to the lowest floor, where cells carved out of the stone walls were home to a dozen men.

Nathan said a few words to the jailer, who eyed Ben suspiciously, but then walked away, shuffling keys on a metal loop.

The servant waited with Ben and listened to a cell door being opened and a second pair of footsteps joining the first.

Ben watched the jailer pull Fable's father down the long hall. When they moved under the light of a wall torch, Ben was once again struck by the brightness of hope in Ashmore's eyes, shaping his smile. Ben was immediately reminded of Fable and breathed out a longing sigh.

He stepped forward when the jailer handed Ashmore over and wasted no time in heading for the stairs.

"Who sent you?" Ashmore asked him as he hurried up the stairs behind Ben.

"An old woman called Lizzie Black. She claims to be your aunt many generations removed—and…your daughter."

At the mention of the old woman, Ashmore had no reaction, but when Ben spoke of the man's daughter, Ashmore stopped and stared at him. "Which one?"

"Fable," Ben told him, trying to ignore the feeling of loss surging over him like the waves of an angry sea.

"Fable," the earl said in a quavering breath. "You found her?"

"She found me," Ben told him, and as he told him about Fable and her lonely life hidden from the world outside the city streets of the homeless, tears streamed down her father's face and hooked Ben in his heart. Thoren Ashmore had never had the chance to get to know his daughter—either of them, or make their lives better. If he was hanged by order of King George, any chance he had would end.

Because of what his own heart felt for her, Ben understood the pain of what it would be like not having her in his life.

When they reached the main floor and stepped into the hall where Ben's parents were waiting, Ben stopped and waited for Fable's father to stop as well. He didn't know if Ashmore would disappear the moment the pocket watch was back in his possession, or if Lizzie would pull him back before Ben had a chance to speak with him—and there were things he wanted to say.

"I would have you know—" he began.

"I haven't had a chance to thank you, and it should have been the first thing I said to you."

Ben stared at him, his gaze warming on him. There was something familiar and light about the Earl of Dorset. He resembled Fable, grateful with a charming air about him.

"Truly," Ben let him know. "I did nothing but agree to come."

"Your sacrifice, no matter how insignificant you think it was, saved my life. You saved Fable's life, as well. I will forever be in your debt."

"You owe me nothing," Ben told him, "for your daughter saved not only my life, but my soul. I would have you know that she is the reason I breathe."

"You love my Fable."

His Fable? No, Ben thought, she wasn't Ashmore's anymore. She had become an adult with no help from her father or anyone else, and she'd joined her life to Ben's. "If she wishes to come back to me, please do not stop her."

"Benjamin," his father called out, interrupting whatever else Ben wanted to say. "That was quicker than we expected. The king must truly hold you in the highest regard."

"That's why I'm here," Ben reminded him then introduced his parents to the earl.

"Dorset," his father said with his wife at his side, "we were told about you. I admit that I do not like the fact that you are a sorcerer—"

"A sorcerer?" the earl echoed with a slight smirk. "If I was a sorcerer do you think I would have needed your son to save me?"

The Lt. Colonel was quiet for a moment. "What are you then?"

"A father," the earl answered earnestly.

Ben looked away. What if her father wouldn't allow her to return to Ben? *I was a fool.* He thought. He should not have left the future without her.

"Captain," Ben uttered in a low voice blended with warning and plea. "Let her return to me."

"And if she doesn't wish to return to you?" her father asked, matching his tone.

"She will. Let her. I beg you." He didn't sound like he was begging. But the proof was in his eyes. He would beg on his knees if he had to. There was no place for pride in love.

"I've waited twenty-four years to see her again."

Ben swallowed his argument and nodded with a pit lodging in his belly and tethered to his heart. He said nothing and bit back the wave of emotion overtaking him. She would come to him. He knew she would find a way.

But what if she chose to remain with her father? Ben would do his best to understand her wanting what had been taken from her her whole life. He wanted her to be happy more than he wanted her to make him happy and come to him. So, with a heavy heart, he said nothing when the Lt. Colonel handed over the pocket watch and Fable's long lost father returned to her.

THOREN ASHMORE STOOD on the polished, wooden floor of a large room with sofas of various sizes and an old woman sitting in a chair by the window. When she saw him, she stood and crossed the room to him.

"So, here you are, child," she said, reaching her hand out to touch him.

He moved back like a flickering flame, just outside of her touch. "Where's my daughter?"

"She went out for lunch with Bernadette and Harper. She'll return shortly. Why don't we sit and chat."

Thoren took a better look at her. He knew her. She had visited Ashmore Castle when he was a child, her and another woman…Tess. He cared less about who they were and more about something else. "What year is it?"

"2024."

His cerulean eyes settled on her, then he sat on one of the sofas. "What are you doing in the twenty-first century, Old Lizzie?"

She cast him an amused smile and held out her hand. "The watch?"

"You'll get it after I'm reunited with Fable and not an instant before."

"We saved you, Thoren," the old woman said.

"We? You mean you and the Duke of Colchester?"

"No, of course not. He has no gifts."

Thoren shrugged. "I disagree." And so, according to Colchester, did Fable. Was her heart lost to the duke? If it was, what would he do? Could he give her up after a lifetime of trying to find her?

"What do you know of my daughters? What of Magnolia?"

"Since you sent her there, you can now visit Graven Fortress in the physical realm and try to find her. She has disappeared."

His blood drained and his heart sank. "What do you mean, she has disappeared?"

"Just that. We suspect she used an object to travel to another time in the past."

He should be used to this, but Thoren wasn't. It had taken him years to find Magnolia, and it was after he'd died, so it was that much more torturous. Now, he was alive and she was gone again!

He wouldn't take the chance with Fable. "Tell me, where is Fable so I can go get her?"

"Excuse me."

The dulcet voice coming from behind him stopped Thoren's heart. He closed his eyes for an instant before he turned to see his daughter.

The Duke of Colchester's voice rang through his head. She'd had no home, no father, barely a mother, no one else to care for her, and very few meals.

He turned and smiled as his heart swelled with love that threatened to burst through his eyes. For many years he wondered what she and Magnolia looked like. He breathed as one who was on the brink of death and was finally healed. Fable looked like him, save that she had her mother's hair tied up in a tail behind her head. It was as fiery copper as it had been when she was two. Her eyes, the same color as his, were wider and shaped with wonder as he said her name.

He took a step toward her, but paused when she moved back like a butterfly about to fly off. He wondered how she and the young duke got along when they both denied touch.

"It's so good to see you, daughter."

Her delicate smile didn't reach her eyes, so she lowered them.

"I'm sorry you missed me for so long."

"My beloved daughter, I'm the one who separated the three of us and you are apologizing to me? Let that be the last time."

She lifted her gaze and he saw the thread of warmth pass across her eyes.

"We'll leave you two to get reacquainted," Old Lizzie said and pulled the other two girls off with her.

Alone, Thoren decided he would be grateful just to stare at his daughter for the remainder of his days. But he didn't want to frighten the poor girl away. He wanted to take her in his embrace and never let her out of it again, but he had to remember she wasn't used to having a father.

"I was told your life was quite difficult," he said, biting back the heavy waves of emotion trying to escape him.

She moved a step closer, her brows lifted in curiosity. "Who told you?"

"The man who saved my life," he told her, "the Duke of Colchester."

He listened closer. Was that her pounding heart he heard, or his own?

"He told me he cared for you," he admitted, watching for her reaction.

"He did?"

He nodded, taking note of her breathless anticipation of hearing more about the duke. "He asked me to send you back to him, but I'm too selfish. I want to spend time with you, Fable. I want to learn who you have become and imagine that we haven't lost so much."

"If what I have now was the prize for enduring a difficult life," she told him, her eyes like twin oceans, "then I have much to be thankful for."

He let out a soft, charmed laugh and shook his head at them both. "You comfort me when I should be comforting you."

Her smile widened like a breathtaking sunrise, reaching her eyes this time. "I'm glad I could comfort you. I'm comforted by the fact that my father isn't a monster tyrant, or a detached ogre. You tried to find us for twenty-four years. Is it true you never took a break from your search for us?"

"Even after I..." he stopped for a moment remembering the rope around his neck and the lever to release part of the platform was pulled. He wasn't sure what killed him. He briefly remembered his neck breaking, and then he was free. "Even after I died, I continued searching. It was how I found your sister, but I could never find you. Now I have, and I—

"Ben agreed to not seeing me for two weeks."

The duke agreed. Thoren felt a hook in his side. Who or what was Colchester to her?

"After that I wish to return to him."

"You share his feelings then?" he asked.

"Yes, maybe even more so. And Father, I'm sorry but I don't want to return to sixteen-eighty whatever. I don't want to start over, or change my past. I won't. It took twenty-six years to become who I am. I won't do it over and risk becoming someone I don't like."

"I'll speak to Miss Black about it," he promised, sounding sorrowful even to his own ears. He cleared his throat and put on a smile. "How about we freshen up and have dinner together?"

He was infinitely thankful when she nodded her head. The more time they spent together, the more she would get used to having him as her father and he could work at changing her mind about leaving.

Chapter Twenty-One

*B*EN DISMOUNTED AND *looked at the door to his house. For the first time in seventeen years he was happy to be home. Fable was inside, beyond those walls. He'd been away from her all day, and every hour that had passed was like another hour in the dry wilderness. He should be cursing himself for allowing her to traipse across his defenses, smashing them to pieces with the light touch of her slippered feet, but all he could think about was if she ate supper yet?*

He smiled recalling what she told him it meant. She was his beloved wife. He practically ran to the doors.

Not to be outdone by his friend, Sudbury used his long legs to reach the doors at the same time. They laughed as they pushed them open.

Ben saw his sister and scanned the halls for the woman he was most anxious to see.

Feeling her gaze on him, he shifted his eyes to his sister. She wore a glum expression. Edith stood behind her, wringing her skirts.

His thoughts brought him back to that day when the news had come that his mother and father had been killed by Jacobites.

"Word arrived that the Jacobites attacked...your mother...your father were slaughtered." Slaughtered. Slaughtered.

"What is it?" he asked now. His heart pounded for a whole different reason.

"Benjamin," his sister answered. "Your Miss Ramsey is gone. She is gone."

Ben sat up in his bed in a cold sweat. He covered his face in his hands recalling his dream. "Please, no. Do not leave me,

Fable. I beg you."

He swung his bare legs over the side of the bed, forcing himself to rise up and see to the new day. Another day without Fable. Would she return today, the thirteenth day? Would she ever be allowed to leave the twenty-first century and return to him?

He groaned and crossed his chamber in five strides to wash up and get dressed. *She might return to me today.*

When Stephen arrived, he helped Ben choose a midnight blue velvet doublet with a white shirt beneath and black hose and boots. His old friend tied his cravat in a triple knot while his dressers combed his hair back at his nape.

With a great sigh and a terrible, nagging voice in his head telling him she was gone.

"What will I do if she doesn't return?"

Stephen looked up at him while they stepped out into the hall.

"I can do nothing!" Ben let out. It was more of a soulful lament than a shout.

"She will return to you, my lord."

"I don't think her father will allow it."

"Her heart belongs to you. She will find a way back."

Ben was thankful for Stephen's encouragement. It was so much more than he received from Old Lizzie for saving Thoren Ashmore from the noose. Ben expected to hear something from the seer as a blasted courtesy. It was as if none of it had been real.

Fable was real. She was his wife and the master of his heart. He couldn't sleep in peace without her. He couldn't control his thoughts of her while he tried to practice his swordplay. He ate enough not to starve himself but he had no appetite.

When he entered the Colchester House's dining hall, his heart felt lighter seeing his parents at the table with Prudence. Their reunion was tearful for everyone. Ben was happy for his sister, who hadn't stopped smiling for the last fortnight. He knew what having his parents back meant.

The only thing that would make this happiness complete was

if Fable were sitting at the table with them.

He missed her carefree smile, hearing her silky laughter like a siren's song laying claim to him. Indeed, she made him too weak to fight her guileless wiles. He longed to hold her again, to tell her every day what she meant to him.

Swallowing his heart, he smiled and took the seat his father left open at the head of the table.

"You look radiant this morning, Mother," he complimented as his porridge was set before him. He pushed the bowl away and scanned the fruit on the table; grapes, cherries, peaches. Nothing appealed to him.

Feeling his mother's gaze on him, he reached for a piece of black bread. She snatched it from his hand and slathered butter and honey on it, then handed it back to him.

"Benjamin," she scolded, "if you don't eat you won't be here when she does return."

He bit into the bread and cast his sister a resigned smirk. Her Grace Dorothea West was still unhappy with her son's choice of a wife, but at least she didn't voice her displeasure at times like this—when he felt as if he was treading on unsteady ground and at any moment it could all fall away.

"I heard you met Lady Charlotte of Nottingham," his mother brought up while he chewed.

"That's true," he let her know.

"You threw her out of Colchester."

He slid his gaze to hers. "Yes."

"All right," she said with a frown. "I heard Lady Margaret is kind-hearted and beautiful."

"Mother—"

"Please, Son," she whispered, reaching her fingers to his cheek. "Meet the king's niece at least and if you decide—"

"I have met her. I do not want her for a wife. I already have a wife."

His mother turned to Prudence. "Has he met Lady Elizabeth Dra—"

Ben slammed his palm down on the table. "Enough! Please. There is no one I wish to meet. I have met them all already." One corner of his mouth rose with a snarl of distaste. "None of them pleased me. My plan was not to marry but to rejoin the king's army and die on the battlefield."

"Benjamin!" his mother and sister shouted in unison.

He settled his gaze on his sister. He was sorry he'd misled her. He knew she would have fallen apart when he told her. She didn't fall apart now. In fact, she calmly popped a grape into her mouth then slipped her gaze to him. "You were correct not to tell me. So...do you feel the same way now?"

"No."

"Because of her?"

"Yes," he confirmed in a low voice. "Because of her."

Prudence spread her warm gaze over her parents. "When she returns, let us welcome her as a sister and a daughter."

Ben's father nodded his head and kept his gaze on his shoes.

"Mother?" his sister surprisingly continued, "Give Ben your blessings. I know Fable. She makes him happy. She brought a light I thought long dead in Benjamin back to life. She's quite thoughtful, but goes so far as to invite servants to sit with her and Ben. Just...be prepared."

His mother's eyes opened wider as she echoed two words—*"be prepared*?

"She thinks differently than the people of this world," Ben's father intervened. "You of all people should understand, Thea. You spent seventeen years learning to think the way she thinks."

"I only want what's best for him. He needs—"

"I need Fable," Ben told her. "Mother, pray for that."

"She found you, Mother," Prudence reminded her. "No matter what kind of power those *witches* have, they could not find you. I think she belongs here."

Ben had heard and eaten enough. With a slight bow to his parents he started for the door.

His sister's fingers closing around his wrist stopped him.

"Benjamin, Mother and Father want to see Simon's parents, so he is escorting us to Sudbury two days from now. You should come. You need a few days away."

"You are assuming Fable will not return," he said, sounding more hurt than angry.

"No, Brother. If I assumed that, I would have suggested we leave tomorrow. I'm praying that she returns by tomorrow."

Prudence had forgiven Fable everything when she learned that Fable was the reason their father and then their mother were finally reunited and were able to return home. Ben couldn't be more relieved that his sister finally stopped badgering him about marriage.

"I need a few days away from Mother's stepping into your footsteps."

Prudence screwed up her face and whispered. "Was I that bad?"

He smiled and nodded.

She didn't hold him back when he turned away and continued out of the dining hall. Her recently betrothed stopped him instead.

"Chess?"

Ben tossed him a sedate stare. "So you can beat me again?"

Sudbury grinned. "This is the only time I get to do it. Will you deny me?"

Ben shook his head in mock disgust. "You take shameful advantage of your closest friend when he is not at his sharpest."

Sudbury threw his arm around Ben's shoulder and led him to Ben's private solar. But even trying his hardest to beat his friend, Ben's thoughts were filled with the sound of Fable whispering his name.

FABLE CAME AWAKE from a dream of laughing in bed with Ben,

leaning in and whispering his name in his ear.

She sat up. It was the fourteenth day. Her last day here in 2024 with her father. She didn't want to leave him. Over the last two weeks they had spent a lot of time together. Her father couldn't do enough to make her happy, as if he needed to make amends for her past. He didn't need to and she let him know it. It made them more comfortable with each other and helped them fit better into each other's life. With his playful laughter over the smallest thing, his wide, easy smiles, as well as his pouting surrender when he couldn't beat her at chess, Thoren Ashmore was easy to like.

He was honest to the core, letting her know that he wasn't altogether innocent of piracy. He had, after all, popped onto that pirate ship when it was losing to the king's navy. He saved the crew and made his way to land—to the garden of Colchester House.

"The first thing I knew I had to do," he had told her, "was bury my treasure. So, that's what I did. I had nothing to do with the Wests finding it." He found amusement in the tale, and she, being his daughter, after all, had laughed with him.

They'd visited Bernadette and spent more time talking with Old Lizzie, learning about their family. Thanks to some curse, Fable's grandparents had to fight a demon. Thoren was the first child born to the Blagdens and Ashmores. The first and only male.

"I don't know what any of it means," her father had vowed. "And I don't care. You're all that matters to me. Help me find your sister and we can—"

"Dad—" Nothing had changed for Fable. "I'm going to Ben. But we don't have to separate. I don't want us to separate. Come with me."

He had shaken his head. "I have to find Magnolia."

She groaned. That was yesterday. Would he or Lizzie give her a hard time about going? She hoped Lizzie would keep her word. If everything went her way, she would be with Ben today.

She wiped away a bittersweet tear and got out of bed.

She left her room and padded downstairs in her pajamas and slippers. She headed to the kitchen and was happy to find her father cooking with old Aunt Lizzie.

He looked up from a frying pan where bacon sizzled and popped. "Good morning, my daughter."

It was what she had always wanted. A bed, a warm meal at a family table. A family.

Nothing was mentioned about returning to Ben. They ate in silence but neither hesitated to share a smile across the table.

While they ate, she eyed her father and thought about how handsome he was. "What was Mother like?"

He smiled, remembering her. "She was a spirited woman with hair like yours and a temper to match."

Fable remembered the men in her stepmother's life while she was growing up and the ones who'd lifted their hands to Kittie Ramsey. "You didn't mind her spiritedness?"

He shook his head. "How could I be angry with a flame?"

She gazed at him, wishing for the thousandth time since she met him, what a good father he would have been to that little homeless girl who'd never understood what security was. "Send me home today."

Lizzie was the first to open her mouth, but Fable quieted her as a cold blanket covered her. "Keep your word, Lizzie. You told Ben you would abide by my wishes if he saved my father. Keep your end of the bargain."

"It won't be me who keeps you here, Child," Lizzie told her and cut her glance to Thoren.

Yes. The powerful male heir of the Ashmore and Blagdens. Fable looked at him. "Come with me."

"I cannot."

"Swear to me you'll send me to him today."

But he shook his head and offered her a repentant look. "No."

"No?"

He appeared to be choking a bit on his word. "Fable, please—"

"Come back with me!" she shouted at him. "Don't give me everything and keep from me the only thing I truly want. Find Magnolia and then come spend time with me. You can do it. You don't need the pocket watch, just as she—" She pointed to Lizzie standing close by.—"doesn't need to use it. You're more powerful than she is. You're Lord Thoren Ashmore, only son of—"

"Child," Lizzie interrupted, pointing at her. "Let your father have what he desires for once. All he asks for is time with you."

Wonderful, Fable thought scathingly. Just what she needed. Guilt. Her cold stare made the older woman bristle.

"It seems I was right never to trust anyone before *or after* Ben," Fable told her.

She didn't feel tears burning her eyes until she turned them on her father. "I'm sorry that the pocket watch exists and that it took you away from me and Magnolia. But you were gone for so long. We had to grow up without you—or anyone even remotely like you. Benjamin West is the first person I remember loving, trusting, and feeling safe with. Are you truly going to come back to me—thanks to him, no less—and take him from me? Please don't." She sniffed and wiped her eyes. She was done crying. "I don't know what either of you are used to, but I'm not going to cower."

"Fable," her father protested gently. "I have no intention of asking you to cower. I didn't want to be a father who forced his selfish restrictions on his children. Now that I found you, I certainly won't do it. I'll send you back today."

Fable and Old Lizzie were quiet while they stared at him. Fable swallowed and blinked first. Did he just agree so easily? "You will?"

"Yes." He smiled but Fable could see the disappointment behind the veil in his eyes. She thought about what she could do besides taking hold of him when she was leaving and dragging him back to 1718.

"I won't have you hating me," he murmured with a pout. He caught her in his arms with a laugh when she threw herself into them.

"Thank you!" she exclaimed after a kiss to his cheek. He saved her from fighting whoever she needed to fight with whatever powers she possessed. She didn't want to fight. She wasn't made for fighting.

"Would you hate me if I told you how your joy feels like a kick in the guts?"

"Of course I wouldn't hate you for that," she assured her father happily.

"He doesn't even know what he's doing," Lizzie pointed out. "He's likely to send you somewhere in the thirteenth or nineteenth century." She shrugged her seemingly frail shoulders. "Could be anywhere."

"Then will you keep your promise and do it?" Fable asked her.

Lizzie looked away from her nephew and nodded. "If that's what you want."

"That's what I want. I want to go home to Ben."

"I'll do it on one condition," Lizzie told her. Before Fable could protest, she held up her hand. "Today I will send you to your Benjamin West. The condition is that I will not tell you when you're going." She turned her pale gaze to Fable's father. "Treasure each moment together."

Fable didn't protest. She was thankful she was being given the chance to treasure moments with her father. "Come on!" she beckoned her father with a wide grin and a tug on his sleeve. She led him outside and down the street.

She smiled because he didn't ask her where they were going. He didn't care. Was it possible to love someone you've only known for two weeks?

She brought him to a park where children played under the watchful eye of their mother or father. When she hurried to the swings, unfazed by any disapproving glance that came her way, her father followed.

"I used to hang around parks while my mo—Kittie panhandled," she told him. "I'd always see little girls on the swings with their fathers pushing them." Before she said anything else, he went behind her and gave her a push.

They laughed together and Fable hoped she didn't disappear in that moment.

But, she did, in fact, leave her father although not in her body. Physically, she remained swinging on the swing. Only her laughter had stopped. Her sudden silence brought her father around to the front of her. He knelt before her and called her name.

Fable held out her hand to the red-haired woman with earth-colored eyes looking back at her. She smiled at Fable and reached for her. They shared blood. Magnolia.

Her father called her name, and touched her face. His heartbeat drew her back.

No! Wait!

Magnolia, where are you? Tell me.

Fable let the sound of her father's voice pull her back. The sound of children laughing and calling their friends filled her ears and replaced her sister's rhythmic breathing in her ears. What happened? Was this one of her abilities? Spirit telepathy? Could she 'find' others or did she know when her sister was because they were twins?

"Dad."

Before he let her speak, he made certain she felt herself again. "What happened, Daughter?"

"I don't know but I saw Magnolia. I know where she is."

"Tell me," her father said.

"She's in the year—" She began to disappear. No! Not yet.

Child, you cannot tell him where to find her. Fable felt Lizzie's voice more than heard it.

"1424," Fable said as quickly as she could. She hadn't been raised with rules, and she didn't care about them either. She would give her father back his daughter. "Graven Fortress."

Her father reached out for her, but before another instant passed, he was gone.

CHAPTER TWENTY-TWO

BEN WATCHED SUDBURY move his knight and capture Ben's bishop.

Today was exactly a fortnight since he had said farewell to Fable and left her in the future. Fool! He raged inwardly. Why had he left her? Why had he believed the old witch when she'd promised to send Fable back to him? A thought occurred to him and he rose from his seat.

Sudbury's gaze followed him up. "What is—?"

Did Fable choose not to come to him? Was a pair of weeks too short? Would she stay longer and then come home? How much longer? How would he know?

"Ben?" Sudbury's voice broke through his haunting thoughts.

"Forgive me. I am not in my proper frame of mind to think or play."

"The day is young, Brother," his friend pointed out. "Your beloved will return to you."

Ben wanted to smile and reassure Sudbury that he was fine. But he wasn't, and he couldn't hide it anymore. "How do you know?" he asked, almost pleaded.

"Because she will never find a man as good as you," his friend told him.

Ben would never find a woman like her, delicate and fierce, able to flip him flat on his back, a woman who was not looking for what else she could gain, but rather grateful for what she had—though it was not much of anything. The hint of a warm smile softened his expression while thoughts of dancing alone with her in her room after his sister's ball invaded his mind.

"I want to eat with her again."

Sudbury gave him a doubtful look. "Did you say eat with her?"

Ben nodded and then turned for the door. Being around others while they tried to make him forget what day it was, would be as difficult as trying to win at a game of chess. He needed to be alone.

He had his parents back. It was a miracle and Ben was more than thankful for it. He should feel more elated, but instead he felt as if he were being swept away on waves of anxious insecurity and sadness. He needed an anchor. Everything he'd known that had to do with his parents, all that he'd believed, and the way he lived—by killing others on the battlefield—had changed almost in the blink of an eye. His head was still spinning. At least while he believed his parents dead, and before a woman had brought him back from the brink of self-destruction, he had a single purpose and that was revenge. It's what had driven him. Now he had no purpose.

He needed his anchor. He needed Fable.

He walked the halls and left the house when he reached the doors. The afternoon sun shone in his eyes. He held his hand to his brow for shade and headed toward the garden to try and clear his thoughts.

A robin singing in a tall birch almost brought a smile to his face. It would be a perfect day if—

The sound of a cat meowing stopped his foot before he took his next step. It wasn't a cat…

Ben came upon her kneeling in front of the memorial where he'd found her the first time. He was afraid to move, lest he wake up and the dream be shattered.

"Please. Oh, please, Lord," she prayed fervently, her long waves hanging to her waist, "let me stay here in the eighteenth century. I'll do anything. And please don't let Ben's parents hate me. It scares me—"

"Fable."

She bounded up on her feet and turned to see him.

He opened his arms and she ran into them, proving that she was real. The refreshing scent of her filled his nose and went to his head. He closed his arms around her tighter and buried his face into her hair. He didn't know if he wanted to hold her or if he needed to kiss her.

"Were you missing me, Duke?" she teased.

He lifted his head to look at her. "Yes, my love. I feared I would die without you."

She smiled and he was sure his heart stopped. He would be thankful to die with her smile being the last thing he saw.

"I wouldn't let you die without me," she told him as he leaned down to kiss her.

He wanted to devour her, to brand her so that she would return to him from any century, but he pressed his lips to hers with restraint stiffening his muscles. Still, he couldn't help but run his tongue over her lips to taste her. To hold her closer with tender strength.

"Fable..." he wanted to carry her off somewhere they could be alone.

"Fable? Miss Ramsey, is that you?"

Fable leapt from his arms. He tried to catch her, but she hopped away.

Ben turned to his sister and returned her smile.

"I knew you would return to him," Prudence told her as she slowly closed the distance between them. "He doubted you would."

"I did not!" He snapped his head around to Fable. "I never doubted you."

His sister gave his reply a short laugh. "You trudged around here, pining for her as you had lost her. Am I not telling the truth?"

It didn't matter that she was right about him. She made him sound like a pitiful sot—and he didn't want to admit to that.

"Am I?" Prudence insisted with a glint of affection for him in her eyes.

"N—" He sighed then began again. "Yes, it's true."

Both women smiled at him, and then at each other.

"Welcome back," Prudence said to her. Then, "You are his wife now. Welcome back, Sister."

Fable appeared flustered by Prudence's new behavior. Ben liked it.

"Come inside and see my parents."

Ben took Fable's hand and led her into the house.

They met Stephen, who called out for Edith in between his wide grins. By the time all the servants were gathered around her to welcome her home, Ben's parents arrived to see what all the celebration was about.

"It's good to see you again, Daughter," his father greeted her first, looking happy and relieved for his son.

His mother offered Fable a practiced smile. Ben was happy she appreciated the importance of it and practiced it for his sake. She didn't know Fable. Once she did, Ben was sure she would love Fable as much as everyone did.

"You have made my son a very happy man today, Miss Ram—" She stopped and corrected herself. "Fable. Was your family against this?"

"I won't let anyone keep us apart," Fable let her know with a confident smile.

"We are happy to hear that," the Lt. Colonel said. "Our son is a fortunate man to have a wife who will defend their marriage."

Ben nodded slightly. His father had spent time with her. It was clear that he liked her. But he didn't care who accepted her or not. He was hers.

They ate together at the large family table in the dining hall. Ben wasn't sure if there was a moment when his beautiful wife wasn't smiling. She laughed with Sudbury and even Prudence.

She toasted with his father, and asked his mother what her favorite things were. Any favorite things; food, plants, flowers, etc. Ben suspected Fable would think of something kind to do for his mother. It made him love her all the more if possible.

When she took a moment to whisper in his ear that his mother wanted a grandchild, he would have cheered his mother's answer if he thought it would not embarrass Fable.

"I'm eager to make one," he whispered back. He'd dreamed of the night on the floor with books scattered around them when he had begun to teach her to read. And then with eyes painted by talented artists watching them. He missed her. He wanted to kiss her, touch her, breathe her in…

She slapped his fingers away when they reached for her thigh under the table but he was close enough to see the pulse beat at her throat quicken. He stretched his arms up and yawned, bringing Stephen to his feet. The steward hurried to Edith and they both left the dining hall.

"We should help," Ben said to his wife, looking after his steward and her servant. He took Fable's hand and stood with her. He bid everyone at the table good night and barely gave her time to curtsey before he pulled her away.

She blushed on the way out of the dining hall, but they ended up laughing together as they hurried up the stairs. They didn't speak, for words were forgotten in place of desire. They kissed up the last four steps and almost tumbled back down all of them, but Ben found his balance and they laughed again as they approached their chamber door.

When they entered the chamber in each other's arms, Stephen smiled and quickly grasped Edith by the elbow and pulled her toward the door.

"Good night, my lady," Edith bid, digging in her heels and refusing to be moved just yet. "I cannot tell you how happy I am…we all are that you are back. Mayhap tomorrow you will tell me about the world you came from?"

Fable gave her a warm smile. "Of course."

After another warning look from Ben, their friends left and he was finally alone with his wife. He couldn't wait another moment to be with her, to tell her with his body what she meant to him. He pulled and tugged at her futuristic clothes but couldn't get off the contraption covering her bosom.

"Will you burn that thing tomorrow?" he asked as she bent her arm around to her back and with a seeming snap of her fingers, set her breasts free—and into his hands.

"Do you know how much I love you, my fair wife?"

She smiled at him as he carried her to bed. "Yes, I do. You tell me every time you look at me."

"And yet your smiles tempt me to say it every time I see one."

"Then I'll smile often," she told him huskily.

He lowered her to the bed and breathed against her lips, "I love you, Fable."

She cupped his face between her hands when he finished kissing her mouth. "I love you, Ben," she told him. "I waited fourteen days to tell you. Thank you for letting me fall into your arms that first day in the garden. I woke up untouched in your kitchen and knew you were a good man. I know there are good men out there in the world, but in my world I hadn't met any until you."

He kissed her again, thrilling in her words and in the acceleration of her heartbeat against him. They undressed without leaving the bed and breathed hard against each other as passion engulfed them. He pressed himself down atop her, between her open thighs and took her between whispers of his love and swift kisses to her face and throat.

Her scent—faintly vanilla—went to his head, conquering every frightening thought, every doubt. Her lips against his chest, up the column of his neck, all while she moved beneath him and drove him mad. When he approached his peak he didn't stop or slow down. Why should he? He had so much more to give her. He let her do as she wished until he came in spurts of trembling passion. Almost immediately, he was roused again by the scent of her desire. He moved upon her like a surging wave, gazing into her eyes, then kissing her hungry mouth while he moved inside her. When he took her by the hands and held her arms over her head, she let him have his way—and he took it, bringing her to climax that made her cry out and grind him harder, until they found release together.

They lay in each other's arms, with Fable's head resting in the crook of his shoulder. There were things he wanted to ask her about her father and her family—but those things could wait. No longer did she haunt his thoughts. Here she was in his arms! That was all Ben cared about. It was all he needed. He hadn't been alive before her, and when centuries separated them, he knew he would die without her.

They didn't sleep but they stayed awake held tightly in an embrace that provided everything Ben needed. He would never let her go. He realized she was an Ashmore with gifts inherited from her father, the sole male born since the seventeenth century. Her family might want her back. How would he stop them? He was glad he began studying herbs and flowers. Certain mixes were said to stop the powers of a seer, or anyone using magic.

He didn't care about other seers, just Old Lizzie Black. If she used her power to try to snatch Fable away, he would use his most potent mix to stop her. He would make certain no one dared to touch his wife.

Finally, he closed his eyes and a smile appeared on his face where there had been a frown for the last fourteen days. She had chosen him. It still made his heart flip. He pulled her closer and listened to her rhythmic breathing. She was asleep.

"Fable," he whispered, "you showed me the truth in the light. It wasn't my parents, it was you and getting lost in your fire. You showed me how to love and breathe again *before* I got my parents back. Thank you for rescuing me, my love."

HE SOON FELL asleep and Fable opened her eyes. She remembered her father calling her mother a flame and she breathed easier for the first time in her life. She had a mother and a father. As the truth dawned on her again, she swallowed back a wave of grateful tears. For the first time, she felt grounded in something. And Ben was the one reason. "Ben," she said in a barely audible whisper. "I love you, my dearest.

EPILOGUE

THE WEDDING CELEBRATION was in its fourth hour and Fable's head was still spinning. Her marriage to Ben in the church while they were in the future was legitimate. But his mother wanted something huge to send her son off to wedded bliss. Everyone in Colchester House ate, laughed and danced together. Fable tried to remember every detail of her wedding day, but much was lost in the whirlwind. She'd remained agreeable to everything her husband was doing for her, but she wouldn't wear a wig. That was where she had to say no. Nope. No thanks. It didn't help that the wigs were ridiculously high. She laughed looking at it in Edith's hands.

With the duke's approval, sought and given via a quick-footed messenger, Edith sent for four more of the best hairdressers in the house. Everything Fable needed or wanted was supplied.

Except one thing.

"Dad, I'm waiting for you," she'd whispered. She didn't mention to her father her private empty void where her family should be.

"I think you owe me a dance."

Fable looked up to see husband's welcoming smile. She held out her gloved hand and he took it.

When they began their dance and their eyes locked in a loving gaze, the air turned blurry. Fable saw it and stopped dancing.

"Someone is coming."

They all watched a man appear in the middle of the dance hall, and then a few moments after him, another figure appeared.

"Father!" Fable cried out. "Magnolia!" She moved to run to them, but her husband held back.

"We do not know what they want," her husband explained his action.

He was right. What if they came to take her away? "What brings you here?" she asked. Her eyes moved over her sister's pretty face while she waited for his answer. The first time Fable had seen her was in a spiritual realm of some kind. Her sister's features weren't clear. Fable could see perfectly well now. They weren't identical. They had the same color hair but that was it. Magnolia must look like their mother.

"I learned how to transport," her father explained. "I found Maggie—" he stopped and turned to offer his other daughter his most radiant smile. "We practiced moving through time and all to visit you." His cerulean gaze swept over the wedding celebration. "It seems we chose the right day to visit."

"Yes, you did," Fable answered, going to him and slipping her arm through his, unhindered now by her husband. "You've already met His Grace Duke of Colchester, Captain of the king's army Benjamin West."

"Of course," her father smiled amiably. "The man who saved my life."

The men got along well, so Fable took the opportunity to pull her sister away.

They shared stories of growing up and wept in each other's arms for a bit. Maggie told her what she had been doing in the fifteenth century. It was where she had recently fallen in love with her man.

Fable liked her sister very much and they promised to visit each other once they grew more settled in their new lives. Before she left, Maggie agreed to their father spending the next two weeks with her and Ben at Colchester House.

Ben was happy about the news, as was the Lt. Colonel—and a gaggle of various ladies attending the celebration.

"He's charming," Ben remarked to her while even his own mother seemed unable to stop staring at their guest. "Like you, he doesn't seem to be aware of it."

"You think I'm charming?" she asked, grinning up at him.

"And beautiful," he answered, smiling back at her.

Fable didn't know any fairy tales but she felt as if she were living in one. Every day with Ben was the most perfect one whether they were in the eighteenth century or the twenty-first. She couldn't wait for the celebration to be over so they could be alone. She wanted to kiss him. To kiss him for all time.

The End

About the Author

Paula Quinn is a New York Times bestselling author and a sappy romantic moved by music, beautiful words, and the sight of a really nice pen. She lives in New York with her three beautiful children, six over-protective chihuahuas, and three adorable parrots. She loves to read romance and science fiction and has been writing since she was eleven. She's a faithful believer in God and thanks Him daily for all the blessings in her life. She loves all things medieval, but it is her love for Scotland that pulls at her heartstrings.

To date, four of her books have garnered Starred reviews from Publishers Weekly. She has been nominated as Historical Storyteller of the Year by RT Book Reviews, and all the books in her MacGregor and Children of the Mist series have received Top Picks from RT Book Reviews. Her work has also been honored as Amazons Best of the Year in Romance, and in 2008 she won the Gayle Wilson Award of Excellence for Historical Romance.

Website:
pa0854.wixsite.com/paulaquinn

www.ingramcontent.com/pod-product-compliance
Ingram Content Group UK Ltd.
Pitfield, Milton Keynes, MK11 3LW, UK
UKHW021526240125
4287UKWH00046B/511

9 781965 539798